Piccolo

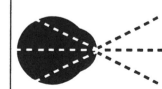

This Large Print Book carries the
Seal of Approval of N.A.V.H.

Piccolo

A Novel

James Baddock

Thorndike Press • Thorndike, Maine

Library of Congress Cataloging in Publication Data:

Baddock, James.
   Piccolo : a novel / James Baddock.
     p. cm.
   ISBN 1-56054-589-5 (alk. paper : lg. print)
   1. Large type books. I. Title.
[PR6052.A3128P53   1993]   92-33397
823'.914—dc20   CIP

All the characters and events portrayed in this work are fictitious.

Thorndike Large Print® General Series edition published in 1993 by arrangement with Walker Publishing Company, Inc.

Cover design by James B. Murray.

The tree indicium is a trademark of Thorndike Press.

This book is printed on acid-free, high opacity paper. ∞

Many grateful thanks are due to the following for their assistance and patience in the writing of this book: John Kennedy Melling and Paul Biddle for their background information; Peter Rubie and Barbara Godfrey for their faith in me; and, especially, Melanie, as always, for being there.

Part I

One

Barrow-In-Furness

Inspector Calvert of the Cumbrian police was standing at his office window when the silver BMW 525i turned into the car park below him. With the habit born of twenty years in the police force, Calvert noted the car number almost unconsciously — it was only one year behind the current registration — and knew intuitively that this was the man he had been told about on the phone that morning: Inspector Steven Redmond — of Special Branch.

The deputy chief constable had told him no more than that Redmond was to be given every co-operation during his stay in Barrow. The DCC had not said why Redmond had suddenly been wished upon them by New Scotland Yard, but it was not difficult to deduce the reason; when a computer expert working on a weapons guidance system for nuclear hunter-killer submarines decided to blow his brains out in his bedroom, there was bound to be some interest generated within the security services.

Even so, Calvert found it vaguely insulting,

as if London did not trust the local police to deal with the investigation, but there was damn-all he could do about it. With any luck Redmond would not be around for too long because there was little doubt Phillips's death was a straight case of suicide.

The BMW had parked about thirty yards from the entrance — Redmond had carefully avoided the spaces reserved for visiting VIPs, Calvert noted — and a slightly built man with brown hair cut fashionably short climbed out. He would only just have made the minimum height requirement of five feet eight inches, Calvert realised, wondering how Redmond had coped during his time on the beat. Not that he would have been on it for very long. Calvert watched Redmond take an expensive-looking briefcase out of the car's boot and walk briskly towards the main entrance, locking the car with a remote control fob as he went. Redmond had Accelerated Promotion written all over him, because he could only be in his early thirties at most yet was already an inspector — Calvert had just celebrated his forty-second birthday and knew he was unlikely to rise any higher. Redmond was in Special Branch as well — and they were pretty choosy as regards their recruits. . . . He was probably looking at a future chief constable, Calvert decided morosely, a fucking whizz-kid, which was all he needed. . . .

As Redmond moved out of sight below, Calvert moved back to his desk and pressed the intercom button.

"Front desk," boomed a distorted, unrecognisable voice.

"Calvert here. If that's Inspector Redmond just arriving, get someone to bring him up here and have some coffee laid on."

"Will do, sir."

Calvert flicked off the intercom, stared at it with a faint expression of distaste, then sat down at his desk. It was always a pain having people descend on you, whether it was from Divisional HQ or from New Scotland Yard, but it was worse when Special Branch — or the Branch as its officers called it — was involved. They would only tell you what they thought you ought to know, which in some cases was damn-all, and a lot of the time, they weren't investigating criminal activities at all — unless you counted being involved in a Greenpeace rally or organising a boycott of South African goods criminal (which Calvert didn't); they weren't pursuing what Calvert saw as real police work, the maintenance of Law and Order.

A knock on the door interrupted Calvert's reverie. "Come in," he said briskly and looked up as Redmond entered. The thought crossed

11

his mind that Branch officers were supposed to be able to blend into whatever social group they were working with: if that was the case, then Redmond, with his expensive leather jacket, aviator-style sunglasses, and designer stubble, must have been investigating yuppies for some time. Yet his clasp as they shook hands was firm enough, Calvert conceded reluctantly.

"My name's Redmond," the other man said emphatically. "Inspector Calvert, I take it?"

"I am," Calvert said awkwardly, vaguely aware that Redmond had in some way already seized the advantage. He tried to place Redmond's accent. It was almost pure Home Counties, refined without being overdone, but there was the faintest trace of a North Country burr as well. "Grab a seat." He indicated the chair in front of the desk.

"Thank you." Redmond sat, removing his glasses and tucking one of the earpieces into his breast pocket so that the lenses hung down from it. Somehow, that one gesture seemed to crystallize Calvert's impressions — he did not like Redmond one little bit.

"I take it you've come about Phillips?"

"Yes," Redmond said slowly. He shrugged. "I was in Glasgow, they needed someone on the spot in a hurry, so here I am." He smiled faintly, as if to say, nothing to do with me.

"Glasgow?" Calvert echoed thoughtfully. "How much do you know about Phillips's death then?"

"I received a fax giving me all the background details, the scene of death report and so on, but that's about all." He shrugged again. "All I know is that he worked for a computer firm under contract to the Ministry of Defence."

Calvert nodded. "Comelec. They've been developing some sort of computerised guidance system for use aboard submarines, but that's about all we know. Phillips was under contract to them, but part of his work apparently involved going aboard the subs in the Vickers yard, so he had quite a high security clearance."

"Which is why they want me to take a closer look, presumably," Redmond said thoughtfully, almost to himself. He looked at Calvert. "So why did he do it?"

"Top himself, you mean?" Calvert shrugged. "He didn't leave a note or anything, but apparently his contract was to be terminated at the end of the month. That could have done it, I suppose, but given his qualifications and experience, I wouldn't have thought he'd have had much difficulty finding another job."

"If he was that good, why was Comelec getting rid of him?"

Again, Calvert shrugged. "You'd have to ask Comelec that. All they've said so far is that they're closing down one of their projects here and he was on it. They're getting rid of five or six people on top of Phillips, most of them computer specialists or technicians of some sort."

"But Phillips's work involved the nuclear subs?"

"Yes. They're built here and they return here periodically for refits or modernisation. Comelec has offices in the dockyard, which is where Phillips worked."

Redmond nodded absently, his eyes unfocused as he stared out of the window. "Phillips was divorced, wasn't he?"

"Yes — eight years ago."

Redmond grimaced. "So it's unlikely that he was brooding about that, not after all this time."

"His colleagues said he never mentioned his wife at all, but then he was a bit of a loner, by all accounts, and he'd only been in Barrow for six months, so nobody really knew him that well anyway." Calvert spread his hands in a gesture of helplessness.

Redmond nodded pensively, then said, "Are there any indications at all that it wasn't suicide?"

Calvert shook his head. "There was no evidence of a forced entry into the house, or of a struggle. The only fingerprints on the shotgun were his own, and they were consistent with his holding it up to his mouth and squeezing the trigger. The gun was his own — he went shooting with a local club about once a month." Calvert sighed. "Nothing was stolen, no sensitive documents are missing from Comelec, nor were any found at his home. No, it looks pretty definite that he came home, had his tea, went upstairs, got the gun out, sat on the bed, and killed himself."

Redmond frowned. "Just like that? He hadn't had a drink?"

"There were no traces in the bloodstream, no."

"Was he teetotal?"

"No, but he only drank occasionally. Is that significant?"

"I think that if I were about to blow my brains out, I'd want a stiff drink first, even if only for one last time — but no, I don't suppose it is significant." Redmond pursed his lips, his eyes fixed on the desk top with that unfocused look that Calvert decided was characteristic of him, then grimaced suddenly. "I suppose I'd better talk to his boss at Comelec — Gilroy, isn't it?"

"Gilroy, yes," Calvert nodded. "Maybe you'll get more out of him than we have. He keeps quoting the Official Secrets Act at us."

"Understandable, I suppose, if his firm's working with nuclear submarines." Redmond's tone was noncommittal, but Calvert suspected that the other man fully approved of Gilroy's reticence, even when it made a standard police investigation unnecessarily difficult. Redmond would go far in the Branch, Calvert decided: he was bright, capable, and would toe the party line, come what may.

Calvert pulled himself up short. It wasn't his concern, after all. "Okay," he said briskly. "I'll give Gilroy a ring and let him know you're coming."

Redmond glanced up at the lowering sky as he went back out to his car and grimaced as he felt the first drops of rain: there was now no trace of the bright sunshine in which he had driven down from Glasgow. It looked as though the forecasters were going to be right for once. That's all I need, he thought glumly, stuck in a godforsaken place like Barrow-In-Furness on a bloody dead-end assignment with it pissing down with rain. He used the remote control to turn off the alarm and unlock the car, then climbed in, wondering why he had been asked to look into what seemed to be a pretty clear-cut case of suicide. Had it simply been because he had been handy — in the minds of those in Whitehall, Glasgow and Barrow were virtually next door — or had someone got it in for him down there? Or maybe, just maybe, there was more to this than anyone had told him so far. . . . He snorted derisively. Fat chance.

He turned on the ignition and a blast of rock music came pounding out of the car's speakers as he pulled on his seat belt and drove away. His fingers tapped out an unconscious rhythm on the wheel in time to Led Zeppelin, but he was only half listening, still brooding about the instructions he had been given to look into Phillips's death. That had been all he had been told, no indication as to what to look for, whether there was any hint of a breach of security — or what kind of report they wanted in London. As a result, it was difficult to know how to play it. Did they want an exhaustive, in-depth probe lasting several days and involving up to half a dozen officers, or were they simply looking to have the file officially closed as soon as was decently possible — a whitewash job, in other words? Tricky, because if he read it the wrong way, it would not do his standing at the Yard much good. The fact that he had been given so little

guidance implied the second alternative —
they just wanted him to go through the motions — but it might mean someone in London, one of his rivals, was digging a trap for
him to fall into. There would be several who
would not mind seeing him come a cropper.
. . . He rubbed his chin thoughtfully, then
grimaced at the stubble: he hadn't even had
a chance to shave yet.

His attention was brought back abruptly as
he turned into the street leading to the dockyard gates. To the right of the gates was a
small group of people, most of them carrying
placards, who were being kept in place by half
a dozen or so uniformed policemen. As he approached, Redmond could see what was written on the banners: RIGHT TO WORK, NO
DOCKYARD CUTS, and JOBS NOT PROMISES.
Vaguely, he recalled hearing news reports
about possible cutbacks in the dockyard now
that contracts for two hunter-killer subs had
been cancelled, so presumably the demonstrators were protesting about that. There was
a BBC camera crew with a reporter holding
a microphone in front of one of the protesters,
but it seemed peaceful enough. Redmond
brought the car to a halt and wound down
the window to show his warrant card to the
Navy sentry on duty at the gate.

As the rating studied it, a memory forced

its way into Redmond's mind, a similar scene that had taken place years before, but outside the gates of a colliery in a Yorkshire mining village. The Coal Board had just announced it was closing the pit, and a crowd of angry miners had gathered outside, demanding to speak to the area manager, who was supposed to have been inside. The mood had been ugly — and there had been only two policemen confronting them, one of them trying vainly to make them see reason, but then a stone had come hurtling out of the crowd, dislodging his helmet, and a moment later, the mob had surged forward, pushing him and his colleague into the wire-mesh gate as they forced it open. Both policemen had ended up in hospital, the one who had tried to talk to them with two broken ribs, extensive bruising, and a concussion.

That policeman had been his father. . . .

"Right, sir," said the sentry, returning the card. "You'll find Comelec about a hundred yards along the road here, to your right."

"Thanks," said Redmond, returning the card to his pocket. He was just about to drive on when he saw one of the demonstrators pointing towards him, and, in a flash of intuition, he knew exactly what was running through the other man's mind. Expensive car, ID pass — that's one of Them, the employers, the Government, the Establishment, whoever. The protester turned and shouted something; the next moment, the police line buckled as the demonstrators pushed forward, one of the constables stumbling and falling, pulling his arms up over his head to shield himself as he went down. Redmond slammed the car into first and drove off, accelerating through the opening gates. Almost immediately, he felt a wave of self-disgust and eased his foot off the throttle, but as he glanced in his mirror and saw the gates swinging shut behind him, he could not help letting out a small sigh of relief. Not that it would have mattered, he realised ruefully — the pickets had not even reached the gates, but had been forced back by the rest of the police line. For a moment he wondered if any of them had used their truncheons — never a good idea with cameras present — but then dismissed the thought as he drew up in front of a two-storey office building with the initials CE in a logo design above the door.

Gilroy was a lean, intense man, almost completely bald, whose desk was totally devoid of any papers or other encumbrances beyond a large desk blotter in front of him. To his left was an IBM PC terminal to which he could push himself on the castors of his chair, but that was the only hint that this was the office of a senior manager in a computer firm.

"Inspector Redmond," said Gilroy, shaking his visitor's hand and showing him to a seat. "You've come about Phillips, I take it? London told me to extend every cooperation to you." He shook his head. "Terrible business. Came as a shock to all of us." He didn't sound either shocked or upset.

"I can imagine," Redmond replied.

"So — what can I do for you?"

"Firstly, I'll need to look at Phillips's personal dossier, then I'd like to talk to those colleagues who were closest to him."

Gilroy nodded. "Of course. I feel I should warn you, Inspector, that Phillips did tend to keep very much to himself in a social sense. I'm not sure that any of us really knew him that well. He had only been here six months, after all."

"What exactly was he working on here?"

Gilroy hesitated, then said carefully, "The nature of his work does fall under the heading of classified information, Inspector."

Redmond bit back an exasperated retort and instead said patiently, "Mr. Gilroy, I'm not one of your local bobbies, I'm in Special Branch, remember?" And I've probably been privy to more Official Secrets than you've had hot dinners, sunshine, he added silently. "I need to know what Phillips was working on. It may have a bearing on whether this was suicide — or murder," he finished, wondering whether he was overdoing it with the melodramatic pause and emphasis on the last word.

"I see," Gilroy said, with the look of a man with a nasty taste in his mouth. "Very well," he added with obvious reluctance. "Phillips's work involved developing a computerised guidance system using lasers that could be used either by submarines for underwater navigation or by torpedoes to home in on their targets. The project consisted of about a dozen people, most of them systems analysts or programmers. Phillips was the deputy head of the project."

"He'd been working on it for six months? How long had the project been running altogether?"

"Just under a year, all told."

"Where had he been before that?"

"On a similar type of project, I believe, certainly one using a laser guidance system, anyway."

"A Comelec project?"

Gilroy shook his head. "No. Phillips worked for us on a contract basis, but his transfer here was arranged through the MOD."

Redmond nodded. It was by no means an unusual arrangement in the field of Ministry of Defence computer research. There were dozens of experts like Phillips who, because they had been given a high security clearance, were shunted around from one project to another at the ministry's behest. "So he would have had access to the submarines themselves?"

Gilroy shook his head. "Actually, he hadn't. Obviously, developing such a system would involve some knowledge of the design of submarines, especially the nuclear ones, but his would only have been minimal. His brief was to test the system itself via computer models, not to install it." Gilroy smiled thinly, as though enjoying cutting off that line of enquiry. "He would not have been in a position to pass on classified information about the nuclear submarines that have been built or refitted here, if that's what you had in mind."

"Quite," Redmond replied, trying to cover the fact that this was exactly what he had been thinking. "Was he good at his job?"

"Excellent. First-rate."

"So why was his contract being terminated?"

"The project itself was terminated."

"Why?"

"Lack of progress. We kept getting malfunctions. Whitehall decided to cancel the funding and so the project was no longer viable."

"Were all the people working on it sacked?"

"No," Gilroy admitted slowly. "Phillips and five others were made redundant."

"Why those five and not the others? If Phillips was that good —"

"Not my decision, Inspector," Gilroy interrupted smoothly. "It came from head office in London. I can only assume that there weren't really any niches for him in any of our other projects, so . . ." Gilroy allowed his voice to trail away.

So you gave him the boot and he went home and stuck the barrel of a shotgun in his mouth and left his brains spattered all over the wall behind him and you really don't give a shit, do you? Redmond thought, but his face remained impassive. "I see," he said neutrally. "It would have come as rather a blow to him, though, wouldn't it? I mean, he was forty-seven years old and other computer firms would have been looking for younger men, wouldn't they?"

"He would have been given excellent references by us . . . but yes, you're probably right," Gilroy conceded. "As I said, it was not my decision," he added defensively.

No, but you didn't exactly fight tooth and nail to keep him, did you? "No, I don't suppose it was. Very well, Mr. Gilroy, we'd better press on. If I could have a look at Phillips's file, then I'll have a word with some of his

24

colleagues, if I may."

"Certainly, Inspector."

London

The Metropolitan Police Special Branch, to give it its full title, is very much an organisation set apart from its peers. Although its members carry the same warrant cards as any other police officer and are ultimately answerable to the Metropolitan Police commissioner, the Branch's role differs from that of the police in general in that its brief is the protection of national security rather than that of investigating crime. Amongst its many and varied duties are guarding cabinet ministers and visiting politicians, vetting every application for British citizenship, mounting a round-the-clock watch on all ports and airports, providing security for foreign embassies, maintaining records on overseas visitors and immigrants, carrying out surveillance on organisations adjudged to be subversive, and executing arrests under the Official Secrets Act. To help carry out these duties, computer files on over two million individuals are kept at Jubilee House at the southern end of Putney Bridge, but the Branch has its headquarters on the top floor of New Scotland Yard itself. The permanent staff, as well as any visitors, have to wear ID badges displaying their photographs and names and franked with a computer bar code; these codes allow or prevent access to the higher security areas on the floor.

It was one of these badges that Redmond was pinning to his lapel as he emerged from the lift and headed across the open-plan main office towards his own "office," a ten-by-ten cubbyhole divided from its neighbours by glass partitions: he often thought of them as goldfish bowls. He nodded to a few acquaintances on his way, but did not pause to speak to anyone, even though he had been away for several days. As he pushed his office door open, the internal phone on his desk began to ring — surprise, surprise, he thought and picked it up. "Redmond."

"Selvey here. Come on in, will you?"

Superintendent Bill Selvey, with his powerful frame and broken nose, looked more like a rugby prop forward than a top-echelon policeman — he had indeed played regularly for the Met in his younger days — but anyone tempted to dismiss him as being more brawn than brains would have been well advised to look more closely. You did not rise as high and as fast as he had — a superintendent at thirty-eight — without being a very capable police officer. Yet, even now, after working with Selvey for nearly four years, Redmond still had to remind himself that there was an incisive, first-class brain under his boss's hail-fellow-well-met exterior.

"Sit down, Steve," Selvey said absently. "Just got to finish this off." He waved the sheaf of documents he was reading, but without looking up. With anyone else, such a gesture would have been a simple case of playing power games, but Redmond knew that Selvey had no time for such things.

He sat, glancing quickly around Selvey's office. Being a superintendent, Selvey was entitled to a separate office, not to mention a window overlooking the city. One day, Redmond thought, as he made himself comfortable. One day . . .

Selvey scribbled an illegible signature at the bottom of the circulation slip, then tossed the bundle of papers carelessly into his out tray. "Sorry about that. Okay — Phillips. Suicide?"

Redmond smiled faintly — Selvey never was one for beating about the bush. He paused momentarily before answering, wondering again if Selvey knew something he didn't, then took the plunge. "I'd say suicide, sir. There's nothing to indicate anything else."

Selvey nodded. "While the balance of his mind was disturbed, you mean?" His voice was faintly ironic as he intoned the almost ritualistic coroner's phrase.

27

"He'd just got the sack," Redmond pointed out. "At his age, he probably thought he'd never get another job, although, given his qualifications and his security clearance, I'd have thought he wouldn't have had that much trouble. The thing is, did he know that?"

"True," Selvey agreed.

"His colleagues all thought he was a bit morose at the best of times. Kept pretty much to himself, didn't have much of a sense of humour, that sort of thing. They didn't exactly describe him as a manic-depressive, but apparently, he was hardly a bundle of laughs either. I'm pretty sure the jury will return a suicide verdict."

"Any security implications?"

"Not so far. He was in a White File, of course, but that was all." Redmond stared at Selvey — had the question been as casual as it had sounded? "I could do a follow-up check if you like, sir," he suggested tentatively.

"You might have to," Selvey replied, leaning back in his large swivel chair. "Let me put you in the picture. Phillips is the fourth computer expert involved in MOD research work to have died in the past six months and someone in Whitehall seems to be getting a little worried about it. Presumably, they think some rogue KGB hit man who hasn't heard of *glasnost* or — God forbid — the IRA is going around knocking them all off or something. Anyway, the Branch has been asked to look into it. Or, rather, you have."

"I see," Redmond said noncommittally. "Four deaths, you said?"

"I did." Selvey reached into the top desk drawer on his left and took out a manila folder. He opened it and held up the top page inside. "Number one — Peter Hayward. Found dead in his car in a locked garage with the engine still running. Number two — Robert Barclay. He had a tyre blow out at seventy and wrapped his car round a tree. Number three — Mark Inchmore. Gas explosion in his home. Phillips was number four. Each one was, or had recently been, involved in research for the Ministry of Defence, and all of them were computer experts. Nothing to indicate foul play in any of their deaths, but none of them died of natural causes either — so someone upstairs wants it checked out. Lo and behold, we have Project Mandrake — that's the code name for the investigation."

"And I drew the short straw?" Redmond asked heavily.

"Afraid so."

"What exactly do you want?"

"A detailed report. One that'll satisfy whoever it is that wants it looked into. Go through each of them with a fine-tooth comb, see if there are any common factors — there could be, because nobody else has tried looking yet — or if there's anything to all this beyond pure coincidence."

"But you don't think there is?"

Selvey smiled faintly. "Let's just say I don't think you should bust a gut trying to uncover some dastardly plot. Sure, if you turn anything up, that's fine, but, reading between the lines, I don't think anyone's expecting you to perform miracles, so don't lose too much sleep over it."

"Message understood. What sort of help do I get?"

"Three officers, I should think. Hodge and Lennox be okay?"

Redmond nodded; he'd worked with both before. "They'll do fine."

"Anyone else you especially want?"

Redmond thought for a moment then said, "If we're going to be looking for common factors then I want someone who knows their way around computers."

Selvey nodded and scribbled a note on a pad. "I'll get someone from Records assigned to you. Anything else?" he asked, his tone of voice implying that there had better not be.

"I'll let you know if there is, sir."

"Right." Selvey passed the folder across to

Redmond. "It's all in there. Keep me posted."

"Will do, sir."

Redmond was deep in thought as he headed back to his own office. This was the kind of job everybody hated, the "whitewash" report, calculated to reassure the powers-that-be everything was under control, but which could come back to haunt its compiler if subsequent events proved him wrong. It would be his name on the report if it all blew up, thought Redmond sourly. I could have done without this. Why the hell did Selvey have to choose me?

The answer, he realised, was simple: he had happened to be available when Phillips shot himself. But even if he found something, Redmond would still gain no kudos for it; this was a strictly no-win situation, with the distinct possibility of serious damage to his career prospects.

Redmond decided he'd make damn sure he covered himself on this one. It was his neck on the line, after all.

Two

Redmond finished reading the last of the files he had requested, then leaned back in his chair, rubbing his eyes. The gesture was more one of frustration than tiredness because there was absolutely nothing in any of the deaths as far as he could see that gave even the remotest indication that they were not what they appeared to be — accidents or suicides. He had been through the reports and inquest transcripts in minute detail and the only thing out of the ordinary was the fact that they had all occurred within a time span of twenty-three weeks. This was, presumably, why someone had decided a closer look was in order — they had been working on the adage "Once is happenstance, twice is coincidence, but the third time, it's enemy action." That was fair enough, but that was still a long way from proving that the four deaths were, in fact, linked. At the moment, there did not seem to be any evidence at all to suggest that this was the case.

Apart from being involved in MOD computer research work, the four men had little in common. Phillips had been a specialist in guidance systems, Hayward in detection and target acquisition, Barclay had concentrated on database and retrieval systems, while Inchmore had been developing a scrambler decoder. None of them had been to the same university or college and, although their paths had crossed occasionally over the years, as was almost inevitable given the fact that they had worked for the same ministry, there had been no apparent social contact. The deaths themselves had nothing in common, either.

Barclay had been on his way home after work when a front tyre blew out as he approached a sharp corner. He had lost control on the wet road and had smashed into a tree, breaking his neck: dead by the time the ambulance arrived. The tyre had been examined but there had been nothing to indicate that it had been tampered with. There had not been too much doubt about the verdict of accidental death, which had also been the case with Inchmore. He had returned home after a dinner party (some sort of departmental do, apparently) and had then been killed in an explosion caused by a gas leak, probably after turning the light on. The inquest had heard how there had been several leaks along that street in recent years, including one in that same house four years before; the verdict had been a virtual formality.

As regards the two suicides, each one seemed fairly clear-cut. Hayward's bank account had gone quite heavily into the red, and his wife had admitted that he had been quite worried about it during the weeks leading up to his death. An expected promotion at work had not materialised and it had been announced that the next year's poll tax would be increased by over a hundred pounds per adult. With a mortgage well in excess of a hundred thousand and with the bank making noises about clearing the overdraft without delay, Mrs. Hayward had found her husband sitting in his car in a locked garage with the engine running and a hosepipe attached to the exhaust that ran into the car itself. There had been no note left, but there had been no other realistic verdict for the inquest to reach.

The same applied to Phillips, Redmond decided — that had also been a pretty clear-cut case — but the problem was that each death could have been faked, and if you took all four together, you had to at least consider the possibility that they were not all they seemed. Which, in turn, meant that he would have to mount a very detailed, persuasive argument in establishing that this had been nothing more than a particularly unfortunate run of unconnected deaths.

Which was all it was, he was certain. Quite

apart from the fact that, because of their MOD involvement, each death had been very closely investigated without finding anything suspicious, there was also the consideration that the alternative, that they had all been murdered, was even more unlikely than a random series of deaths. Who would be behind it, for one thing? Again, he could see how the mind of the unknown instigator of this investigation was working: this could be a plot by what was left of the KGB to sabotage the UK's hitech defence research projects. There were at least two major objections to this theory as far as Redmond could see. Firstly, although the KGB was still active to some extent in the fields of intelligence gathering and espionage in the West, it was just not in the market for this kind of "wet" operation any more. They were too preoccupied with matters inside what had once been the USSR to mount such an operation.

The second objection was that it would just not be worth it. The victims were hardly top-ranking figures in their field, and so their deaths were not really harming the MOD research effort to any great extent. If the KGB really were to mount such a sophisticated, high-risk project, they'd be going for the top names, not the foot soldiers. No, KGB involvement just did not make sense.

This second argument also applied to industrial espionage — the victims just weren't important enough, even if, for the moment, he accepted the outrageous notion that a computer firm was employing a hit man to kill their competitors' experts. For the same reason, you could also rule out the IRA or any other terrorist group, quite apart from the fact that there had been no statements claiming responsibility for the deaths.

What it boiled down to was that there did not seem to be any reason for these four being singled out for execution.

A knock on the door interrupted his wandering thoughts. He called out, "Come in," and stood up, closing the file as a slim young woman with reddish blond hair cut stylishly short came in, nodding briefly at him. There was a slightly defensive air about her, but her gaze seemed steady enough as she said, "Sergeant Harper reporting, sir." Her voice was a slightly husky contralto.

"Er — right, Sergeant," Redmond replied, trying to conceal his surprise. Okay, so dossier photographs were never very good, but hers had done her considerably less than justice. Gail Harper was an attractive twenty-seven-year-old woman, in marked contrast to the rather plain-looking face that had stared back at him from her file. For a moment, he felt a brief glow of anticipation at the prospect of working with her and at the possibilities it raised — the "working" lunch, the meeting in the pub after work to discuss some aspect of the case — then pushed the thought aside, although not without regret. Complications like that he could do without, thank you very much. . . . "Do sit down," he added, wondering if she had noticed the hesitation.

"Thank you, sir." She took the seat in front of the desk, placed the folder she had been carrying on the desk top, then waited for him to begin, her features calm, composed — and aloof, her entire body language stating that this was strictly business. Fair enough, thought Redmond.

"You've read the file?" he asked, nodding at the folder she had brought with her. It had MANDRAKE stencilled on it in large letters.

"Yes, sir."

"Any thoughts about whether the deaths are connected?"

"Not really, sir," she replied without hesitation. "Beyond the obvious correlations, there don't appear to be any common factors."

"Okay. What I want you to do is to see if there are any buried in the files, anything at all that might link them, so you'll need to do a full-scale search on each of them."

"How deep do I go?"

"I want everything we've got. Background, previous career, qualifications, wives, girl-friends, bank accounts, medicals, what they did in their spare time, membership of clubs or societies, holidays abroad — anything you can find."

"You want to see if there's a pattern to the deaths, you mean."

"Exactly."

She stared speculatively at him with a directness that he found disconcerting. "Am I being told everything?" she asked bluntly.

"What do you mean?"

"Is there anything to find? I mean, do you have any reason to believe that the deaths are linked or is this just a case of running it through the computer to see what comes up? Am I going to spend days looking for something that isn't there?" There was a hint of impatience in her voice, an expert who suspected that her time was being wasted.

Which it probably was, Redmond thought suddenly. The realisation that she was thinking along the same lines as he himself a few minutes ago made him bite back the angry retort that he had been about to deliver. "I don't know," he said evenly, then added, with the barest perceptible edge in his voice now, "We won't know one way or the other until you do your stuff with the computer, will we?"

There was a momentary flush of anger in her blue eyes, instantly suppressed. "No, we won't — sir." Again, she met his gaze steadily. "How long do I have?"

"There's no time limit. Get as much data as you can."

She nodded. "What level access do I get to the files?"

"What's your present level?"

"Three."

Redmond raised his eyebrows slightly in surprise. Three was unusually high for a sergeant, even one who was serving her post-qualification year as a sergeant before a virtually automatic promotion to inspector — no mean achievement for a woman so young. "I'll get you access to level two," he said.

"I'll need a password."

"Rosebud. That'll get you into the files." It was his own password, chosen as a kind of tribute to the film *Citizen Kane* in one of his more whimsical moments.

"Rosebud," she echoed, nodding slightly as she committed it to memory, but there was no sign that she was aware of the reference. "And if I come across any 'Access Denied' messages?"

"Leave them be," he said firmly.

She nodded again as if this confirmed what she had already suspected, that this was just an exercise in going through the motions.

"Right, sir, I'll get started. How often do you want reports?"

Redmond hesitated, torn between the desire to keep a close eye on the investigation and the realisation that if he did, he would have to wade through piles of computer printouts. "Just let me know of any common factors you turn up, but record everything for the final report."

"Understood, sir," she said briskly. "I'd better get started." She rose to her feet, evidently eager to be gone. "Unless there's anything else?"

"No. Just be sure you don't miss anything." Now why the hell did I say that? he asked himself. I've put her back up enough already. . . .

"Don't worry, sir," she said frostily. "I won't."

Redmond sat staring at the door for several seconds after she had gone, then shook his head slowly. Working with her was not exactly going to be a bundle of laughs by the looks of it. In a way, he could not blame her resentment at this assignment, because it matched his own. She, too, was earmarked for greater things and, like himself, almost certainly felt that this investigation was a potential career damager. The thing was, if she let her feelings show as openly as she had, she would not get very far in the Branch, no matter how good she was at her job.

Redmond shrugged and picked up the top file again. That was her problem, not his.

Once she was back in the Computer Room, the large office that was separated from the main area by a short corridor, Gail sat in front of her computer and turned it on. She began to access the relevant files, but with only half her mind on what she was doing, because she was still thinking about Redmond and his unspoken attitude towards Mandrake. It was obvious that he shared her view that it was all a huge waste of time, but there was nothing either of them could do about it; they were stuck with it, like it or not, so she would just have to make the best of it. And the trouble was, she had hardly got off on the right foot with him, if she were honest about it.

She had heard of Redmond, but knew little more about him other than that he was on his way up — and fast. He was generally held to be ambitious, capable — but not much liked; a bit of a "crawler," a sycophant, really, but she would have to work with him for the next few days at any rate. At least he did not seem to be as patronising as other male officers in the Branch, who tended to be chauvinistic to a greater or lesser extent.

With an almost conscious effort, she focused her attention on the VDT display and inside a few minutes, she was totally absorbed in her work. For her, hunting through computer files and accessing records had its own peculiar pleasure. This was what she had done as a teenager, "hacking" into programmes and protected files with almost contemptuous ease before leaving her "calling card," an instruction or message written into the file that might not be discovered for weeks or months. Now, she was doing it with official approval — and to a higher level than before — but the game still held its old seductive fascination.

At first, everything went smoothly, but after ten minutes or so, she ran into a "Restricted Access" flag while working through Hayward's biographical details. Next to the flashing message was the instruction "Refer to Olympus," which she had never seen before. Nevertheless, she knew what it meant — the details of that particular part of Hayward's career, covering six months last year, were contained in the Olympus files, which, as their name implied, were the most secret in the Branch's records. Access to them was far above her, or Redmond's, level. Exasperated, she pressed on only to swear again five minutes later when she found the same thing in

Inchmore's dossier. She was about to hit the exit key in annoyance before she stopped herself and looked at the display again. As with Hayward, the restricted-access flag covered a period of time last year, although it was only three months in this case and did not overlap with Hayward's "gap." There had been nothing in Barclay's file, however, but she was still aware of a sense of anticipation as she called up Phillips's file — and there it was. The same reference to the Olympus files as with Hayward and Inchmore, only this time, the gap covered almost a year — and overlapped both of the others at different times.

"You still at it, Gail?" said a voice suddenly from the office doorway. "It's nearly half past six." The voice belonged to Inspector Ellis, the records supervisor.

"Is it?" she said, startled. "Bloody hell, so it is. I'm supposed to be going out at eight. I got a bit caught up." She stared at the glowing VDT screen, then, reluctantly, cleared it and turned the computer off.

"Trying to sort out a problem?" Ellis asked.

"Sort of," she replied evasively. "But it'll have to wait. I must dash if I'm not going to be late for my date."

"Okay, okay, here's the tenner," said Roger Stone resignedly, handing Redmond a ten pound note as they emerged from the squash court changing room.

"Like taking candy from a baby," Redmond grinned, pocketing the note.

"Dunno why I keep agreeing to it," Stone grumbled good-naturedly. "I'll be bloody bankrupt if this keeps on."

"You? Don't make me laugh. You're rolling in it."

"I wish I was. I've got a wife and two kids around my neck — you want to try it some time, instead of being footloose and fancy-free."

Stone had not been looking at Redmond while he had been speaking and so he did not see the shadow that had passed momentarily across the other man's face, but when Redmond spoke, his voice was light and bantering still. "Your own fault, Roger. Now if you'd stayed single . . ."

"Don't remind me," said Stone, grinning.

"Now don't give me that — you love every minute of it."

"Don't bank on that," Stone replied as they reached the foot of the steps that led up to the Leisure Centre bar. "Anyway, this first lager will slide down a treat." Redmond had the impression he'd only said that to change the subject.

The stairs emerged into the centre of the

bar, which was predictably furnished — modern and plastic, with a window along one entire wall overlooking the swimming pool.

"Steve! Roger!" a voice called out. Redmond turned and saw Julie Curren waving to him from a table by the window. She was beckoning him over, indicating the empty seats at the table. Next to her was another woman, tall, blond, and slim, who was regarding him with obvious interest.

"Now who is that rather tasty piece with Julie?" asked Stone. "I could go for that."

"Down boy," Redmond grinned. "I saw her first. Anyway, you're a married man. Get the drinks in, will you?" He handed over the ten pound note. Stone headed towards the bar, while Redmond made his way over to the two women. As he approached, he could see that the other woman was attractive enough in an overdone way — she wore too much make-up, for example — and, in all honesty, was still not as good-looking as Julie, but she'd do, no doubt about that. . . .

"Steve, this is Sandra. Sandra, this is Steve."

"Hi," said Redmond, sitting down next to Sandra.

"Pleased to meet you," she replied. "Julie tells me you're a policeman."

"Afraid so," he admitted wryly, fighting down the momentary annoyance he always felt

45

at being forced to reveal his job; when possible, he did not. Was it because he was vaguely ashamed of it, or because it tended to put people on the defensive? Or didn't it suit the image he tried to project of himself?

"You certainly don't look like one," she told him, smiling invitingly.

"That's the nicest thing anyone's said to me today."

"We were watching you playing squash. Do you always play like that? As though your life depended on it. It's only a game, after all."

"Games are only worth playing if you play them to win." He grinned. "I'm not sure Roger has the same view."

Stone appeared with the drinks, but did not stay long, because Julie finished her drink fairly rapidly and asked him if he could give her a lift home. The two of them left, Julie smiling at Redmond as if sharing some secret with him.

"Are they having an affair or something?" Sandra asked, as they went out.

Redmond seemed genuinely amused. "What — Roger and Julie? Hardly. She just wanted to get him out of the way." He looked intently at her. "I suspect she's playing Cupid."

"Quite possibly," she admitted. "I get the impression you and she have known each other for a while."

"We have," he said, nodding. "Julie and I go back quite a few years. She's a good friend. A very good friend," he added, almost to himself, then smiled at Sandra. "Look, come on, what are we doing talking about Julie? I mean, she's done her damnedest to make sure we've been left to ourselves, so the least we can do is make the most of it."

"I'll go along with that." She chuckled throatily. "What do you suggest?"

"That I offer you a lift home."

She stared appraisingly at him. "You don't waste much time, do you?"

"Nope," he said, grinning mischievously. "Unfortunately, I have my car with me."

"In that case, I'll follow you home."

Her eyes held his, then she smiled slowly. "Okay," she said huskily. "You're on."

"Penny for them? Or is the food that bad?"

Gail looked up apologetically from the ravioli she had been toying with for the past ten minutes or so and shook her head. "Sorry. It's delicious. It's just — something's come up at work. It's bugging me."

"So I see. You've been off in another world all evening. I thought it was something I'd said."

"No, really, it isn't you, Alan." She reached

out and put her hand over his, but the gesture felt awkward, artificial. "I'm just not very good company tonight, I'm afraid." Suddenly, unaccountably, she found herself thinking of Redmond.

"Then we'll have to cheer you up, won't we? How does Stringfellow's grab you?"

Stringfellow's did not grab her at all, but she forced a smile onto her face and a brightness into her voice. "Sounds great."

"Okay, let's go."

If it had been Don or Mike, she reflected, someone she knew better, she would have told him the truth — that she just wasn't in the mood — and he would have understood. But she had only been out with Alan three times and they were still at the stage of getting to know each other. She liked what she had seen of him so far and was fairly sure that he'd be a considerate lover; in fact, she'd had vague plans about finding out about that tonight, but not now. . . . The point was that she did not want to put him off altogether — so she went along to the nightclub with him. Yet, even there, with the pounding disco beat and flashing lights, the thought of those restricted-access flags kept nagging at her. It was not unusual for people working on high-priority projects, but for it to have happened on three of the Mandrake subjects was curious, to say the least. Oh, come on, she told herself as Alan pulled her close for a slow dance, it's probably nothing at all. . . . Forget it!

It was well after midnight when he brought her home, walking up with her to the door of her second-floor flat in Chelsea. She let him kiss her, but when she felt his hand on her breast, she knew that it just wouldn't work, not tonight. Gently, she disengaged herself. "Thanks for the evening, Alan. Sorry I've been such a wet blanket."

"I never noticed," he said gallantly. "Don't I get invited in for a nightcap this time?" There was more than a hint of disappointment behind his boisterous tone.

Yes, she had invited him in last time and she'd been very tempted to let him stay the night as well, she remembered. For a moment, she felt sorry for him; he must have been expecting the whole works tonight. "Look, I'm sorry, Alan, but I really am bushed. I didn't finish work until after seven and I've got to be in early tomorrow. Maybe next time?" she finished, injecting a note of invitation into her voice.

"Yes," he said, not bothering to hide his disappointment now. "Maybe next time. I'll call you tomorrow, okay?"

"Okay."

She felt a pang of guilt as she closed the

49

door and had a sudden premonition that he would not call her tomorrow or any other day. I really blew that one, she told herself. A pity — I rather liked him. For a moment, she cursed Redmond — why had he landed her with an assignment that would interfere with her love life? — but then shook her head, frowning suddenly, wondering why she was thinking about him again. Then her eyes came to rest on her computer terminal on its desk under the window. She hesitated, glancing at her watch, then went over to it, switched it on. Again, she paused, as she considered what she was about to do, then, rapidly, deftly, she started keying in instructions, closing her mind to the likely consequences if she made a mistake. The excitement of the hunt, of hacking into forbidden areas, had gripped her once more, the patient stalking through the electronic labyrinth as she eased her way into the system and began to track down her quarry. Time and again, she stared at the screen in impotent frustration as she came up against an "Access Denied" message, but each time, she cleared the screen and tried again. Patience; that was what a hacker needed most.

It was almost three-thirty before she found what she was looking for.

Three

Redmond tried unsuccessfully to stifle a yawn as he emerged from the lift and caught a momentary expression of amusement, instantly suppressed, on DC Wilkinson's face as they passed in the doorway. Bloody hell, thought Redmond, divining the reason for Wilkinson's reaction, do I look that bad? Very probably, he decided, aware of the dull headache throbbing away just behind his eyeballs. If he still looked anything like the gaunt, hollow-eyed wreck that had stared back at him from the shaving mirror that morning, then it must be apparent to everyone that DI Redmond had a hangover. Hardly surprising, of course, as he had not returned home until nearly four that morning, exhausted by Sandra's enthusiasm for sex. An almost feral grin crossed Redmond's face as a vivid image of her kneeling astride him flashed into his mind: Jesus, what a lay . . . And almost the best part about the whole thing had been the fact that there were no strings involved. As far as she was concerned, they'd had their fun and that was it — if he wanted to repeat it, he knew where to find her. When he had dressed and left her just slipping off into sleep, it had been without any feelings of guilt or encumbrance. Ships in the night, which was just the way he wanted it.

It hadn't always been like that, though, had it? Not when Elaine . . . With an effort, he shut off that avenue of thought. Far better to think of Sandra bending over him, her hair brushing softly across his groin, or of her urgent, panted instructions as she approached her orgasm, faster, faster, that's right, oh God, yes. . . .

There was an undeniably smug expression on his face as he sat down behind his desk, but it disappeared as soon as he saw the handwritten note that had been left there. It was from Sergeant Harper, asking him if he could drop by when he arrived. He looked at his watch, wondering if there had been an implied criticism in the message, but he was only about ten minutes late — what time had she come in, for God's sake?

The Computer Section was at the far end of the building and Redmond paused on his way to buy a coffee from the automatic vending machine. There were one or two irritated glances directed at him as he went into the section and he remembered that they did not like food or drink to be taken anywhere near their precious machines, but he pressed on regardless, sipping from the Styrofoam cup as he went over to Gail Harper's station. She looked up as he approached, her eyes flickering momentarily to the cup, then nodded briefly at him. There was no visible reaction on her face to his appearance — either she hadn't noticed or did not think it important.

"You got my message then, sir?"

"I'm here, aren't I?"

"I've turned up something in the files that hasn't been mentioned so far." She was typing in instructions on her terminal keyboard as she spoke.

Redmond drew up a typist's chair and sat next to her. "Go on," he said, taking another sip of coffee.

"This came up in three of the personal dossiers." She nodded at the VDT. On it had appeared the words HAYWARD INCHMORE PHILLIPS: PICCOLO.

"Piccolo?" Redmond asked, mystified. "What the hell's that?"

She shrugged. "I was hoping you might be able to tell me. It must be an MOD research project or something, because all three of them were working on it at one time or another." She pressed another key and the three names appeared again, this time with dates next to them. "Hayward was on it for six months, Inchmore for three, and Phillips for a year

53

or thereabouts."

"So I can see," Redmond said. "But what is it?"

"Like I said, I don't know. Even using level two, I still can't get any information. All I get is 'Access Denied.' I think it's classified Olympus."

"Which means it is very important," Redmond said, half to himself. He hesitated a moment, then reached over and, with a dexterity that surprised Gail, rapidly keyed in the password "Rosebud" followed by "/*7". "Strictly speaking, I'm not supposed to know that code," he murmured to her as they waited for the display to reappear. He typed in ACCESS PICCOLO, then swore softly as "Access Denied" appeared once more. "Shit," he muttered. "It must be Olympus. . . ."

His voice trailed away as he realised the implications. If Piccolo was important enough to be stored in Olympus, then he was getting out of his depth. He glanced at Gail and saw something in her eyes that brought a jolt of realisation. "You've already done this." He pointed at the screen.

She hesitated, then nodded. "I didn't use the same password — but yes, I did. That was where I found the reference to Piccolo. It isn't mentioned on level two."

Redmond drew in his breath, then glanced

quickly around at the other computer operators. "Outside," he said curtly. "Now."

She pressed the reset key on her machine, then followed him out, her face set in an impassive mask.

As she emerged into the corridor, Redmond said icily, "Just what the hell were you doing hacking into level one files? You're level three, remember, with temporary access to two."

"I was simply carrying out your instructions, sir." She stood rigidly to attention, her eyes fixed on a point somewhere beyond his left shoulder.

"I never told you to hack into level one files, for God's sake!"

"With all due respect, sir," — she sounded anything but respectful — "I didn't actually 'hack' into anything, as you put it. I merely gained access to level one to see if I could come up with any further information. There were gaps in the biographical details on level two, so I was trying to see if I could fill those gaps — they could be significant. All I could find on level one were these references to Piccolo. You did tell me to try and dig up any data I could find on the victims, sir," she pointed out.

"Within limits, for God's sake. I —" He broke off as someone came through the double doors ten yards away and hurried past, casting a curious glance their way. Redmond saw an open doorway opposite and went over to it, sticking his head round the door. Inside was a bank of printers but no people. "In here," he snapped. Inside, he glared at her for several seconds. "Right," he said slowly. "A few simple and, I would have thought, self-evident facts for your consideration, Sergeant Harper. You were given authority to use level two file — that was all. You exceeded that authority the minute you gained access to the level one databanks. I don't give a damn what your motives were — you were way out of line. And you know it — right?"

"Yes, sir," she said sullenly. She swallowed then added, "I apologise, sir. It won't happen again."

Redmond stared at her. "It had better not." Then, he nodded briefly. "Very well. Just make sure there isn't any repetition. Is that understood?" For a moment, Redmond was struck by his pomposity and he realised why senior officers so often resorted to it when admonishing a junior: it was the only alternative to letting rip with every vile obscenity and insult they could summon up.

"Understood, sir." She was still gazing steadily beyond his shoulder.

He shook his head, almost in exasperation. "All right, Sergeant, relax."

"Thank you, sir," she replied formally, her voice distant. Beyond letting out her breath and adopting a slightly less rigid posture, however, she did not unbend appreciably.

More calmly, Redmond said, "Okay, let's get back to this Piccolo connection, now that you've uncovered it. You said three of them were working on it at some time?"

"Yes, sir."

"But not at the same time, if I remember the dates correctly?"

"There was some overlap between Phillips and the other two, but Hayward and Inchmore were at different times."

"But Barclay had no connection with it at all?"

"No, sir. Not that I could find."

"It's not exactly conclusive, is it?"

"With respect, sir," Harper began, still with that maddening formality in her voice, "three people who worked on this Piccolo have died within six months of each other." She became more animated, evidently trying to persuade him. "We're talking about something that's in the Olympus files, sir. Surely that's significant?"

"What about Barclay?"

"Maybe he was a real accident."

Redmond nodded slowly, conceding the point. "Maybe he was. Or maybe they were all accidents or suicides."

"Are you saying we shouldn't follow this up, sir?"

He thought for a moment then replied, "No, I'm not saying that. If there is a link then we need to look into it." He looked intently at her. "But before you start going walkabout again through the computer files, check with me first, understand? See what you can find about Piccolo, but no more hacking — got that?"

"Understood, sir." Again, her voice was icily correct. "I'll do everything by the book."

Redmond glanced sharply at her, wondering if he had imagined the hint of irony in her voice. Arrogant little bitch. "Just be sure you do," he snapped.

Detective Constable Hodge, a youthful-looking man with very dark hair, was waiting in the office when Redmond returned. He gave a faxed message to Redmond. "We've got another one, sir. Guy called Henry West — suicide by the look of it."

Redmond stared morosely at Hodge. "Terrific."

The next day, Gail finished reading the police reports on West's death and placed them on Redmond's desk. "So, another suicide?" she asked.

Redmond shrugged and looked at the third person in the office, DC Hodge. "You spoke to the local woodentops — what do they reckon?"

"The Letchworth police are more or less convinced West topped himself, and given that evidence" — Hodge nodded at the reports Gail had been reading — "I would imagine the inquest will agree. There's no evidence of any forced entry to the house. Nothing was taken, by the looks of it, and nobody saw anything suspicious. West came home at the usual time, probably had two glasses of sherry, got in the bath, and slashed both of his wrists. Death would have occurred within minutes — end of story."

"No note, though, was there," Gail pointed out. "No indication that he was unhappy or under stress — no more than usual, anyway."

"Apparently things were going well at the lab, actually," said Hodge. "That's why his colleagues haven't been able to give any reason for his killing himself."

Redmond rubbed his chin thoughtfully. "Okay, Hodge, get a report typed up, will you?" He waited until the door had closed behind Hodge, then turned to Gail. "Anything in West's file to tie him in with the others?"

She shook her head in evident reluctance.

"Not that I can make out, anyway."

"What about Piccolo?"

Again, she shook her head. "No," she said quietly. "He was never involved in it."

"So that's two who weren't now," Redmond pointed out. "Tends to make this Piccolo connection look a little insubstantial, doesn't it?"

"Unless West was a genuine suicide —"

"— and also Barclay," Redmond finished for her, a weary note in his voice. "We've been through all that. You can't just pick the ones that suit your theory and ignore the rest."

"I know that, sir — but this one does follow the same pattern as Hayward and Phillips," she continued doggedly. "No note, nor any great indications of depression. There isn't even an apparent motive for West killing himself, is there?"

"No, I'll grant you that. The thing is that we still don't have anything to go on beyond this vague Piccolo hint — and for all we know, half the computer experts on the MOD list have worked on it at some time or another."

"I suppose so," she said, sounding far from convinced.

"We're going to have to find a lot more than this if we're going to recommend an extended investigation."

Gail rose to her feet. "In that case, I'd better carry on looking, sir." She turned to go, but

Redmond stopped her.

"You think there really is something to all this, don't you?" His disbelief was evident.

She hesitated, then said, "I don't know, sir. It's more a hunch than anything, really."

Redmond shook his head, smiling faintly. "You're going to need more than that to convince our elders and betters to change their minds if they've decided not to do anything."

She stared at him. "I see, sir. All the same, there are some lines of enquiry I haven't followed up yet."

"Okay, off you go."

As the door closed behind her, Redmond shook his head in wry disbelief. Barely four years in the police and she was talking about hunches, the kind of intuition that went with years of catching criminals. . . . Redmond chuckled to himself, but his amused expression died away as a thought struck him.

He had only been in the force for eight years himself — and a mere two of those had been spent catching crooks in the accepted sense of the phrase. He was a fine one to be talking about intuition.

Four

"Come in!"

Redmond pushed open the door and went in, glancing quickly around the office as he did so. There was only one man in the large, well-appointed room, Chief Superintendent Bryceland, who was seated behind his desk. He looked up as Redmond came in and genially waved him into a chair. Bryceland had always been muscular but now he was tending to overweight, his face beginning to sag into fleshy jowls. His eyes were still as shrewd and alert as ever, though, and as Redmond sat down, he reminded himself that Bryceland was one of the closest associates of the Deputy Assistant Commissioner — the head of the Branch; he was not a man to be treated lightly.

"You asked to see me, sir?" Redmond said.

"I did, Redmond, I did." Bryceland paused, his eyes fixed intently on the younger man's face. "This Mandrake thing — how is it going?"

Redmond hesitated, but there was absolutely nothing in Bryceland's expression to indicate which answer he was seeking. When in doubt, honesty was often the best policy.

"Frankly, not very well, sir."

"I see. How much longer do you intend spending on it?"

"Difficult to say, sir," Redmond temporised, wishing he knew what the hell Bryceland wanted.

The chief superintendent leaned back in his seat, interlocking his fingers in front of his face. "The reason I ask, Redmond, is that I may have an assignment coming up for you. Something that may be rather more up your street than investigating a series of unconnected deaths." He paused, then added slowly, "Especially as your investigations seem to be taking you into rather — ah — sensitive areas, shall we say?"

"I see, sir." *Piccolo.*

"Let me offer you some advice, Redmond." Bryceland's tone was conciliatory. "You're very highly thought of around here and there is no reason why you should not have an outstanding career in the Branch, but you must learn to distinguish between dogged persistence and pure pigheadedness. I appreciate your desire to submit a thorough report in this instance, but we both know that there is nothing to find, so why waste time looking? Do enough to cover yourself, by all means, but don't go treading on anyone's corns. Do I make myself clear?" There was a sudden steely edge to the last question.

"Yes, sir. Perfectly."

"I hope I have, Redmond." Bryceland suddenly beamed expansively. "And as regards the other assignment, I'll be in touch with you within the next few days. I think you'll find it rather more exciting — and rewarding. Just to whet your appetite, I can tell you this much. It concerns a new Provisional IRA Special Action Unit operating here in London."

"I see, sir. Thank you."

Bryceland waved his hand dismissively. "Don't thank me, Redmond — you're the best man for the job. Just get this other thing out of the way and we'll get started, shall we?"

As he emerged from Bryceland's office, Redmond glanced at his watch — almost a quarter past five — then began to walk rapidly towards the Computer Section. If Gail had not left yet, he might just catch her. . . . The Provisionals: now that was more like it — and working under Bryceland as well. Any operation against the Provos was a high-profile one within the Branch, especially if it took place in London, while Bryceland was higher up the pecking order than Selvey, much more in a position to make or break inspectors. In any case, Bryceland was right, there was nothing in these deaths, and it was purely a waste of time trying to dig up something that just wasn't there. . . .

Gail was alone in the room in front of her console when Redmond walked into the Computer Section. The section was only manned from nine to five. At any other time, computer enquiries were handled by Jubilee House. Redmond was obscurely pleased to find her alone.

"Still at it?" he asked, leaning against a desk.

She looked up, surprised. "Oh, hello, sir. Yes, I am." She looked at her watch, then grimaced. "I didn't realise it was this late. I was trying to track down some leads."

"Yes, well, that was why I came to see you," he said. "You won't have to worry about that now. I'm closing down Mandrake. We've got enough to put in a report."

She stared incredulously at him. "You're not serious, are you?"

"Of course I'm serious," he retorted, his affability evaporating. "We're not getting anywhere, are we? All we've got is this Piccolo link and that's tenuous, to say the least. Apart from that, we've come up with nothing. We're wasting our time — there's nothing there."

"I haven't finished my computer search yet," she protested. "There may be other factors —"

"We could go on looking from now to doomsday hunting through the databanks and

65

we'd still find nothing, because there isn't anything to find and you know that as well as I do. We have to call a halt sometime and that's what I'm doing."

"Pulling the plug," she said flatly.

"If you want to put it that way, yes," he snapped. "But in case you've forgotten, Sergeant, I'm in charge of this investigation and it is my decision that we've spent enough time on it already. We've both got better things to do."

"I bet you have," she said icily.

"And just what the hell do you mean by that?"

"I would have thought it was perfectly obvious what I meant — sir." The contempt in her voice was unmistakable. She switched off the computer with an almost savage gesture, then rose to her feet. "You're just going to be a good boy, aren't you? Hand in the report they want and get a nice big pat on the back, right? You're more interested in toeing the line than in trying to find out if something's actually happening."

"Sergeant, I suggest you watch what you're saying. You're letting your faith in your so-called hunch get the better of you. We have absolutely no evidence —"

"No, and you're determined not to find any, aren't you?" she said angrily, her eyes flashing.

"Five deaths in six months, three of them of people who worked for a project so secret it's in the Olympus files and you're giving it a whitewash. You haven't given this a proper shot and you know that as well as I do. Dammit, we've only had West's file for forty-eight hours, the inquest hasn't even been held yet, and you're ringing the curtain down already." She gestured angrily in disgust. "Hasn't it occurred to you that if there's something going on, then people are getting killed out there? Doesn't that matter to you?" She glared at him, then shook her head. "No, I don't suppose it does. You're just the same as all the others. Okay, if that's all you want, go ahead. Get your promotion. It's all you're really interested in anyway, isn't it?"

She snatched up her handbag and stormed out, yanking the door shut behind her — but the hydraulic catch slowed it so that it closed with only a soft click.

Redmond raised his eyebrows and blew out his cheeks, shaking his head almost disbelievingly as he wondered why he hadn't let her have it with both barrels there and then. She had certainly done more than enough to merit a tongue-lashing, yet he had done virtually nothing. Even now, he was not conscious of any great feeling of anger or resentment at her outburst, more . . . more like the way he had felt when his mother had caught him helping himself to her birthday chocolates and had torn him off a strip — a conviction that he had deserved it.

Perhaps he had, he thought, staring at the closed door.

Four hours later, Gail stood outside the door of Redmond's flat, staring at it almost fearfully, her hand strangely reluctant to reach out and press the doorbell. It had been like this all the way over, a sense of foreboding that had increased with every minute. Yet there was no rational reason for it, because Redmond was no ogre, that she already knew. A bootlicker, perhaps, but not vindictive . . . she hoped, anyway. Okay, so she might be in for a right bollocking — which would not be undeserved, she admitted — but that was not her chief concern. What was causing her to hesitate was the realisation that she was going to have to apologise, even though she was still convinced she was in the right. Because, when it came right down to it, her career was important to her, and she had come within an ace of throwing it away. So, like it or not, she had to go through with it. . . . It's not as though you're going to seduce him or anything, she told herself.

She hoped. . . .

Come on, get on with it! With a sudden, almost involuntary jerk of her arm she pressed the doorbell and fought down a momentary impulse to turn and run for the lift. There was a delay that was probably no longer than ten seconds but seemed more, then the door opened and Redmond, wearing an open-neck shirt, faded jeans, and Hi-tec trainers, stood in the doorway. His surprise at seeing her was obvious.

"Sergeant Harper." His expression became carefully neutral. "What can I do for you?"

"I've brought a peace offering." She reached into the off-licence bag she was carrying and took out a bottle of Mouton Cadet. "Er — may I come in?"

He hesitated a moment, then shrugged. "Sure." He stood aside, his face wary now. She went through a small lobby and into the living room, looking quickly around. She was impressed; two rooms had obviously been knocked through into one large living area that was well-furnished, although rather too futuristic for her taste. Nevertheless, the furniture and fittings had clearly not been cheap, and the overall effect was one of comfort and style.

"You'll have to excuse the mess," he said, gesturing vaguely in the general direction of the sofa. "I haven't got round to tidying up yet." He sounded defensive, awkward, and she guessed that he wasn't used to visitors dropping by unexpectedly. He looked at the bottle she held. "Okay," he said, his voice firmer now. "What is this all about?"

"Like I said, sir — it's a peace offering. I was a long way out of line earlier on and I wanted to apologise. I shouldn't have said what I did." She was aware of a sense of relief as she finished speaking: there, it was done, it was said, and now she could let events take their course. Mentally, she braced herself for his response: moral indignation, condescension, a diatribe, whatever.

In fact, he did none of these things. Instead, he stared opaquely at her for — how long? Ten seconds? Longer? Then, slowly, he nodded. "Apology accepted," he said quietly. He looked quizzically at her, then added, "I don't suppose that was very easy for you, was it?"

"Well, no," she admitted. "But I felt I ought to, you know, clear the air as soon as possible."

He looked down at the bottle she was still holding. "You didn't have to do that."

She was puzzled by his responses. It was almost as if the incident in the Computer Section had not happened, he seemed so calm and detached about it all. "The least I could do," she said and held the bottle out to him. "Please — I'd like you to have it."

He seemed to hesitate, then nodded and took it from her. "Okay — but only on condition you have a drink as well now you're here."

Oh, shit, she thought. Maybe he does want me to seduce him after all. Maybe that'll be his price for not wrecking my career. . . . He could go to hell, if that was the case. Apologising was as far as she was prepared to go. "Okay," she said. "If you insist."

"I'll get some glasses. Make yourself at home — grab a seat or something. Won't be long." He disappeared through a door that she presumed led to the kitchen.

She wandered about, musing to herself that if he called this a mess, then what did he mean by tidy? The flat was, in fact, very neat and well-kept: she reflected that if he could see her place sometimes, he'd know what a mess really was. She looked at the rows of books along two shelves above the stereo and saw that he was evidently a science fiction fan, which surprised her somehow, although she didn't really know why. Mixed in with the books by Clarke, Asimov, Niven, and Pohl were several naval history texts, but there was not a spy novel or police thriller to be seen. There was an impressive number of records lined up below and on each side of the stereo system, mostly consisting of "progressive" rock bands from the seventies, but there had to be at least a couple of hundred LPs in all, arranged carefully in alphabetical order of the artists' names. You could learn a lot about people by looking at their book and record collections, she thought, then wandered over to a large sideboard. There was a large group photo on top, whose background she recognised — the Training Centre at Bramshill. There were twelve people in the photo, all but two of them men, she noticed sourly, and Redmond was standing in the back row, right at one end, looking awkward and uncomfortable. Perhaps he didn't like having his photograph taken, she mused, then picked up a second, framed, photograph of a blonde woman, aged about twenty-five and very attractive. Was that his wife? she wondered. There were conflicting stories about her in the Computer Section: some said she had died in a car crash several years before, others that there had been a messy divorce.

Suddenly, she became aware of Redmond standing in the kitchen doorway, a glass in each hand. . . . He was not looking at her, but at the photograph, and there was a look of wistful sadness in his eyes for a moment before the shutters dropped. Hurriedly, she replaced the photo, wondering what to say, but before she could think of anything, he held out one of the glasses.

"Here," he said quietly.

"Er — thanks."

"Do sit down," he said awkwardly.

She did so, relieved at the chance to move away from the photo and that moment when it seemed she could read the thoughts that were so plainly written on his face.

"Cheers," he said, his voice still sounding artificial.

"Cheers," she echoed, and silence fell as they sipped at the wine. "You — you've been very good about this," she said nervously.

"Well, the thing is, you were right," he said bluntly. "We probably do need some more time, at least to check out West's death. So . . . I'll give it another two days. If we turn up anything by then, fair enough. But if not, I call it off. Understood?"

She nodded. "Understood, sir. And . . . thank you." She was sitting perched on the edge of her seat, wondering how soon she could decently leave.

He stared down at his glass and shrugged. "Must be getting soft in my old age," he muttered, almost to himself. The silence fell again between them and she took a couple of sips from her wine before suddenly draining the glass. He noticed the movement and said, "Another glass?"

She shook her head and rose to her feet. "No, thanks. I really ought to be going."

"Well at least take the bottle with you. You didn't have to bring it, you know."

"I'd rather leave it here, sir — really."

He shrugged. "If you insist." He put his glass down and showed her to the door with, it seemed to her, an air of relief. He was as keen to be rid of her as she was to be gone. Nevertheless, she paused in the doorway and turned back towards him. "Thank you again, sir — for the forty-eight hours."

"Don't get too excited. I don't suppose it'll make any difference in the end."

She forced a smile. "You never know, though, do you?"

There was a suspicion of a wry grin on his face. "True."

"Good night, sir."

"Good night, Sergeant."

As she waited for the lift to arrive, Gail could feel the tension gradually draining away from her. She'd been lucky, no two ways about it. Redmond might be a pompous creep, but he wasn't all bad, she supposed.

She'd still rather be working for someone else, though.

Redmond stood in the lobby for some seconds after closing the door, then walked slowly back into the living room. He picked up his glass of wine and stared at it, a bemused expression on his face. Now why the hell had he given her the extra time? What he should have done was slammed her on report for insubordination — God knew, she had deserved it. She would not have had a leg to stand on in the disciplinary hearing. Obviously, that was why she had come round to apologise, to save her career, so why the hell had he let her off? And without making her sweat for it?

The thing was, as he had said to her, she had been right. He *had* called off Mandrake too soon. Bryceland had unnerved him. But despite what Bryceland had said, the signature at the bottom of the report would still be "Steven Redmond." Best just to make absolutely sure there was nothing suspicious in West's death before terminating Mandrake.

Redmond shook his head slowly and drained the glass. As he turned towards the kitchen — might as well have another, seeing she'd left the bottle — he caught sight of his reflection in the wall mirror and paused, peering intently at himself.

He wasn't sure he liked what he saw there.

"Death was caused by the fracturing of the second and third vertebrae, which in turn snapped the spinal cord. Death would have occurred almost instantaneously."

Redmond nodded, still looking down at the lifeless face on the slab. Even with the bruising and contusions, it was apparent that Elizabeth Kirk had been an attractive woman — but what difference did that make now? he wondered moodily, then looked up at the police pathologist, a short rotund man with sparse sandy hair and freckles. "What you're saying is that she broke her neck, right?"

"Yes — that would be the way a layman would describe it." The pathologist returned Redmond's look with one of thinly veiled condescension.

"Caused by her falling down the stairs?"

"The evidence would seem to suggest that, yes. It's up to the inquest to decide, of course, but the injuries were certainly consistent with such a fall."

"Injuries?"

"Bruises and contusions to the head, neck, and body."

Redmond nodded again and looked down at the dead face once more before he pulled the sheet over it. He stared thoughtfully at the covered head for several seconds, then said, "How likely is that? She seemed pretty fit — went for a workout at the gym at least once a week. Is it likely that she broke her neck just by falling down stairs?"

The pathologist smiled tolerantly. "I'm afraid it is feasible, Mr. Redmond, very much so. If the head were to strike the wall or the floor at the wrong angle, the weight of the entire body would be concentrated on that particular point."

"That wasn't what I asked, Dr. Evans," Redmond said, trying to keep the impatience out of his voice, not altogether successfully. "What I asked was how likely it was for a healthy woman of her age to break her neck under such circumstances. Does it happen often?"

"No, not often," Evans admitted. "It does happen, however."

"Dr. Evans, I want you to think very carefully about this. Was there any chance that her neck was broken immediately before she fell down the stairs? Would you still get the bruising we see here?"

Evans rubbed his chin thoughtfully, then said reluctantly, "It's possible, yes. Her neck could have been broken and she could then have been thrown or pushed down the stairs, I suppose."

"And would it be possible to tell in which order it happened?"

"No, not with any certainty. But I would remind you that the police found no evidence of any forced entry to the house, while her husband has a cast-iron alibi. They certainly are not treating this as a murder investigation."

"I'm aware of that, Dr. Evans," Redmond snapped, irritated beyond measure at the other's air of superiority. "Thank you for your time," he said with exaggerated politeness. "You've been most helpful." He spun on his heel and stalked out, wondering at his display of temper. True, Dr. Evans was insufferably smug and patronising, but that did not matter, he was also a damn good pathologist. Why had he let Evans rile him so much? Especially when he was only providing evidence that would enable Kirk's death to be entered as accidental: another nonsuspicious death.

Except that it was number six in less than seven months; they were happening almost once a month now, and it was becoming more difficult to accept the series of deaths as just a freak actuarial run. . . .

He was just emerging into the car park when his portable phone rang in its clip on his belt. He detached it and flicked it on. "Redmond here," he said and leaned against the side of his car.

"Sergeant Harper, sir."

Redmond's lips compressed themselves into a thin line. Somehow, he knew what she was

78

going to say and he did not like it one little bit, because that would really complicate things. "Go on," he said.

"It's about Elizabeth Kirk."

"Don't tell me," he said resignedly. "She worked on Piccolo — right?"

"Yes, sir. For over six months, up to seven months ago, when she was transferred. That makes four out of six, sir."

"I can count, Sergeant."

"Sorry, sir. She was also a radar and guidance systems specialist, like Phillips, so there's a possible link there. There are a couple of other things — I don't know whether they're significant or not, but . . ."

"But what?"

"She left Piccolo less than two weeks before Hayward died."

Redmond's lips compressed themselves momentarily. "Could have been coincidence."

"Absolutely, sir. The other thing is that she was apparently a brown belt at judo. I'm not sure how high that is, but —"

"It's only one step down from a black belt," Redmond said absently, his mind racing ahead as it evaluated the implications.

"In that case, she must have been pretty good at it. Don't they teach people how to fall properly in judo training?"

"It's a very important part of it, yes."

"So if she did stumble at the top of the stairs, wouldn't she have known how to fall without hurting herself too much?"

"She'd have had more chance than most people, yes," Redmond agreed slowly.

"We're back to the old cliché again, sir, aren't we? Did she fall or was she pushed?"

Five

When the knock came on his office door, Redmond called out, "Come in!" but did not pause in his reading of Elizabeth Kirk's file. Not that it was yielding anything new.

"Sir?" It was Gail Harper; he might have known, he thought, as he leaned back in his seat and gazed impassively at her.

"Yes?" he asked as she took a seat.

"Something's turned up, sir. I'm not sure if it's important, though."

"Go on," he said resignedly. One thing you had to say about her, she left no stone unturned, but her persistence did produce a lot of false trails. This would probably be another one.

"I've set up a search programme in the database to tell me whenever anything connected with our victims or their various companies or projects comes up. This morning, I got a flag on a Stuart Mackinnon."

Redmond frowned. "Mackinnon? Who's he?"

"He's the one who took over Hayward's job at SysCom."

"So why has his name cropped up?"

"He's been transferred to a Red File, sir."

Redmond stared at her, taken aback. The Branch kept three main categories of files on the individuals in whom it took an interest. Anyone involved in secret work or who was connected in any way with "suspect" organisations went into a White File, simply for notification. A number of these would then go into a Green File, especially if they were involved in high-security work or if they were known to be active supporters of, say, CND or Greenpeace. The Red File was for actual surveillance, which meant that there were almost certain to be substantial grounds for suspicion. So what had this Mackinnon been up to? "Was he in a Green File before?"

She nodded. "Up until yesterday."

"Any indication why he was upgraded?"

"No, but it was on Chief Inspector Prentice's authority."

Redmond nodded thoughtfully. Graham Prentice was an able, experienced officer, so there was probably more to it than a simple knee-jerk reaction to a faintly suspicious situation. "Okay, so Mackinnon's regarded as a security risk. Where do we come in?"

"He was Hayward's replacement, sir," she reminded him. "Suppose there's a connection? Suppose Hayward was killed just to get Mackinnon that job? He's working with classified material, after all."

Redmond shook his head. "SysCom is working on a computerised tracking system, if my memory isn't playing tricks on me, but it isn't exactly world-shattering as regards the technology being used there. We run into the same old problem — why go to all the risk of knocking off Hayward just to get hold of some second-division material? It doesn't add up."

"No, I know it doesn't," she agreed glumly. "Unless we're not getting the full picture. The point is, it does seem funny that Hayward's replacement is now classified as a security risk — although I'm damned if I can see its significance."

"I know what you mean," Redmond said thoughtfully. He shook his head. "You know, the deeper we get into this, the less sense it makes."

"But you think there's something there?" she asked, a note of anxiety in her voice.

"I'm starting to think there's something bloody peculiar going on, yes," he said slowly and caught a momentary glimpse of surprise and puzzlement on her face. It was not the first time she had looked at him like that over the past couple of days — since Elizabeth Kirk's death, in fact — and he was sure he knew the reason why. It was because he was finally beginning to take Mandrake seriously and she could not figure out why. That was hardly surprising — he was not really sure himself what had happened, but there was no denying the fact that he was finding it difficult now to swallow the idea that the six deaths were completely unconnected. It wasn't just the sequence of accidents and suicides that was stretching the idea of random chance, it was also the doubts raised over Kirk's death in particular; what would have been a somewhat freakish accident anyway now seemed even more unlikely as an explanation. There was also the consideration, illogical though it might be, that the last victim had been a mother of two as well as a scientist — and an attractive one at that. Of course, that should not have made any difference at all, but it did, for entirely irrational reasons; her death had made more of an impact on him than the others. Then there was Gail's scathing accusation: *People are getting killed out there.* It had come back to him more than once, unbidden, to prey on his mind — what if she were right?

Mind you, he thought sourly, she probably thinks I've seen some career benefit in keeping the investigation going now. And, if he were absolutely honest about it, the notion had occurred to him as well. If there was something

84

going on and he uncovered it, he could probably do quite well out of it if he played his cards right.

For some reason, the thought left him feeling vaguely depressed. "What do you want to do about this Mackinnon thing?" she asked, cutting across his daydreaming.

"I don't know yet. I'll go and have a word with Prentice."

"Mackinnon?" Prentice asked, a few minutes later. He looked shrewdly up at Redmond from his seat. "Why are you interested in Mackinnon?" he asked.

"He works for SysCom," Redmond said blandly. "I'm investigating everyone who works for them, sir. Chief super's instructions." He shrugged.

Prentice nodded and rubbed his nose. "Okay," he said eventually. "You're cleared for this level of information, I suppose, so why not? We put him in a Red File after we searched his flat and found a Soviet-made miniaturised camera hidden in the false bottom of a bureau drawer, along with a roll of microfilm. Seems a good enough reason to me."

Redmond grinned wryly. "You could have a point there. . . . What got you on to him in the first place?"

"We found out he was a screaming poofter."

"When?"

"Week or so ago."

Redmond nodded. It was, sadly, typical of the mentality of many Branch and MI5 officers. The mere fact that Mackinnon was a homosexual was enough for Prentice to obtain authority to break into Mackinnon's home and search it. Okay, so they'd found incriminating evidence, but it would have been just the same if Mackinnon had been as pure as the driven snow — his place would still have been turned over. Even if nothing had been found, he would have been finished in secret work, innocent or not. Had he been a married man having it off with any woman he could find, nothing would have happened; Prentice would probably just have silently wished him good luck and let him get on with it. But Mackinnon was gay and that had been enough — he had been branded.

It was pointless getting uptight over it, though, because there was no way he could change anything. . . .

"So what are you going to do with him?" he asked.

"The usual. Put him under twenty-four hour surveillance and wait for him to make contact."

Redmond thought for a moment, then said,

"Sir, could you keep me in touch with what goes on with Mackinnon? It might well have a bearing on my investigation."

Prentice nodded. "Be glad to."

Watford, Hertfordshire

Several days later, Prentice and Redmond were walking slowly across the grass in Cassiobury Park, occasionally pausing for one of them to throw a ball for Prentice's Jack Russell terrier, which had been brought along as cover. Redmond had to admit it was a neat touch, effectively dispelling suspicion, as did the cover adopted by DC Farnham and WDC Rollins, who were walking hand in hand some thirty yards away seemingly oblivious to everything but each other. Other Branch officers were dotted around the area, some in hiding, others apparently eating their lunches or just enjoying the fine spring day. It was all going very smoothly and had done so ever since Redmond had received Prentice's phone call telling him that the SysCom security guard he had alerted a week ago had seen Mackinnon photocopying the documents that Prentice had ordered specifically planted. The information they contained was bogus, but tempting, and Mackinnon had fallen for it. When he had left at lunchtime, Farnham had tailed him to the park and Redmond had arrived with Prentice only a minute or so after Mackinnon had left his car to eat his sandwiches on a nearby park bench. Now all they needed was Mackinnon's contact, the courier who would collect the envelope. Once he — or she — was identified, they could tail him in turn so that he would lead them to the next link in the chain.

"Looks promising," Redmond commented; Prentice nodded in agreement.

The dog dropped the ball at Redmond's feet and looked up at him, its tail wagging expectantly. Redmond grinned, picked up the ball, and threw it, watching the dog as it raced off in pursuit. Prentice's quiet voice brought his attention back to the car park.

"The bloke in the red anorak."

Redmond nodded. "I see him."

A brown-haired, slightly overweight man was sauntering towards Mackinnon's Escort, his hands pushed deep into his pockets. As he reached the car he looked quickly around, then took something from his pocket. His body hid what he was doing from Redmond and Prentice, but, within two or three seconds, he had unlocked the Escort's passenger door.

"We could be in business," Redmond muttered. Both he and Prentice watched intently as the man reached inside the car and picked up the envelope. He straightened, stuffed the package inside his anorak, and had just slammed the door shut when a voice called out from the park gate:

"Oi, you! Just hold it right there!"

Redmond looked over towards the gate and groaned inwardly as he saw a uniformed policeman running across the car park. "Oh, shit," he murmured: now they'd have to pick the courier up, like it or not. Why did that policeman have to interfere?

The man looked around then broke into a run, heading away from the policeman but at an angle to Redmond and Prentice. The two of them took off in pursuit and their quarry veered away from them, hurling the package to one side, his face panic-stricken as he glanced over his shoulder at them. Within seconds, it was obvious that they were gaining on him, and it was Redmond who brought him down with a diving rugby tackle. The two of them sprawled on the ground, the other man underneath.

"Okay, okay!" the man gasped breathlessly as Redmond grabbed his right arm and pulled it up his back. "I'll come quietly!" His voice was pure cockney, Redmond noticed — and that was when he began to suspect something might be wrong.

"Come on — on your feet!" he said as Prentice and the uniformed policeman arrived.

Prentice was showing the constable his warrant card and there was a look of puzzlement on the PC's face at this sudden appearance of Special Branch. Then, the policeman saw the face of the man Redmond was holding and his eyes widened momentarily.

"Micky Slater!" he exclaimed. "I should have realised it'd be you."

"You know him?" Redmond asked before he could stop himself: it was a pretty stupid question, under the circumstances.

The constable stared at him, but then, with a glance at Prentice, he nodded again. "Micky's been thieving things from cars for years — when he's not nicking the cars themselves. That right, Micky?"

"I'm saying nothing till I've seen my brief."

Redmond and Prentice exchanged despairing glances, then Redmond looked away to where Mackinnon was being brought back to the car park by Farnham and the WDC; Mackinnon was evidently under arrest. But, instead of his courier, all they'd got was a bloody car thief.

Mackinnon looked up quickly as Redmond walked into the interview room carrying an envelope, and the fear in the prisoner's eyes was only too evident. Yet there was also resignation, as if he had known all along that it would come to this, a bare room in an anonymous safehouse, confessing everything. The final shame. Redmond stared down at him for almost half a minute, saying nothing until he saw Mackinnon swallow nervously. With an almost imperceptible movement, Redmond nodded to the young DC by the door and the officer left.

Redmond sat on the far side of the table that, along with the two chairs, formed the only furniture in the room. He opened the envelope, took out the documents that Mackinnon had copied, then stared levelly at the other man. "Recognise these?" he asked, his voice icy cold.

Mackinnon licked his lips. "Who — who are you?" he stammered hoarsely.

"Never mind that. Answer the question."

"I — I want to know who I'm talking to." The attempt at bluster was pitiful in its transparency.

"Mackinnon, you are not in any position to be making demands. You are in deep shit, so don't make it worse. I'll give you one more chance to answer the question. Do you recognise these documents?"

Mackinnon hesitated, then nodded slowly. "You know perfectly well I do."

"How long have you been handing over information?" Redmond asked.

"Eight months," Mackinnon said sullenly, still staring at the damning evidence on the table.

"Before you got your present job, you mean?"

"Yes."

"Who are you working for?"

"The Russians, I suppose."

"What do you mean — 'I suppose'?"

"I was never told exactly who I was working for, but I assumed it was them."

Redmond nodded slowly. "How do you make contact?"

"What do you mean?"

"How did your contact know you would be delivering documents today?"

"I telephone a number, let it ring three times, then I hang up."

Redmond took out a notebook and looked expectantly at the other man. Mackinnon hesitated, but then gave a telephone number, which Redmond duly noted. Not that there was any need, for in addition to a video camera mounted high up in one corner, the room was wired for sound so Prentice's team would already be trying to trace the number. "You phone this number — when?"

"In the morning," Mackinnon muttered, almost inaudibly. "Then I go to the park at lunchtime and leave the envelope in my car while I have my lunch. When I come back, it's gone."

Redmond's face was impassive, but he was inwardly disappointed. Mackinnon was describing a classic cutout, an arrangement whereby he never saw the man who collected the envelope. "How many of these deliveries have you made?"

Mackinnon murmured something.

"Speak up."

"Seven or eight — I'm not sure. About one a month."

"Dates?"

Mackinnon shook his head. "I don't know exactly. The first was sometime in July last year."

"Always the same place? In the park?"

"Yes."

"Did you ever receive specific instructions as to what information to look for?"

"Only at the beginning. They said they wanted anything connected with the radar research we were doing."

"But nothing after that?"

"No."

Redmond looked at Mackinnon. "So now we come to the important question — why?"

Mackinnon stared mutely at his feet, his cheeks colouring.

Redmond nodded slowly to himself. "Okay,

93

let me guess then. Photographs, was it? Of you and a good-looking young man from the Russian or Czech Embassy? Was that it?"

"Damn you!" Mackinnon hissed, startling Redmond with his unexpected vehemence. "It's easy for you to feel superior, isn't it?" As suddenly as it had come, his anger faded. He shook his head. "You don't understand."

"No, I don't," Redmond agreed. Mackinnon looked up, surprised by the gentleness in Redmond's voice. "Try explaining it to me."

"What does it matter now?"

"It matters a great deal. The more you help us, the better it will be for you in the end. You know that."

Mackinnon did not answer immediately; he seemed to be gathering his thoughts. Then, he said softly, "It was only a brief relationship. We met twice — once at the Turkish Baths, the second time at his flat. And yes, he was Russian."

"You knew that at the time?"

"No, not until later. He told me he was Austrian."

"And they said you'd lose your job if the photos were produced?"

Mackinnon nodded. Redmond stared at him almost pityingly. It was virtually the oldest trick in the espionage book, but still one of the most effective and one of the most difficult to prevent. Someone like Mackinnon — lonely, guilty, terrified of being exposed — would be ideal for the Russians. "Who showed you the photographs?"

"Nobody did. They arrived in the post one morning, then someone telephoned with instructions."

"What sort of voice was it on the phone?"

"A man's voice — his accent was central European, but I wouldn't recognise it again, if that's what you mean. It was months ago, and he only ever telephoned once."

Very neat, thought Redmond. There was absolutely no way that Mackinnon could identify anyone except the lover, who had probably returned home months ago. He tried another tack. "This present job of yours at SysCom — it's the highest level of classified project you've worked on?"

"Yes."

"So they had to upgrade your security clearance?"

"Yes."

"Yet you still gained the post ahead of at least two other candidates who would appear to have had better qualifications — and who also had higher security clearances anyway. Can you explain that?"

"I don't see what this has —"

Redmond interrupted, "Just answer the question. How did you get the job?"

"Well . . ." Mackinnon hesitated. "To be honest, I think I might have had a little help behind the scenes."

"What makes you think that?"

"Originally, I wasn't too sure about applying for the post, but I was told that if I did, I wouldn't have to worry too much about the interview."

"Who told you this?"

"Miles Farrington."

"And who's he?"

"He's the head of the Research Co-ordinating Unit at the Ministry of Defence."

Redmond stared at him. "What exactly did he say to you?"

"He said that if I applied for the job, he'd put in a good word for me."

Redmond nodded. It was by no means uncommon for the MOD to "recommend" people to the firms who had won contracts to carry out research work for them; it was all part of the "old boy" network. "Would you have applied for the post if you hadn't been told that?"

Mackinnon shrugged. "I don't know. Probably not."

"So why should Farrington show you any

favours? Were you at the same school or something?"

"No, but . . ."

"But what?"

"Well, he didn't actually say anything, but when he left, he gave me a Masonic handshake."

"And you're a Mason."

Reluctantly, Mackinnon nodded: it was almost as if this last admission had cost him more than anything he had said so far. Maybe it had, Redmond thought. "Right," he said briskly. "Now we get down to business. I want to know exactly what you gave the Russians. Every last document, the lot."

As the image of Mackinnon's face dissolved into snow on the TV screen, Redmond reached over and turned off the video player, before turning to face Gail, who had been watching the recording of the interrogation with him. "So there it is," he said briskly. "Any comments?"

She was still staring thoughtfully at the blank screen. "Interesting, sir," she said eventually. She hesitated then continued, "All the same, I'm not sure if it ties in with Mandrake."

"Go on."

"Mackinnon is obviously passing on classified material, apparently to the Soviets, and

97

has been for a while. That doesn't mean there's any connection to Hayward's death, though, does it, sir? You said it yourself — why kill Hayward just to get Mackinnon into SysCom?"

"Okay, I agree it doesn't seem to make a lot of sense. Mind you, we don't actually know for certain it was the KGB he was passing information to. Thanks to that car thief, we never got a sight of his contact — and he or she'll have been warned off by now. I would imagine the lover's long since disappeared and there's no way we can trace the voice on the phone, so all we've got are some central or eastern European accents. He might have *thought* he was working with the KGB, but it could have been anybody." He rubbed his nose tiredly. "Perhaps if we knew who Mackinnon was working for, some of this might start making sense."

"Assuming it is linked to Hayward's death," she repeated. Redmond glanced at her sharply, wondering momentarily at her change of attitude, then realised that she was only doing what any good subordinate should do in this situation, acting as devil's advocate, trying to pick holes in any theory. She continued, "It could just have been opportunism on someone's part. Mackinnon was recruited before he moved to SysCom, so maybe someone decided to put him into a higher classification project. Or he simply got the job anyway and it happened to be a bonus for them."

"Yes, but supposing it wasn't just chance? What if someone did arrange for him to get the job at SysCom?"

"Farrington, you mean?"

"Why not?" Redmond asked, leaning back in his chair and steepling his fingers in front of his face. "It would seem he did use some influence to get Mackinnon into a job when he wasn't really the best applicant."

"You heard what Mackinnon said — they were both Masons." She suddenly looked uncomfortable, and Redmond knew she was recalling the accusation that she had made about him being a member himself.

"No," he said firmly. "What he said was that Farrington gave him a Mason's handshake. That doesn't prove anything. I know the handshake, but —" he grinned suddenly — "despite what you believe, I'm not a Mason."

"All the same, it does happen — they do help each other get jobs, don't they?"

"Yes, they do — and we're hardly in a position to throw stones, are we?" Redmond said heavily. Despite several attempts to lessen their influence, there was no doubt that there were still too many senior police officers in the Metropolitan Police who were also Masons and who used their authority to further the careers of fellow lodge members. Redmond himself had been invited to join, three years before, but had declined: ambitious he might have been, but, even then, he had not been prepared to go that far. "Okay, so maybe that was all there was to it — Farrington was simply helping a fellow Mason. But maybe he wasn't. All we know is that a senior civil servant used his influence to secure a position in a research project sponsored by the Ministry of Defence for someone who was passing on secret information. We can't really afford to ignore that, can we?"

"No, I suppose not, sir — but we still haven't established whether there's any connection with Hayward or the others, have we?" she persisted.

Redmond grimaced wryly. "Okay. Let's assume that someone is knocking off these computer experts. Putting aside the obvious question of why, which we can't answer, they would need to have someone on the inside to identify the victims, wouldn't they?"

"Seems reasonable."

There was something in her voice that made him look sharply at her, just in time to catch that puzzled expression on her face. It disappeared so rapidly that he wondered if he had imagined it. She was obviously still wondering where he stood on this investigation — hardly surprisingly, perhaps. . . . He said, "This someone would have to have access to both personnel and project files so that he could identify the prospective victims and then provide the killer with the necessary information to carry out the hit. Both sorts of files are kept in the Research Co-ordination Unit over at the MOD — Farrington's outfit. Farrington could be the — I don't know, the controller, the one who either decides who's next for the chop or sets them up once someone else has chosen them. Does that make sense?"

"It could do, sir, but there are at least a dozen people with access to that kind of information, plugs — I don't know — probably another twenty or thirty who could find it out without too much difficulty."

"I know," Redmond admitted. "I don't like the coincidence, though. Hayward dies and is replaced by a security risk with the help of someone who could have been in a position to provide the sort of information Hayward's hypothetical killer would have needed. See what I'm getting at?"

She nodded, but there was still a trace of bemusement in her eyes. "I think I do, sir."

"Good." Redmond picked up a pen from

the desk and twiddled it restlessly in his fingers. "Okay, this is what I'd like you to do. Get me everything you can find on Farrington and his unit. If we're going to chase this particular wild goose, we might as well do it properly."

Redmond answered the phone on his desk without looking up from the file he was reading. The voice at the other end said:

"Selvey here. Come on over, will you?"

Redmond stared at the phone; that had sounded ominous.

Selvey looked up as Redmond knocked and entered. "You've been summoned."

"Summoned? Who by?"

Selvey chuckled and shook his head in mock sorrow. "I don't know — what do they teach in these universities these days? 'Who by?' It's 'By whom?' laddie. In answer to your question, the eminence who wishes to see you is none other than Sir Ronald Mayhew."

"Oh, bloody hell . . ." Mayhew was the deputy director general of MI5.

"Indeed," Selvey agreed heavily. He stared thoughtfully up at Redmond, then said, not unsympathetically, "I'd say you were in deep shit, old son."

The first thing Redmond noticed about

Mayhew's Whitehall office was the oak panelling. All four walls were covered in it, from floor to ceiling and, combined with the luxurious leather armchairs that faced each other on each side of the large fireplace, the room looked as though it belonged in an exclusive London club — White's, perhaps, or the Athenaeum — rather than being the office of the second-in-command of MI5. As Mayhew was a member of both clubs, however, this was hardly surprising, Redmond thought as he took the chair in front of the desk in response to Mayhew's gesture.

"Can I get you anything, before we begin?" Mayhew asked courteously. His voice was pure Oxbridge, deep and resonant, reminding Redmond of the late Richard Burton in some ways. "Cigar? Cigarette?" He pushed a large cigarette case across the desk top.

"No, thank you, sir. I don't."

"Very wise. Some coffee, then, perhaps?"

"Again, no thank you, sir. I only had some half an hour ago."

"Quite. Good of you to come across to see me at such short notice."

"You said it was important, sir."

"Quite," Mayhew said again. The two men eyed each other for several seconds. Redmond had met Mayhew once before but only briefly, so this was his first chance to study him. He

103

saw a man aged fifty or so with brown hair that was fading to grey and receding from the temples and very clear blue eyes that showed nothing but polite interest at the moment. He projected an affable enough facade — but he was still the deputy DG of MI5. Suddenly, Mayhew began to speak, taking Redmond a little by surprise. "The reason I wanted to see you, Redmond, is to do with this Mandrake investigation of yours."

"I see, sir," Redmond replied cautiously. Technically, Mayhew had no authority over him whatsoever, but in practice, it would be extremely unwise for any mere inspector to cross him.

"Along with several other senior figures both here and in the MOD and Home Office, I'm rather concerned about the amount of disruption that your investigation has caused," Mayhew said. "Now, I'm aware that I have no jurisdiction over you, but your enquiries have apparently upset a number of people working on various research projects that do fall within MI-five's brief. I've also had a memo from the head of the Research Co-ordinating Unit at the MOD, complaining about exactly the same thing — unnecessary interference and harassment of research workers. In addition, you have apparently been making enquiries about the Piccolo Project and it is this that is also causing concern. It is a highly secret project, and your investigation is posing a threat to its security that we can well do without. To be blunt, Redmond, you are causing a good deal of trouble all round — and for no good reason." There was a steely glint in his eye and, despite himself, Redmond swallowed nervously.

"I'm sorry about that, sir, but I was asked to compile a complete report and —"

"Your dedication is commendable, but surely you've had enough time now, Redmond? Frankly, I'm surprised at you. It was perfectly obvious what was expected of you, so why are you being so awkward about it? To be honest, it was a mistake to ask anyone to look into it — there is clearly nothing to be found, after all — but since someone obviously decided to go through the motions, then why the devil haven't you done what was required of you?"

"There have been one or two somewhat suspicious circumstances," Redmond pointed out. "I'm not entirely satisfied that —"

"Redmond, you're not listening, are you?" Mayhew snapped. "I see I am going to have to spell it out for you. I am speaking on behalf of the Ministry of Defence and the security services in this. We do not want your investigations to proceed any further, because if they do, they could cause a serious breach of security in one of our most important research projects. We want Mandrake terminated — immediately. Is that clear?"

"In that case, why not simply close it down?" Redmond asked, vaguely surprised at his small display of defiance.

"Because now that it has been initiated, we need the negative report at the end of it — I would have thought that was obvious. But you are being willfully obtuse as far as I can see in refusing to do what is expected of you. You're a sensible man, Redmond. Just do what is necessary and everyone will be happy." Mayhew paused, then added, with an edge in his voice, "If you don't — if you continue to drag your heels over this, you will regret it, Redmond — do I make myself clear?"

Redmond licked his lips. "Yes, sir."

"I trust I do." Mayhew stared across the desk at him for a second or so longer, then pulled a folder towards him. "That will be all."

Six

West Yorkshire

Redmond paused for a moment to catch his breath and looked around, trying to make it appear as though he had only halted to admire the view. It was certainly well worth stopping for with the bleak moors all around him that always made him think of *Wuthering Heights* — Cathy and Heathcliff rushing towards each other as the wind lashed at them — while below was the reservoir, its water a slate grey reflection of the sky; but in truth, the impressive panorama was not why he had come to a halt. Put quite simply, he was knackered. His legs were aching and his feet were killing him: even the hiking boots he had remembered to dig out from the back of his wardrobe had only postponed the discomfort because all he wanted to do at the moment was bathe his feet in hot water for at least three hours. Time was when a five-mile jaunt like this was nothing. Steven old son, he told himself, you're getting soft.

Which could definitely not be said about the stockily built man fifty yards ahead of him, still striding effortlessly up the hillside, his stamina belying his sixty-plus years. As Redmond watched him, shaking his head in rueful admiration, the older man stopped and looked back. He was too far away to see his expression, but Redmond had no doubt that he would be grinning hugely.

"Now coom on, Steve. Tha's no son o' mine if tha can't walk a few miles afore loonch." The Yorkshire accent was deliberately thick, laid on with a trowel. Redmond knew his father loved playing the part of the dour Yorkshireman, even to the point of self-parody. "Eeh, when I were tha age, I could walk twice this far and still have enough puff to roon t' last mile." Despite the distance and the wind, his voice carried easily to Redmond. "Course we were real men in them days, not poncified townies."

"Yeah sure, Dad," Redmond called back. "You forgot the bit about having a ferret down your trousers and having to live in a shoe box."

"Shoe box?" his father called out, laughing. "Them was for toffs. We 'ad to live in a hole in t' ground."

Redmond chuckled and shook his head. The thing was, he thought as he began to trudge up the slope, his dad had not been so far off the mark as regards the distance he could walk.

For as long as Redmond could remember, his father had set out every Sunday when he was not on duty to walk across the moors above the mining village where he had lived almost all his life. First as a boy, then as a teenager, Redmond had gone with him until he knew the bleak hillsides like the back of his hand. He had learned to identify the call of the curlew and dozens of other birds, had watched hawks plummeting majestically downwards, straight as an arrow, seen lambs staggering about, less than an hour old, smelled the fragrance of the wild mountain thyme. . . . It seemed like another world now; alien. He'd lived in the city too long and was no longer at ease in the country. The decision had been made years ago to leave behind these surroundings, and although he had experienced the odd twinge of nostalgia, he had not really missed the moors; they were no longer a part of his life.

Now, for the first time, the thought saddened him.

"Had enough?" his father asked, grinning, as Redmond came up to him.

"Me? No . . . of course not," Redmond replied, still breathing heavily and oozing insincerity. "Could go on for hours yet." He shook his head and blew out his cheeks. "Just find me a hole to crawl into and die and I'll be a happy man."

"Too much city living," his father assured him. "Still," he admitted, "I'm not as spry as I used to be. We'll take a rest, then head down to the Colliers' Arms for a jar." He eased his knapsack off his shoulders, opened it, and took out two cans of beer, handing one to Redmond. "Not as good as the draught stuff, but it'll do to be going on with."

"You bet," Redmond said, opening the can. Normally, the only time he drank bitter these days was when he visited his father — in the village pub, only "southern poofters" drank anything else. Funny how you forget things, he thought. . . . Real Yorkshire bitter; tasted bloody good, even when you weren't dying of thirst (as he was now). Yet, in the clubs and wine bars of London, if you drank beer at all, it had to be lager or Pils — which is what he drank when he did not fancy a vermouth or whisky.

The two of them sat in companionable silence while they took occasional sips, staring down the hillside. Momentarily, the sun broke through the scudding clouds overhead, transforming the reservoir into a gleaming mirror, but almost as quickly the sun disappeared and the moment was gone.

"Okay, Steve," his father said quietly. "Spit it out. What's on your mind?"

"Why should anything be on my mind?"

"Because you haven't been up here for months, apart from Christmas." The unspoken criticism in the words made Redmond flush; it was true, unfortunately. "Then suddenly you descend on us out of the blue. Not that you're not welcome — your mam and I are always glad to see you, you know that — but I wasn't a copper for thirty years without picking up a trick or two."

"True," Redmond admitted, yet still hesitated.

"Look, come on, Steve, if it's advice you're after, fair enough." He smiled faintly, almost wistfully. "What else are fathers for?"

Despite himself, Redmond smiled and looked at his father, realising, almost for the first time, that, suddenly, he was beginning to look his age. The wispy hair was grey now, with more white than Redmond remembered. The face was more wrinkled, weatherbeaten and he no longer had quite the same burly physique that had flattened more than one brawling miner. He was gradually fading away. . . . From somewhere, a line from a Robert Louis Stevenson poem came into his mind: "I was leaving home, and my folks were growing old."

"It's something at work, Dad," he said suddenly. "I've been asked to put together a report but it's a PR job. They want me to put in a negative report, say everything's okay, that sort of thing."

His father nodded. "Only you think that everything isn't okay, is that it?"

Redmond looked away and stared out over the valley. He sipped at his beer before he said carefully, "I think there are enough suspicious circumstances to justify further investigations, yes." *People are getting killed out there. . . .*

"But if you do that, if you rock the boat, you could be up shit creek, right?"

"Got it in one, Dad. It's been made very clear to me what the likely consequences will be if I don't toe the line."

His father shook his head. "I've said this before, Steve, but I'll say it again. This sort of thing is bound to crop up with Special Branch."

"I know you don't like the Branch, Dad, but —"

"I've got nothing against the Branch, Steve — it's just that it should never be part of the police force. Spying on people, tapping their phones — that sort of thing should be left to MI-five. No, what I mean is this. Special Branch doesn't deal with evidence the way policemen ought to, because you deal in suspicion and rumour. Someone belongs to

CND? Right, put them under surveillance and tap their phones. Somebody once went to listen to a left-wing MP give a speech — right, they must be a prime candidate for recruitment by the KGB." He shook his head. "We had enough of the Branch round here during the miners' strikes — that's when the pit was still open, of course. They wanted me to identify people in photos they'd taken of picket lines or on marches — people I'd gone to school with in a lot of cases. I knew damn well they were putting the names into files when all they were doing, the people they were photographing and who they wanted me to shop, all they were doing was trying to save their jobs. Most of them wouldn't have known what a Marxist tendency was if it had hit them over the head with an empty beer bottle."

He paused, then grinned wryly. "Sorry. There I go again, getting up on my soapbox. What I was originally going to say was that you're in an organisation that doesn't deal in black or white and that tends to tell its lords and masters what they want to hear. I don't suppose most of your colleagues, or you, for that matter, genuinely believe that everybody who goes on a peace march is plotting to overthrow the government, but you still keep files on them all the same, because that's what they want in Whitehall, right? So you compromise yourself. You distort the truth — and that's all you're being asked to do now, isn't it?"

Redmond stared at his father, taken aback by the attack. It had not been delivered with any hostility; indeed, the words had been spoken dispassionately, more in sorrow than in anger, but an attack was what it had been — and it had hurt. It had hurt, because what he had said was absolutely true. "There's more to it than that, Dad," he said quietly. "People's lives are involved."

His father stared at him, then nodded slowly. "Ah, now that's different." He looked expectantly at his son.

Redmond hesitated, then said, "There's been a series of deaths of people involved in military research, all apparently accidents or suicides. I was asked to look at them to see if they were connected."

"And your superiors want you to say they aren't? That they're genuine accidents or suicides?"

"Right."

"So you think they're murders?"

Redmond shook his head. "I'm not sure, Dad. I can't see any motives for murder — but there are some suspicious patterns emerging."

"Enough for you to think it's worth looking deeper."

"Yes."

"But you've been told to drop it."

"Right."

His father nodded again. "So, the choice is for you to go out on a limb for something you're not sure about either way and thereby wreck your career prospects, or play it safe and stay on schedule for a rapid promotion — is that it?"

"In a nutshell."

His father finished off the can, crumpled it, and replaced it in his knapsack. He took out two more, passed one to Redmond, and opened the other. He took a long pull from it, then said quietly, "You've seen what the village is like now. Since the pit closed, the place has been like a ghost town. There's just about nobody left between the ages of sixteen and forty nowadays. They've all moved out — and why not? There's nowt for them round here, hasn't been for years. I mean, I were bloody lucky to get that job when I retired — even if it is only as a bloody glorified nightwatchman."

Redmond nodded slowly. Officially, the job was that of a security guard, but nightwatchman was nearer the mark. His dad patrolled the grounds of a small textiles factory just outside Bradford five nights a week.

"That's why we get so amused with all this bloody fuss about unemployment in the news all of a sudden," his father continued. "We've had job shortages up here for years. Nobody gave a bugger when the pits closed down. The government couldn't have cared less — why should they when we've had a Labour MP round here since before the War? Bloody Tories don't give a damn about anywhere north of Watford — but now they're beginning to panic because they're getting rising unemployment in the southeast for once — where all the Tory voters are. Now, suddenly, they've got to do something about Unemployment, because they've got a bloody general election coming up soon, haven't they?" he asked ironically, then shook his head.

"The point I'm trying to make is that we know what losing your job means up here. It's not something to be taken lightly — I'm not denying that. But there's another side to the argument, which you need to think about. The miners fought like hell to save their jobs — and sometimes they broke the law doing it. I had to arrest people I'd known for years and who'd never been in any trouble before." He looked at Redmond. "I suppose you could say I put my career before friendship. It's not something I'm proud of."

"But they were breaking the Law," Redmond pointed out. "You had no choice. You had to do your job."

His father waited, letting the implications sink in, before he said, "Exactly. That's a policeman's job — and if you're not prepared to do things like that, then you should be doing something else." He looked intently at Redmond. "You've got to ask yourself why you became a copper, Steve. Was it because I was one? Or because you wanted to uphold Law and Order, even if that does sound a bit trite these days, or because you wanted a good career?"

Redmond sipped his can thoughtfully. "It was all three, really."

"Right. So you've got to decide which one is the most important to you now. Okay, so this could cost you your career. It's a bloody awful thing to happen to anyone." He paused, then added quietly, "But some things are worse."

Redmond nodded slowly. "You're telling me to stick my neck out."

"What the hell else did you expect me to say, Steve? You knew damn well what I'd say when you came up here, didn't you? You didn't really need to ask me. . . . Listen to me, son. You're ambitious, I know that. You want to get on. You want to know if this is

117

worth jeopardising your future over. Maybe it isn't — but you're not sure, are you? The thing is, Steve, the question you've got to ask yourself is this: Whatever you do, will you be able to live with yourself afterwards?" He stared at his son for several seconds, his eyes seeming to bore right into Redmond's skull, then, suddenly, he looked away and grinned sheepishly. He lifted the can of beer to his mouth and tilted his head back to drain it. He looked at the tin with exaggerated distaste.

"Come on," he said, his accent pronounced again. "That's enough bloody jawin'. Let's get down to t'Colliers' and 'ave a decent pint."

London

"You wanted to see me, sir?" Redmond asked as he went into Selvey's office.

Selvey nodded. "I did indeed." He had been studying a VDT display on his desktop computer as Redmond had arrived; now he tapped out an instruction rapidly, checked the screen, then pressed the escape key. He swivelled round in his chair as Redmond sat down. "Mandrake," he said without preliminaries. "They're getting a bit impatient over at Curzon Street, by the looks of it."

"I see, sir," Redmond said noncommittally. Curzon Street was the address of the main MI5 headquarters.

"There's been a request through channels for us to terminate Mandrake immediately."

Bloody hell, thought Redmond. Mayhew had certainly not wasted any time. "An official request?"

"Not yet — but that's only a matter of time."

"Under what grounds?"

"Quote National Security unquote," Selvey said sourly. "What other reason is there as far as Five's concerned? The point is that the DAC will have to give way eventually, so it'll look better for you if you close the file yourself before that happens. That's why I asked you to drop by — a friendly warning, if you like."

"And much appreciated, sir," Redmond replied, but with an air of distraction. He knew what Selvey meant, that a definite decision on his part to call a halt would go down better with his superiors in the Branch rather than if he forced MI5 to muscle their way in.

"So — when can we expect your report?" Selvey asked, his tone deliberately brisk. Already, his attention seemed to be wandering back towards the VDT, as if the meeting were almost concluded, with the situation cut and dried. Redmond felt a sudden upsurge of resentment and, almost as if he were listening to someone else speaking, said firmly:

"I want to continue with Mandrake, sir, at least for the time being."

The expression on Selvey's face was almost comical. He stared at Redmond as if he had just uttered a loud obscenity. "You want to keep it open?" he asked, the incredulity in his voice matching that in his face.

"Yes, sir."

Selvey's eyes suddenly became shrewd, calculating. "Are you onto something?"

Redmond hesitated, then said, "Possibly. If this were a straightforward criminal investigation, I'd certainly want to look deeper."

Selvey nodded slowly, and there was something in his eyes that Redmond realised he had not seen for some time: approval — and respect. "Okay — fill me in. Tell me why you want it kept open."

Redmond took a deep breath, then said, "Right. Like I said, there's no conclusive evidence, but — we've had six deaths in as many months. Four of them worked on the same research project, though not at the same time. The project details are in the Olympus files, so, for all I know, these four could have been its entire personnel. The last death had one or two factors that I'd say made a verdict of accidental death anything but clear-cut." Briefly, he explained Elizabeth Kirk's judo ability. "Now, okay, so far we don't have any

120

actual evidence that any of these were murdered, but — well, sir, supposing they were? Shouldn't we be getting a bit worried about it?"

Selvey nodded again, his expression pensive. "If they've been murdered, then yes — but it's a big *if*. What would be the motive? The victims are hardly key members of our research efforts, are they?" He shook his head slowly. "It isn't really much to go on, is it?"

"I know that, sir, but . . ."

"Yes?"

"It's a gut instinct, sir. I just think something is going on — and the more I get told to drop it, the more suspicious I get, to be honest."

Selvey smiled faintly. "I know exactly what you mean there."

Redmond glanced at the other man in surprise.

Selvey stared back for almost a minute, then nodded slowly. "Okay, Steve — we'll play it your way. See what you can turn up. I'll try and keep them off your back, but I don't know how long that'll be."

"Even if Five puts in an official request?"

"We do say no to them sometimes."

"So you think there might be something going on as well, sir?"

"I haven't a clue," Selvey admitted. "Let

me see what you've got so far, then I'll tell you. The point is, Steve, you used to be a bloody good copper until . . . well, I think you know what I'm talking about. I think — I hope — you're about to become a good one again. If that's the case, and you think we ought to keep it open, then I'll back you to the hilt."

Redmond flushed with embarrassment — but also with pleasure. At the door, he paused and looked back. "Sir?"

"Yes?"

"Thank you."

"Anytime. Just come up with the goods, right?"

"Right."

Redmond was still grinning faintly when he reached his office, but then the expression faded as he remembered Selvey's surprise and realised the reason. It had been the unexpected display of backbone that had done it. From Redmond of all people . . . Jesus Christ, he thought, flopping down into his chair, am I really considered to be such a bloody creep around here? You want something done in a particular way, just give it to Redmond. . . . Which was why I was given this assignment in the first place, of course: good old Redmond, he'll do what he's told, he'll know what's good for him. Not anymore, he thought.

★ ★ ★

"There has been another rise in the unemployment figures for the seventh month in succession. Official figures released today show that the number of people out of work rose by twenty-nine thousand during February, bringing the total to —"

Impatiently, Redmond pressed the remote control button to switch channels on the television and found, in rapid succession, a repeat sitcom, a documentary on marine life, and a French film with subtitles. Holding the zapper like one of the phasers on "Star Trek," he aimed it at the TV set and pressed the off button; the screen went dead.

As if on cue, the telephone rang. He gave his number, then tensed as he heard a loud click on the line.

"Hallo, Steve. It's Julie."

"Hi."

"Listen, are you doing anything next Saturday night?"

"Nothing definite, no."

"Fancy a dinner party? I've been invited to one and if I don't take a partner, they'll try and unload this creep of a merchant banker onto me."

"You should know all about those," he commented, trying to make his voice sound natural. "So you want me to ride shotgun on

123

you, is that it?"

"Something like that."

"Be glad to. Anything for a damsel in distress."

"Thanks, Steve — you've just saved my life. I'll get back to you with the arrangements, okay?"

"Okay. See you, Julie."

She hung up, but Redmond stayed on the line until he heard another click, not as loud this time. Slowly, he reached up and slid the switch to "Standby," his expression grim.

His phone was being tapped.

There was absolutely no doubt in his mind at all: he had heard similar telltale clicks often enough when carrying out phonetaps himself. He stared at the handset, then abruptly stood up, still holding the telephone, and went into the spare room, where he kept a large toolbox. Within less than a minute, he had unscrewed the plastic casing and removed it.

"Shit . . ." he muttered, then peered more closely at the tiny disc, less than half an inch in diameter, that was magnetically clamped to the inside of the mouthpiece. It was a miniature transmitter, with an effective range of a quarter of a mile. He knew the type well, because it was used by both MI5 and the Branch.

Carefully, he screwed the casing back into

position and took the handset back to its cradle. Then, he looked slowly around the room and, with a sigh, began to search it, starting behind the picture of a ship under full sail above the mantelpiece.

It took him ten minutes to find the first listening device. It was fastened to the lampstand on top of one of the stereo speakers; the second one was in the bedroom, fixed behind a mirror, and a third was screwed into the shower spray. Between them, they would pick up any sound made in the flat above a whisper and transmit it to a receiver that would not be far away. How long had they been there? For a moment, Redmond felt a cold chill ripple down his spine at the thought of faceless listeners eavesdropping on every noise he made — and, for the first time, he began to have some inkling what it was like to be on the other side of the fence, to be the watched, instead of the watcher. He did not like the sensation at all. . . . Already, he was having to resist an almost instinctive impulse to look over his shoulder.

It was only then that it struck him: this was exactly how they wanted him to feel. He had been meant to find the bugs. He would have had to have been deaf not to hear the clicks on the line — and they were easily eliminated nowadays. The bugs had been in fairly obvious hiding places — he had found all three in less than thirty minutes. Someone wanted him to know he was under surveillance, had made sure he had found out about it. It was very likely that the bugs had only been installed recently — possibly only within the last twenty-four hours.

Since his decision to carry on with Mandrake, in fact . . .

They — whoever "they" might be — were beginning to put on the pressure.

Seven

The red Ford was still there in his rearview mirror and, seeing it, Redmond compressed his lips into a grim line. There was little doubt about it — he was being tailed. He had spotted the Ford almost as soon as he had set out this morning and, although he had deliberately made a fairly substantial detour from his normal route, it had been behind him ever since. True, sometimes it had dropped well back and at others had closed up, but it had not been out of sight for longer than about ten seconds. For a moment, Redmond was tempted to put his foot down and start dodging around the back streets or run a few red lights just to throw off the shadowing car, but it would be pointless: they knew where to find him anyway.

So now he knew, he thought grimly. He'd had a vague suspicion he was being tailed on several occasions over the past few days, but this was the first time he had definitely picked out the shadowing car. It gave him a distinctly uneasy sensation, a tingling at the back of his neck. The boot was now quite emphatically on the other foot, he thought — but who the hell was following him?

The thing that also bothered him was that the Ford today had been almost childishly easy to spot, so much so that it looked as though he had been intended to pick it up. If so, they were playing the same game as with the listening devices, letting him know he was under surveillance. The *why* was fairly obvious — it had to be linked to Mandrake. Someone did not want him probing any further — which implied he was on the right track. But how much more pressure would they exert if he carried on? That was what all this was about; they were letting him know they could get at him at any moment, whenever they chose. The unspoken message was simple: call off Mandrake and we'll call off the watchers.

But who were "they?"

More to the point, how far were they prepared to go?

Redmond was still brooding on the incident when he walked into his office and found Gail already there, waiting. He was still edgy from the shadowing and her presence somehow seemed to make it worse — perhaps it was the realisation that he wanted some time to absorb the implications and now was not going to get it.

She held up a typed report. "I've just got this from Hodge," she said. "He's been supervising the surveillance on Farrington."

"I know," Redmond replied with a hint of impatience.

She glanced at him sharply, then went on. "Apparently, he's been mixing with John Ledsham quite a lot — socially, I mean."

"Ledsham?" Redmond echoed, frowning. "Who the hell's he, when he's at home?"

"The managing director of Comelec," she replied, with exaggerated patience. "It's a computer firm. They do a lot of business with the MOD. Phillips worked for them," she prompted.

"I know what Comelec is," he grumbled.

"I'm glad about that. The thing is that Comelec relies a good deal on contracts with the MOD — they get most of their business there — and so having their MD chatting up Farrington over expensive dinners is hardly ethical, is it? I mean, although Farrington's unit doesn't actually decide who is going to be awarded any research contract, the MOD generally goes along with its suggestions, doesn't it? And Comelec has been doing rather well out of the MOD over the past few years — coincidence?"

Redmond nodded thoughtfully. "So you think Farrington might be receiving back-handers from Comelec?"

"It's possible, sir. Or maybe, if he is taking

money from Comelec, it isn't just for putting contracts their way."

Redmond shook his head doubtfully. "It's pretty tenuous, isn't it? I mean, I know we're getting desperate for a lead of some sort, but I can't really see our elders and betters being too impressed by this. I mean, this is just an offshoot of the Mackinnon thing, when all's said and done — and we don't even know if that's connected."

"No, I suppose not," she agreed glumly. She looked at him quizzically and seemed to hesitate. Then, she said, "How much longer do you think we'll get on this, sir?"

If Redmond was surprised by this sudden change of tack, he gave no sign of it. "I don't know, to be honest. Selvey's trying to hold them off, but apparently Five's made the request to have Mandrake terminated official. Unless we can come up with something rather more concrete than what we've got — I'd say a week at most."

"I see, sir," she said quietly. She looked at him with a curious intentness as if trying to make her mind up about something, then said quietly, "Sir?"

"Yes?"

"Can I ask you something?"

"Depends on what it is," he said warily.

"You can tell me to go to hell if you think

it's none of my business, but — why did you change your mind about Mandrake?"

Redmond stared at her, then shook his head slowly, chuckling softly. "You certainly don't beat about the bush, do you, Sergeant?"

"I — I was just curious, sir. You seemed so determined to close it down, then all of a sudden, you go in and say you want to keep it going. Was it Elizabeth Kirk's death?"

"It was a lot of things, Sergeant," Redmond said, with no inflection at all in his voice. He shrugged. "But as you yourself said, it's none of your business — okay?"

She smiled briefly and nodded. "Okay, sir. Fair enough. But . . . I'm glad you decided to stay with it. I'd like to thank you for that."

"Thank me?" he asked incredulously.

"For giving me a chance to follow up with it." She gestured awkwardly. "In a way, it's the first bit of real police work I've done since joining the Branch. Everything else has just been computer accessing, really. Okay, I know computers are my speciality, so I can't really complain, but — well, sir, I'm enjoying this."

"Glad to hear it," Redmond said, suppressing a grin. Enjoying it? Bloody hell . . . But why not? he thought suddenly. Hadn't he moved over to the nonuniform branch for precisely that reason, that he wanted to be involved in the detection side of police operations? Hadn't he spent hours trying to piece together disparate fragments of evidence and felt a buzz of pleasure when it had all clicked? And how much of that had he been doing recently?

Sod all, that was how much. . . . "You've done well," he said, to cover his thoughts as much as anything.

"Thank you, sir," she replied, flushing slightly.

"Anytime. Okay, back to work," he said briskly. "See if you can find out anything else about Farrington and this Ledsham."

The following morning, Redmond looked up from yet another folder — how many had he read over the past few weeks? — as Gail came in, waving a sheet of printout paper.

"Sir?"

"Yes?"

She perched on the edge of his desk. "I've got something here that might interest you. There was a big pileup on the A-one south of Hatfield last night," she began.

"Yes, I know. I saw it on the news."

"One of those involved was an MOD computer specialist — a Derek Aldridge, a systems analyst with one of Marconi's subsidiaries at Stevenage. He survived the crash and is in hospital with a broken arm. The point is that it was his car that caused the whole thing. He had a tyre blow out and spun across all three lanes. Everybody else braked to avoid him, a lorry jack-knifed and that was it. Four people dead — but not Aldridge. The thing is — he worked on Piccolo as well."

"I see," said Redmond heavily. "You think it could have been a hit that went wrong?"

"It's possible, isn't it?"

Redmond looked up at her, then said slowly, "The problem with staging road accidents is that you can't guarantee they'll work." He pointed to the printout she was holding. "Is that Aldridge's dossier?"

"The Central Registry one, yes. I'll need a bit more time if you want a more detailed one."

"This'll do for now." Redmond stared at the desk for a moment, his eyes unfocused. "I think I'd better go and have a word with Mr. Aldridge," he said, taking the printout from her. "Maybe take a look at his car as well."

There was no denying the fact that the Jaguar had been in an accident, because the front offside wing was spectacularly crumpled, but the rest of the car was relatively undamaged. Paradoxically, the rain at the time of the accident had probably saved Aldridge's life, in that it had allowed the car to spin round, where it might have flipped over on a dry surface. All the same, he had been lucky nothing had hit him; the articulated lorry had come to a halt only yards away, while the Toyota that had been hit by the lorry had missed him by inches.

"Bloody lucky, if you ask me," said the garage proprietor in the doorway as Redmond crouched down to examine the wing. Redmond had shown him a police ID card, but the other man seemed determined not to let him out of his sight, probably thinking the radio would go missing if he turned his back for an instant. Redmond grunted in reply and peered closely at the front offside wheel. The tyre had completely disintegrated, leaving only a buckled wheel rim and no indication as to the cause of the blowout, either.

"Is it usual for the tyre to be completely destroyed?" Redmond asked.

The proprietor shrugged. "Depends on what speed he was doing when it happened and what caused it. If it goes in a big way, then it just rips itself to pieces. You'll probably find most of it scattered across the motorway. The local police will have picked up as many bits as they can for Forensics."

Redmond nodded gloomily; there was nothing for him here.

★ ★ ★

Aldridge lived two miles outside Potters Bar, just off the A121, in a large bungalow that was reached by driving up a gravel drive. It was early evening when Redmond arrived and dusk was just settling. Redmond looked around while he waited for someone to answer the doorbell and found it difficult to believe that he was less than fifteen miles from central London, rather than in the sleepy Cotswolds; the house looked out over a vista of trees and open fields.

Mrs. Aldridge answered the door, a woman of about thirty-five with a long, rather horsey, face.

"My name's Redmond. I telephoned earlier." He showed her his identification.

"Oh yes. Do come in." Her voice was refined, Roedean or Cheltenham, he guessed. She showed him into the study where Aldridge was waiting, sitting in a large leather armchair. His right arm was encased in a plaster cast, supported by a sling around his neck.

"Forgive me for not getting up," he said. "They told me to take it easy at the hospital." He gestured ruefully at the cast. "I can't shake hands either." He was a small man with light-brown hair brushed straight back and a prominent Adam's apple. "Do sit down,

Inspector." He pointed to an armchair facing the door. As he sat, Redmond glanced around the room, noting the large desk in front of the window, upon which was a personal computer.

"Would you like a drink, Inspector?" Mrs. Aldridge asked.

"Er — no thanks," said Redmond. "I have to drive."

"What about tea or coffee?"

"Again, no thank you — but it's very kind of you to offer."

She nodded. "In that case, I'll leave you two to it." She went out, closing the door behind her.

"Right," said Aldridge briskly. "You're from Special Branch. Do you have your ID?"

Redmond nodded and took out his pass again, holding it out to Aldridge, who glanced at the photo, nodded, and returned it to Redmond.

"Right, Inspector. What can I do for you?"

"I'd like to ask you a few questions about your accident the day before yesterday, Mr. Aldridge."

"Now why would that interest Special Branch?" Aldridge looked shrewdly at Redmond. "Or is it that you lot are finally beginning to worry about the death toll amongst us computer specialists?"

Redmond stared at the other man — this was the first hint he had had that anyone outside the security services had noticed that anything was going on. How many others were wondering the same thing now? "We do have to consider all possibilities, Mr. Aldridge," he replied blandly. "You are working on a classified project, after all."

"You mean you think it was no accident?"

"There is absolutely no evidence to indicate that it was anything other than an accident at present," Redmond said, wondering why he sounded so pompous.

"But then you wouldn't tell me if there was, would you?" said Aldridge levelly. He was certainly no fool, thought Redmond — but then he wouldn't be, not with his qualifications.

"I'd just like you answer one or two questions," said Redmond, avoiding the issue. "This is an entirely routine procedure in these cases."

Aldridge shrugged. "Very well. Fire away."

"Did you hear anything just before the tyre blew out?"

"Like what?"

"Anything out of the ordinary."

Aldridge thought for a moment, then shook his head. "All I heard was a bang, then the car veered off to the right."

"Had anyone overtaken you before it happened?"

Aldridge frowned. "What has that to do with anything?"

"Maybe nothing. But did anyone?"

"Well, yes, actually, someone did. He went past me on the inside about a minute beforehand, I suppose."

"Could you identify the car?"

"You think he had something to do with it?"

Redmond stared at Aldridge. It was as if he actually wanted it to be a murder attempt. Didn't he realise that, but for a fluky set of circumstances, he should be dead? "Could you identify the car?" he repeated.

"Yes. A blue Rover."

"Did you notice the registration?"

Aldridge shook his head. "Afraid not, but —" He hesitated.

"But what?"

"I'm not sure, but I think it was the same car that followed me through Hatfield when I took a detour. I couldn't swear to it, though."

Redmond studied Aldridge thoughtfully. Was that true, or was it what the other man wanted to believe? "Did you notice the driver of this Rover at all?" he asked.

"Not really, no. It was dark, after all."

"Do you remember seeing the car at all before the day of the accident?"

"No . . . I can't say that I do."

Redmond nodded, then stood up. "I think that'll be all for now, Mr. Aldridge. Thank you for talking to me."

"Do you really think someone tried to kill me?" Aldridge asked, his voice both fearful and excited.

"As I said, there is no evidence whatsoever that it was anything but an accident — but obviously we had to make sure."

"I see. I'm sorry, but can you find your own way out?"

"Of course." He stood, put his hands in his pockets, then turned to look at a large rubber plant by the door into the hall. "That's a very impressive specimen," he commented and went over to it. "I can never get one of these to grow." He leaned forward to examine it more closely. As he did so, his hand emerged from his pocket holding a tiny listening device. He placed it in the soil at the plant's base and covered it over, his body obscuring what he was doing. "Oh, just one more thing," he said, turning back to Aldridge. "I understand you worked on the Piccolo Project for several years?"

Aldridge nodded, surprised, "Yes, I did. Why?"

"What exactly was it?"

Aldridge stared at him. "Does this have anything to do with my accident?"

"There is a possibility of some connection, yes."

Aldridge frowned. "I doubt it, somehow. After all, the subproject that I worked on closed down a year ago, and the overall project was terminated six months ago, so I believe. I can't say I was surprised — it was obvious to all of us that it was never going to work properly, but —" He broke off and stared suspiciously at Redmond. "Do you have the necessary clearance for this?"

"I don't need to know the details of the project, Mr. Aldridge — just whether it was successful or not."

"I see," Aldridge said slowly; it was evident that he did not see at all. "Well, I suppose I've as good as told you anyway. No, the Piccolo system did not work. It was a failure, and, as far as any of us involved on it could see, there was no way that it was ever going to work reliably. It had too many basic design faults. That was why the project was terminated. Not before time, I would say. If it hadn't been for the support for the project from the States, it would have been closed down at least a year earlier."

"The States?"

"Of course. It was a combined British-

140

American project. Both the MOD and the Pentagon were involved —" Again, Aldridge broke off. "I really think I've said enough. It is an Official Secret, after all."

"Indeed it is, Mr. Aldridge, indeed it is. Well, thank you for your help. You've been most kind. I shan't detain you any longer."

Once he was in the hall, Redmond attached a second bug underneath the telephone table, then let himself out.

Eight

Redmond shifted position to ease a cramp in his leg, then peered through a pair of night glasses at the Aldridge's bungalow fifty yards away. He was vaguely aware of Hodge looking unobtrusively at his watch next to him, but he ignored the momentary distraction, focusing his entire attention on what he could see through the lenses. Which was not a lot, to be honest. . . . The two of them were in an old barn in a field opposite the bungalow and a little way along the lane. Their present vantage point gave them a good view of the front of the house, while there was a third man, Lennox, watching the rear. Between them, they would be able to observe anyone approaching the bungalow from any direction — always assuming that anyone was going to.

He was only too aware of the fact that this was all a long shot, based largely on the assumption that Aldridge's accident had in fact been an attempted murder. Even *if* it had, there was no guarantee that there would be a follow-up attempt, but West and Kirk had been killed since Mandrake had been opened and *if* Aldridge was an intended victim, then three hits had been carried out at a time when it would have been more prudent — and effective — for the killer to call a halt. The deaths had gone on, however, which argued some sort of timetable.

If. The whole bloody situation was built around *if*s, Redmond told himself bitterly. If Aldridge's "accident" had been intentional. If they were in a hurry to see him dead. If there was a killer at all. . . . Was this an act of desperation on his part, because he knew he was running out of time, that Selvey would not be able to hold off the official request for much longer? Redmond knew damn well they needed more evidence — but was this really where they were going to find it? Maybe he should have done the sensible thing and pulled out when he had the chance, because it was beginning to look as though Mandrake was going down the drain. . . .

Along with his career, in all probability. He pushed the thought away and took another look through the binoculars, deliberately concentrating on what he could see through them. Which wasn't very much, but it was infinitely better than worrying. . . . It was too late for that now. Like it or not, he was committed.

He checked his watch; it was 8:15. God, he was bored. He would give it until nine and then leave Hodge and Lennox to it — they would have to stay here until midnight. He looked down at the items they had brought with them — a portable receiver for the bugs he had left, a thermos flask each of coffee, two pairs of binoculars, and a camera that, like the binoculars, was fitted with an infrared image intensifier. Finally, there was a large monkey wrench. This last had been brought virtually as an afterthought: if anything happened they might have to smash their way into the house. He reached inside his jacket, took out a Browning automatic pistol, and checked its magazine for perhaps the twentieth time before returning it to its shoulder holster, smiling grimly to himself as he saw Hodge doing the same. Redmond had spent several hours in the underground target range over the past few days, firing off round after round, but even though the instructor had declared himself pleased with his marksmanship, Redmond still did not feel comfortable carrying a gun: it seemed to smack of failure, somehow. . . . Finally, he checked his watch again, sighed when he saw it was only 8:18, then picked up the night glasses once more.

At exactly 8:30, a Ford Granada came along the lane from the direction of Potters Bar, slowed, and turned into the drive leading up to the Aldridge bungalow. "That must be the insurance salesmen," said Hodge, glancing at his watch. "They phoned last night to arrange it."

Redmond nodded. "Better get their mug shots anyway, just in case."

"Right." Hodge picked up the infrared camera and snapped off photographs of the two suited men that emerged from the car, each one carrying a briefcase. They went up to the front door and rang the bell. Redmond turned up the volume of the radio receiver and heard Mrs. Aldridge open the door.

"Hello, Mrs. Aldridge? My name is Mr. Bryant and this is Mr. King. We spoke to your husband last night. My card."

Redmond saw the taller man hold out a business card, which Mrs. Aldridge took. "Come on in, gentlemen. My husband's expecting you."

Just great, thought Redmond. As if listening to bloody TV programmes isn't enough, now I have to put up with an insurance sales pitch. Idly, he wondered if perhaps the salesmen knew about the accident and were moving in, vulturelike, to boost Aldridge's accident cover, then he flicked the receiver over to the frequency of the transmitter in the study. He heard Aldridge say, "Good evening, gentlemen. Good of you to be —"

A shot rang out from the house, amplified through the receiver. Jesus Christ, thought

Redmond, scooping up the monkey wrench in an almost instinctive action before launching himself into a headlong sprint towards the bungalow. He heard a high-pitched scream that was abruptly cut off by the sound of a second shot as he hurdled the fence into the garden, with Hodge close behind him. There were shouts coming from inside the house, and then there was a third shot as he reached the large bay window, wielding the heavy wrench in one hand, the gun in the other. Holding up his gun hand to shield his face, Redmond swung the wrench at the central pane of glass, which shattered into fragments. Hodge kicked in what was left of the glass and leaped through the window, but the next second there was a deafening roar as someone fired a shotgun, stopping Hodge dead in his tracks as the blast took him in the stomach. He staggered backwards until the backs of his knees caught the low windowsill behind him and he toppled outwards, falling heavily onto the gravel drive, his legs still hooked over the window frame.

Redmond swore, then threw himself through the window, folding his arms protectively over his head. He landed and rolled over, through the middle of the curtains, bringing his gun up as he tried to weigh up the situation.

The taller man, the one who had called himself Bryant, was by the door, ten feet away, standing over Mrs. Aldridge's motionless form, cradling a sawn-off shotgun, while the second man — King — was standing only a yard away from Redmond, staring down at him in astonishment; he too was holding a shotgun. He made no move to use it but, instead, lashed out with his foot, kicking Redmond's gun out of his hand. Redmond twisted around on the floor and came up onto his feet in a convulsive surge, his right hand spearing forward in a straight-fingered karate blow aimed at King's solar plexus. The gunman gasped, but Redmond knew he had not made proper contact. King swung the shotgun at Redmond like a club, hitting him painfully in the ribs. Redmond's hands snaked out, grabbing the gun's barrels. He pivoted round, wrenched at the gun, and pulled King off balance, sending him sprawling on the carpet, but then, out of the corner of his eye, Redmond saw Bryant lining up his own shotgun now that he had a clear shot. Redmond dived behind the desk as Bryant fired, blasting out what was left of the window, before the gunman turned and ran for the door. King scrambled to his feet to follow, but Redmond came out from behind the desk at a run, launching himself at King, his right hand chopping at the other man's throat. King blocked it with his forearm and countered with a punch into Redmond's groin. Redmond barely twisted aside in time, gasping as he took the blow on his hip, but he continued his twisting movement, moving away to his right before he kicked backwards. His foot slammed into King's chest and King staggered backwards, grunting in pain. Redmond moved in, his right fist exploding into the gunman's stomach like a sledgehammer. King doubled up, clutching at his midriff, as Redmond bunched his fists together, raised them high in the air, then brought them crashing down on King's unprotected neck. The gunman dropped like a leaden weight.

Redmond looked around rapidly, seeing Aldridge for the first time, lying on his stomach by the armchair, but then he heard a gunshot outside. He scooped up his gun and sprinted out into the hall, then through the open door onto the drive. As he skidded to a halt, he saw the Granada moving off — straight towards him; he tried to bring his gun up, but then had to leap aside as the car roared past, missing him by inches. He landed heavily, the impact winding him, but he rolled over and came up on one knee, firing off two rapid shots at the escaping car. The rear window exploded into fragments, but then the car slewed round into the lane, its tyres squealing, and accelerated away.

Wincing, Redmond stood up and saw Lennox, lying motionlessly on his back next to the drive. His eyes were staring sightlessly up at the night sky, and there was a massive close-range blast injury to his chest. Redmond shook his head slowly in bitter chagrin, then went unsteadily back into the study, holding his gun on the unconscious gunman as he went over to Mrs. Aldridge, who was lying on her side. She was absolutely still and her chest was a mass of blood, but he felt for a pulse nevertheless. His lips tightened momentarily, then he went over to Aldridge, who was face-down on the carpet in a growing crimson pool — far too much blood, he realised as he placed his fingers against the base of Aldridge's neck.

Nothing.

Redmond sat back on his haunches. "Fuck!" he yelled. He stared down at Aldridge's dead face for a moment, then rose slowly to his feet and dialled 999.

"And you didn't get a good look at the other man's face? The one who called himself Bryant?" asked Inspector Whitham.

Redmond shook his head. "Only a glimpse. The infrared camera might have got a picture, but I doubt it — he had his back turned the whole time as far as I can remember."

"So he's tall, dark-haired, and muscularly built, in his middle to late thirties, driving a dark-coloured Granada, registration F-four-two-two VNP. Right?"

"With a shattered rear window."

"Right." Whitham nodded to the young DC who had been scribbling Redmond's statement down. "Get that lot sent out to all units, along with a warning that the bloke's armed and dangerous."

"Very dangerous," Redmond said grimly.

"Right, sir," said the DC and went out.

Whitham looked around. They were standing in the study by what was left of the window. The bodies still lay where they had fallen, although they were covered by sheets and would be taken away in the next few minutes. A forensic team was patiently combing the room, inch by inch, searching for fingerprints or anything else they could find, while, in the doorway, Collings, the local inspector, was standing talking to a sergeant. He had arrived ten minutes or so before Whitham, whom Redmond had telephoned immediately after the 999 call, and was clearly not happy about Special Branch taking over a murder investigation on his patch. His frustration would be exacerbated by the knowledge that, in all probability, he would never be told the full story of what had happened, and by the realisation that there was absolutely nothing he could do about it either. Once the Branch got its claws into a case, that was the end of the matter.

Whitham looked thoughtfully at Redmond, then lowered his voice, turning away from Collings as he spoke. "You knew this was going to happen, didn't you? That's why you had the place staked out."

"I didn't know for certain, Mike. I just thought it might. That's why I had my men armed — for all the good that did," he added bitterly. "Got both of them killed, didn't I?"

"It looks as though these two were pros, Steve. They certainly weren't messing about, anyway. Just what the hell were they doing here, though?"

Redmond shook his head wearily, then winced at the sudden stab of pain that lanced through his skull; he had a splitting headache. "Sorry, Mike, I can't tell you that, not until I get clearance."

Whitham sighed. "Story of my life, that is," he said philosophically. "Okay, we'll see what we can turn up. You're leaving King, or whatever his name is, at the local nick for now?"

"Yes. We'll shift him to one of the safehouses tomorrow. I don't think he'll be causing any trouble tonight, but if you could lay on someone to keep an eye on him, I'd

151

be very grateful."

Whitham nodded. "Will do. The usual — nobody to see him except for you, right?"

"Well, I suppose you'd better have a doctor take a look at him, but make sure your bloke's with him at the time."

Whitham nodded again. "Okay. I'll get on to it. See you later." He went out, nodding briefly to Collings.

Redmond clenched his eyes tightly shut as a fresh wave of pain surged over him; Jesus, weren't there any aspirins about? Not that having a headache was any great surprise; it was a combination of tiredness, a reaction to the night's events, and a realisation that, for all his preparations, he still had not been able to prevent the murders. That knowledge far outweighed the fact that he had a prisoner to question, or even the fact that now they would have more than enough to keep Mandrake open.

He'd finally found the evidence he'd been searching for — but at what cost?

The man who had identified himself as Bryant flashed his lights twice as he drew up outside a pair of wire-mesh gates, which were immediately opened by a tall, overweight man in a blue anorak. Bryant drove the car on through the gates, the headlights picking out the rusting, crumpled wrecks of cars stacked one on top of another in some kind of surreal landscape. The man — Smethurst, the owner of the scrapyard — closed the gates and then pointed to the right, indicating a passageway between the ranks of cars. Bryant followed him, the Granada lurching over the uneven surface and splashing through puddles until Smethurst held up his hand, signalling Bryant to stop. Smethurst beckoned him on a few feet further, then held up his thumb. Bryant turned off the lights and switched off the engine. He was about to climb out when a figure seemed to materialise from the shadows. With a gesture for Bryant to stay where he was, the newcomer opened the passenger door and sat down. He said nothing at first but simply stared intently at Bryant for several seconds.

"A right fucking balls-up tonight, wasn't it, O'Brien?"

"Look, Mr. Lansky, how was I to know they'd have the place under surveillance?" O'Brien protested in a thick Belfast accent.

"You should have checked. I mean, not only did you screw up the first attempt, you then decide to go in with guns blazing like the fucking Fifth Cavalry. This isn't Northern Ireland! What in hell were you playing at?"

"I wanted it to look like a hit by the boys, you know —"

"Why didn't you leave your name and address while you were at it?" Lansky interrupted scathingly.

"Look, you said he had to be taken out inside a fortnight, right? Given the fact that he had his arm in plaster, it had to be in his home, because he wasn't going to be out much, so faking a suicide or another accident wasn't really on, was it? It was you who said we were in a hurry, for fuck's sake."

"So, instead, you've more or less told everybody what we're up to." Lansky shook his head slowly. "Not doing very well, are you, O'Brien? I was told you were good, but I've seen precious little sign of that. We can't afford mistakes like this — you know that as well as I do." He let his breath out in a long sigh, almost regretfully, then said quietly, "In fact, O'Brien, to be honest with you, we can't afford you anymore."

In that last moment, O'Brien knew what was going to happen and reached frantically for the door handle, but, as if by magic, a silenced automatic appeared in Lansky's hand. There was a soft coughing sound and O'Brien was thrown sideways, clutching at his ribs, his face contorted. He opened his mouth to say something, but no sound came out and he slumped slowly forwards against the wheel, his eyes glazing over as Lansky opened the door and climbed out.

Lansky waved his arm and, immediately, the scene was bathed in light as half a dozen arc lamps came on. Almost instinctively, Lansky stepped backwards into the shadows as Smethurst climbed up into the cab of a large crane. There was a pause, and then the crane's motors coughed into life. Slowly, it rotated, swinging a large electromagnetic clamp towards the Granada. The clamp descended, striking the Granada's roof with a loud metallic clang, its weight making the car rock on its springs. The noise from the crane intensified as the powerful electric current came on, activating the magnet. Gradually, the cable tautened and lifted the car from the ground, swinging it up and round, the swaying motion of the car causing the crane's hoist to jerk erratically. Eventually, the car was suspended above the squat bulk of a mechanical crusher and, slowly, it was lowered down into it. Just before it disappeared from view Lansky had a last glimpse of O'Brien's face staring back at him through the driver's window.

Smethurst climbed down from the crane's cab and walked unhurriedly over to the crusher, where he reached up and pressed a button on the side of the machine. A moment later the crusher started up with a hideous grinding noise.

Lansky stood in the darkness, his face expressionless as he listened to the Granada's death screeches.

Potters Bar Police Station

The desk sergeant looked up as a tall man in a raincoat walked up to the desk, stifling a yawn. The sergeant could sympathise with him — it was not yet five-thirty in the morning and the newcomer looked as if he had only recently been roused from sleep. Any sympathy the sergeant might have felt, however, was tempered by the fact that he had been on duty for seven and a half hours himself and was looking forward to the end of his shift, thirty minutes from now.

"My name's Dean," the raincoated man said, producing an ID card that almost brought the sergeant to attention because not only was it an MI5 pass, but it also had the second-highest security clearance available. "I gather you're looking after a prisoner for us?"

"Er — yes, sir."

"How is he?"

"Seems all right, sir. We've put him in a cell with a Special Branch DS on guard outside."

"Outside?" The man frowned. "He ought to be under constant observation, really.

156

May I see him?"

The sergeant hesitated momentarily — his orders had been only to let an Inspector Redmond in to see the prisoner — but then nodded: Dean's pass granted him virtually unlimited access. "Yes, sir. If you'll follow me?"

The two policemen walked along a corridor with cell doors on each side towards a sandy-haired man who sat in a chair outside the end cell on the right. The man looked up as they approached, a gun in a shoulder holster, judging by the bulge in the left armpit of the jacket he wore.

"Somebody from Five," the desk sergeant explained. "Mr. Dean."

"Morning, Sergeant . . . ?" Dean held up his pass.

". . . Hayes, sir." He inspected the pass much more thoroughly than the desk sergeant, then nodded. "You've come about chummy in there?"

"Yes." Dean turned to the uniformed sergeant. "Thank you, Sergeant." The tone was one of dismissal. He watched the sergeant go, then turned back to Hayes. "You've been keeping an eye on him?"

"Yes, through the peephole. He's been sleeping. The police doctor patched him up, and he's been out for the count ever since."

"I see. Well, let's have a look at him, shall we?"

Hayes hesitated momentarily, but then, evidently remembering how high the clearance had been on the ID card, he nodded and took a set of keys from his pocket. He selected one and unlocked the door, standing aside to let Dean precede him. The man from MI5 nodded curtly and went in, glancing swiftly around as he took four steps into the centre of the cell. He turned as Hayes followed him in and said:

"We'd better have the door closed, Sergeant, just in case."

"Right, sir." Hayes turned away to close the cell door. Dean moved rapidly, raising his right arm high and then bringing the edge of his hand scything downwards with brutal force onto the killing point on Hayes's neck. There was an audible crack, and Hayes collapsed like a deflated balloon. His legs writhed spastically as he crumpled against the metal door; then he slid slowly over sideways and lay still.

Dean spun round, reaching inside his coat, and saw King beginning to stir on the bunk, evidently disturbed by the noise of the falling body. As Dean's hand emerged holding a dart-gun, he saw a look of recognition on King's face, followed rapidly by hope and then horrified despair as the weapon lined up on him.

158

King opened his mouth to cry out, but before he could make any sound Dean fired twice, aiming at King's throat. The tiny darts embedded themselves in his neck and the toxin with which they had been tipped took effect instantly, paralysing his vocal chords and windpipe. His mouth opened and closed desperately as he fought vainly for breath, and then, suddenly, his body arched backwards in agony as the poison reached his heart. His heels and elbows beat a frantic tattoo on the bunk as his eyes bulged and his tongue protruded obscenely before, abruptly, it was all over. His body subsided slowly onto the bed and his head lolled to one side. It had taken less than fifteen seconds.

Dean went to the cell door, gun at the ready as he listened for any sound of an alarm being raised, but there was nothing; the kills had been almost completely silent. Working quickly now, he shoved Hayes's body unceremoniously to one side before he pulled on a pair of rubber gloves so that he could open the cell door and bring in the chair from outside. He positioned it to one side of the door, then manhandled Hayes into it, leaning the body against the side wall, so that all that would be visible through the spy-hole would be his legs. Then, he rolled King over until he was facing the wall and pulled the blankets back over him, before taking one final look round the cell. He picked up the bunch of keys from where they had fallen and went out, closing and locking the cell door behind him. One last check through the spy-hole, then he removed the gloves and walked briskly along the corridor, breathing deeply to drain off the excess of adrenaline.

The desk sergeant looked up as Dean reached the top of the stairs, his expression carefully neutral. "Not much doing, Sergeant," Dean said ruefully. "He's still unconscious. I've asked Sergeant Hayes to stay inside the cell — he really must be under constant supervision."

"I see, sir. Would you like me to post someone outside the cell as well?"

Dean appeared to consider this for a moment, then shook his head. "I don't think we need to go that far — Hayes is armed, after all. But I think he'd appreciate a cup of coffee in half an hour or so, if you'd be so kind — ?"

"I'll see to it, sir."

"Good. Well, I'll be off then. Hayes knows where to contact me when he comes round. Thank you for your assistance, Sergeant." Dean nodded pleasantly and, without any apparent haste, walked out.

He headed for the phone box on a nearby

corner and dialled rapidly. "Beresford?" he said into the mouthpiece.

"Yes?"

"It's Lansky."

"I gather there was some trouble last night?"

"It's been dealt with."

"You're certain of that?"

"Completely."

The harsh, insistent ringing of the telephone dragged Redmond from the depths of sleep and, as he reached across to pick up the receiver from the bedside table, he became gradually aware of a dull throbbing ache in the side of his head where the shotgun's barrel had struck him; he supposed, vaguely, that he ought to see a doctor about it, but then he lifted the phone to his ear. "Redmond," he mumbled, peering blearily at the alarm clock: it was not yet seven A.M.

"Steve? It's Mike Whitham."

"Mike? What —" Redmond suddenly sat up, somehow knowing what Whitham was going to say.

"It's the prisoner you left last night at Potters Bar. He's dead."

"Dead? How, for Christ's sake?"

"Someone got into the cell and topped him — and my DS," Whitham added bitterly.

"Just what the hell is going on?"

"I wish to Christ I knew."

"You mean you're not prepared to tell me, is that it? Well, chew on this as well. We've managed to identify the late Mr. King. His real name is Declan Keenan. He's a member of the Provisional IRA."

"That's him," Redmond said tiredly, pointing to the top photograph on a page halfway through a bulky dossier that he had been leafing through for the past quarter of an hour. "That's Bryant."

"You're sure?" asked Whitham.

Redmond shrugged. "Fairly sure, yes. I didn't really have time to get a good look, but, yeah, I'd say it was him. You could always check with the photos we took."

Whitham shook his head. "No good, Steve. You were right — all you got was the back of his head. So how sure are you?"

Redmond blew out his cheeks, considering. "Eighty percent."

"Okay, fair enough. This character's name is Eamonn O'Brien and he generally works with Keenan. The rest of the description fits as well." He sighed. "O'Brien's one of their hit men. One of their best, actually."

"So Aldridge was killed by an IRA hit team?" Redmond asked, evidently bewildered. "Just what the hell are they doing in all this?"

"All right," said Selvey, holding up his hands in mock surrender as Gail and Redmond came into his office. "You can both say 'I told you so.' "

Redmond glanced at Gail and shrugged. "Nice to be right for once."

"Bloody hell, Steve, you look awful," Selvey said as they sat down in front of his desk.

Redmond touched his bruised cheek briefly. "So everyone keeps telling me."

Selvey looked at the livid mark for a moment longer, then sat back in his chair. "Right. As I said, you were right all along, so it seems. Last night proves it beyond all doubt. We now have to work on the premise that there is a systematic murder campaign being waged against scientists and technicians working on our defence research projects. We have a very highly organised setup in operation here and, judging by the speed with which they located and liquidated Keenan, we have to assume that they do, indeed, have a source either in the MOD or the security services somewhere." He shook his head. "I have to admit that this IRA involvement baffles me. I don't see how they come into this at all."

Redmond shook his head slowly, forcing

himself to concentrate; he still had not really recovered from the night before, either physically or mentally. "Neither do I, sir. There doesn't seem to be any motive for the IRA killing Aldridge. He didn't have any links with Ulster whatsoever — he'd never even been to the place. In any case, what happened to Keenan isn't normal Provo tactics. *Someone* didn't want us to talk to him." He shrugged. "On the other hand, it wouldn't be the first time the IRA's carried out hits for other people. And it would make far more sense than that these blokes were freelancing in this case."

Selvey nodded judiciously. "I agree. So — what leads do we have?"

"Precious few," Redmond admitted. "The police are looking for O'Brien and the Granada, which had false plates, by the way. That registration is for a Vauxhall in Bedfordshire whose owner has a cast-iron alibi."

"They weren't taking any chances," Selvey observed. "And no sign of O'Brien?"

"None at all, sir. He's probably back in Ireland by now."

"What about Keenan's possessions? Any leads there?"

"Not a thing. No driving license, wallet, not even a bunch of keys. His clothes are off-the-peg from Burton's, so you can imagine how

164

easy they're going to be to trace, while the shotgun had its serial number filed off. The lab's trying to pick it out using electron microscopes or whatever, but I don't suppose it'll help us much if we do. They seem to have covered their tracks very thoroughly."

"Yes, so I see. As you said, they do seem to be going to great lengths to preserve their anonymity, whoever they are. Walking into a police station took some nerve, after all. Any leads there, by the way? Surely there must be a description from the policeman on the desk?"

"Oh, yes. Six foot, in his late thirties or forties, muscular build — nothing like O'Brien, in other words. He was wearing a pinstripe suit, but you'd expect that if he said he was from MI-five. Also metal-rimmed spectacles and a moustache. Fair hair."

"Ye-es," Selvey said slowly. "Not doing too well, are we? Have the policemen been looking through the photos?"

"Yes. Nothing yet."

"How did he kill the two of them? Do we know yet?"

"He killed Hayes with a blow to the neck. Keenan was killed by two darts tipped with shellfish toxin. Both killings very quick — and silent. This bloke knew what he was doing."

Selvey nodded. "So I see. And the desk sergeant reckoned the pass was genuine?"

"Yes, he did, but the problem there is that he hasn't actually seen all that many before and he was expecting someone from us or MI-five to show up. Perhaps he didn't look all that closely. On the other hand, Hayes would have spotted anything that wasn't kosher."

"Which means the killer has access to damn good forgeries," said Selvey grimly. "Which implies a leak in the MOD, Steve. That's all we need — another high-ranking mole — and an IRA involvement," he said disgustedly. "They won't like this at all at Curzon Street."

"You mean MI-five, sir?" asked Redmond, exchanging a bleak look with Gail.

"I'm afraid so," Selvey said reluctantly. "I don't think we'll be able to keep them out of it from here on in — it is rather too important to keep to ourselves."

"I suppose so," Redmond said gloomily. He had known this would almost certainly happen, but that did not make it any easier to accept.

Selvey looked sympathetically at the two of them. "I can understand how you feel — and yes, they probably will take over this whole thing, kit and caboodle. But you did your jobs well — I'll see that you get the credit you deserve."

"Thank you, sir," they muttered in unison,

but neither of them with any noticeable enthusiasm. Redmond was trying to tell himself that he was now off the hook, that he had been vindicated, that his future prospects now looked rosy, but all he could feel was a numbing sense of anticlimax.

Maybe it was the headache. . . .

Nine

It was exactly three o'clock when Redmond and Gail arrived at the office of Chief Superintendent Bryceland. He was seated behind his desk and, as they came in, he inclined his head briefly to each of them in turn. "Good of you to come at such short notice."

"You did say it was urgent, sir," said Redmond.

"Quite." Bryceland indicated two chairs in front of the desk. "Do sit down."

They did so, watching Bryceland warily. He gazed impassively at them for a moment, then said, "Firstly, Redmond, I think I owe you an apology. I seem to recall suggesting that you should perhaps not take your investigation too seriously. I had the best of intentions in offering you that advice, but it's probably just as well that you ignored me. I think congratulations are in order. Considering the rather — ah — restricted nature of your investigations, you have made considerable progress."

Redmond and Gail exchanged embarrassed glances. "Just doing our job, sir."

"Quite — but doing it very persistently, if I may say so. However, you do seem to have landed us with a pretty king-sized headache, haven't you? A team of Irish assassins running around killing our computer specialists, at least one Eastern bloc agent infiltrated into our defence research projects, and the likelihood of a mole somewhere in Whitehall." He smiled briefly. "You certainly don't believe in half-measures, do you? On top of that, it looks as though the head of the Research Co-ordination Unit in the MOD has not been conducting himself with the decorum we would like — I know that wasn't what you were looking for when you put him under surveillance, but it's a worthwhile contribution if we do eventually discover him to be guilty of any — ah — impropriety."

"We're still no closer to discovering the mole, though, sir," Redmond replied quietly.

"Quite. However, now that you have uncovered this rather disturbing can of worms, a combined MI-five Special Branch investigation has been initiated and I have been given command of our end of it. We've been given authority to go all out with this — and we will. Obviously, this new investigation will be on a far larger scale than Mandrake and will have access to areas that were denied to you. Hopefully, we will be able to uncover the mole, whoever he is."

"I hope so, sir," Redmond murmured. He

glanced at Gail again, then ventured, "And will we be involved in this stepped-up investigation, sir?"

"Naturally, although I think you will appreciate that you will not be taking quite such a leading role — neither of you are sufficiently senior to be placed in charge of what will be quite an extensive programme. I will have executive authority within the Branch, but Superintendent Selvey and both of you will, of course, be quite definitely involved."

"I see, sir." There was no trace of any emotion in Redmond's voice, but Gail looked sharply at him, sensing his disappointment. Bryceland was taking over the investigation and, obviously, would appoint his own team to take over its running. It would place both Redmond and herself a long way down the pecking order.

Bryceland also stared intently at Redmond, perhaps also divining his reaction. "I'd like you to go to Washington, Redmond."

"Washington?"

"There is a distinct possibility that there is a parallel operation taking place in the United States," said Bryceland, still watching Redmond closely. "Throughout the past few months a number of computer specialists have also died over there in similar circumstances — accidents, suicides and so on — and I'd like you to see if there is any connection. You'll be on temporary secondment to the FBI, which is setting up its own investigation, so it'll be a two-way thing — they'll give you all the information you want while you give them advice on how to set up their operation."

"I see," Redmond said again, his tone neutral. "Do we have any indications that the American deaths are linked beyond what you've already mentioned?"

"No concrete leads, no — but that is why I want you out there, Redmond. If there are, then we really do have a serious situation on our hands."

"Indeed," Redmond nodded. "How much authority will I have to poke around amongst the files the FBI or the NSA let me see?"

"As much as we can get. To that end, we will be moving you up to chief inspector from the first of next month and you will be reporting directly to me. If you have any problems as regards accessing any material, contact me and I'll bring in the big guns."

"Very well, sir," Redmond replied, impassively.

Bryceland turned to Gail. "As for you, Sergeant, I shall want you to set up a collating unit. You'll have access to the files of all the Mandrake scientists, as well as to any other sources you require. I want you to go through those files with a fine-tooth comb and see what patterns you can uncover." He held up his hand. "I know that this is what you've been doing already, but I think you'll find that we can make information available to you that has hitherto been denied. You will be in charge of the unit, with a staff of five or six, I would imagine — which will naturally entail your promotion to inspector being brought forward."

"Thank you, sir," she replied, genuinely taken aback; under normal circumstances, she would have had to wait another five months at least.

"Right," said Bryceland briskly, indicating that the interview was nearing its end. "Gibson downstairs will be in touch with each of you as regards briefing or requirements. I wish you both luck. And, once again — well-done."

Neither Gail nor Redmond said much as they made their way back to his office; both seemed gloomily preoccupied. Gail wandered over to the window, her arms folded across her chest, while Redmond flopped into his chair and began to toy moodily with a pencil. The brooding silence was almost tangible as it stretched out — one minute, two. . . .

Eventually, Gail said quietly, without turning round, "Well, sir — are you going to say it or shall I?"

"Be my guest," he murmured.

"We've been screwed, haven't we?"

"I think that just about sums it up, yes."

She turned round to face him. "I mean, I'm not imagining things, am I? I'm not just being paranoid? Or is Bryceland going to get the credit for uncovering all this?"

"Basically, yes," Redmond said slowly. "We'll get a mention somewhere and a pat on the back each, but the real kudos will go to Bryceland, because he'll be the one in charge when they start making arrests, or start booting out Russian 'attachés.' "

"And, meanwhile, you'll be in the States —"

"Safely out of the way."

"— and I'll still be collating cross-references when I'm not typing up bloody reports."

"Don't knock it — we're both getting promotions out of it."

"Very true — but that's only to keep us both sweet, isn't it? That's part of the deal. We've been bought off."

"Exactly." Redmond sighed and then looked startled as the pencil suddenly snapped in his hands. "But, as the old army saying goes, if you can't take a joke, you shouldn't have joined."

"Is that supposed to make me feel better?"

"No, but let's be honest about it — this sort of thing happens all the time in our business, doesn't it? I mean, there's no way they're going to leave this in our hands, is there? Not something this big. At least we're getting some action out of them — and not before time."

"I suppose so," she agreed reluctantly. She leaned back against her desk. "And maybe you'll turn something up in the States."

"Maybe. If nothing else, I get a free trip over there, anyway."

"Some people have all the luck. Think about me once in a while, ploughing through dusty files in Central Registry, will you?"

Despite his disappointment, Redmond grinned at the thought. "The mind boggles. Anyway, it isn't all bad. I suspect the main reason we're both feeling a bit fed up is because we're not the big cheeses anymore, right?"

She shrugged. "Probably," she admitted.

"This won't do our long-term career prospects any harm at all, really, quite apart from the promotions." Come on, he told himself, cheer up, for God's sake! Chief inspector at thirty-three — that's pretty good going in anyone's book. . . . So why did he feel so deflated? "I mean, hell, you'll get a good report from me, if nothing else."

She smiled awkwardly. "Thanks."

"You deserve it, Gail. You did a bloody good job — and I'll make sure our lords and masters know about it."

She glanced at him in surprise, startled by his use of her Christian name. "Just doing my job. Actually, I rather enjoyed it."

He seemed to hesitate, then said, "As the team of Redmond and Harper is about to be dissolved, what do you say to the two of us going out for a meal to mark the event?"

She smiled nervously. "What will it be, a celebration or a wake?"

"Whatever. Seriously, Gail, I'd like to stand you a meal and a couple or three drinks. My way of saying thank you. Also, we can celebrate our promotions."

"Okay," she said slowly. "I'd love to."

He seemed to relax suddenly. "Right. Saturday night?"

"Saturday night it is."

Redmond passed Gail her vodka and tonic, then picked up his own glass. "There's an empty table over in the corner — see it?"

"Got it. All we have to do is get there." She grimaced at the throng of people at the bar, but it thinned as they headed towards the table. It was next to a window, overlooking the Thames. "Nice view," she commented as

175

they sat. "Cheers." She held up her drink and they touched glasses.

"Cheers."

She glanced quizzically at his glass. "Is that bitter you're drinking?"

"Yes it is — why?"

She shrugged. "I had you figured as a lager or Pils man, somehow. Just shows how wrong you can be, doesn't it?"

Redmond sipped at his beer, but said nothing.

Gail didn't notice his lack of a reply; she was looking around the pub, nodding slowly. "I like this place," she decided. "Thanks for bringing me. And for the meal — it was beautiful."

"Glad you enjoyed it."

"Oh, I did, I did. I'm enjoying the whole shebang tonight, in fact," she chuckled. "I'm glad you suggested it."

"My pleasure, Gail. Like I said — I wanted to show how much I appreciated your help."

"In that case, why am I the only one on the team you've invited along tonight?"

"None of them worked as hard as you did. Apart from that, you were there from the beginning." His face clouded suddenly.

"Hodge and Lennox, you mean?" she asked gently, divining his thoughts.

"Yeah," he said quietly, staring down at his

glass. "They should have been here as well. If I hadn't —"

"Don't start that," she interrupted firmly. "It wasn't your fault."

"But my responsibility," he said. "They were there because of me." He swirled his beer around in the glass, then, suddenly, raised it in a toast. "To absent friends."

"Absent friends," she echoed soberly, raising her glass in response.

There was a gloomy silence before Gail said, "I think maybe we'd better change the subject."

"Let's," he agreed. "Okay, corny question coming up. What's a nice girl like you doing in a job like this?"

"What, the Branch or computers?"

"Both."

"You mean neither is a suitable job for a mere woman?"

"Did I say that?"

"No, you didn't," she admitted. "But there are plenty that do. . . ." She paused as if collecting her thoughts, then said, "I got the computer bug while I was at school. My parents gave my brother a computer for Christmas, but he was too busy playing football, so I used it — and for proper programming, as well. Too many kids who get computers these days are only interested in playing games on them, but they're all aimed at boys and —" She broke off and shook her head, a wry grin on her face. "Sorry — one of my hobbyhorses. The thing is that playing Space Invaders or Pacman never really appealed to me, so I got into the programming side. I found it pretty easy, I guess, so I started hacking as a kind of challenge. Once you've got that bug, you never really lose it — that's why I still like breaking into limited access files."

"And the Branch? Where did that come from?"

"While I was at Cambridge. I'd just got my degree and was about to start on the master's when I was approached. I'd been specialising in security protection for computer systems, you see, so they thought they could use my — ah — talents, I suppose." She paused and smiled faintly at him. "You've probably read all this in my file, anyway."

He said noncommittally, "So what do you think of the Branch?"

She hesitated, then said, "It's not quite what I expected. I suppose I had a glamourised view of it before I joined, but it's not really so different from normal police work, is it? I think I had this vague idea that we'd be hunting all these master spies, but a lot of what we do doesn't have anything to do with spying, really, does it? I must admit I feel a bit uneasy

178

whenever I'm asked to open a file on someone who's only taken part in a CND march or who went on holiday to Yugoslavia. I mean, do our bosses really think these people are security risks or are we just being busybodies?"

Redmond nodded slowly: there had been times when he'd been wondering the same things himself over the past five years. So far, he had been able to push the doubts aside, justifying the actions with the almost ritualistic "In the interests of national security": now, he was not so sure. "So why do it?" he asked. "Why not ask for a transfer? Or get a job in industry — you'd earn a damn sight more with your qualifications."

"True — but I don't think I'm into the rat race approach. Where I am now, I've got the feeling of being privy to confidential information — belonging to a select club, I suppose. On top of that, I'm doing the kind of thing I like doing, digging around in computer files and systems that very few people even know about — and being given official authority to do it. I enjoy most of my work, to be honest, even if some of my colleagues give me the pip. Present company excepted, of course."

"I'm glad about that. Why do they give you the pip?"

"Why do you think? Most of them just treat

me as a glorified secretary-typist — they all look a bit taken aback when I tell them I got a First at Cambridge. They find it even harder to cope with me being a sergeant — God only knows how they'll manage now I'm an inspector. Generally, they try to ignore me if they can. Either that, or they suggest a candlelit dinner for two."

"Like I did."

"I must have missed the candles, then. The difference is that I said yes to you."

"But not to the others?"

"No."

"So what have I got that the others haven't?"

She smiled enigmatically and shook her head. "That's something you'll have to figure out for yourself." She sipped her drink, then said, "Anyway, that's me — what about you? How did you get into it?"

"My dad was a policeman — I suppose I was following in his footsteps. I'd already applied while I was at university and —"

"Studying what?"

He grinned sheepishly. "Would you believe English literature?"

She shrugged. "Actually, yes I would. But you were saying?"

"I got my degree so that I could go on the Accelerated Promotion scheme, but once I was doing my sergeant's year, my CO recommended me for the Branch. The rest, as they say, is history."

"So . . . when are you off to the States?"

"Monday." He looked at his watch. "Exactly forty-four hours from now, in fact."

"Lucky you." She stared intently at him, then said, "Seriously, how do you feel about being sent Stateside?"

"You want the honest truth?"

"Yes."

"I am pissed off about it. I hate the idea of someone else muscling in on Mandrake after we've done all the hard work, not to mention being shunted out of the way. Okay, I know that I shouldn't feel that way and I know that it's too big to be left just to us, but — I'd still like to have seen it through to the end."

"Yes, I know what you mean. Still, as you said, we didn't do too badly out of it — we both got promotions, didn't we?"

"I suppose I knew all along that if we did find anything important, someone else would take over. . . ." He shrugged. "Pointless brooding over it — there's damn-all we can do about it anyway." He grinned. "Except have another drink, I suppose."

"Now that's the first sensible thing you've said for ages."

★ ★ ★

Redmond pulled up outside Gail's flat, but left the engine running. "Here you are, Inspector Harper," he said, grinning. "Home safe and sound."

"Thank you, kind sir." She smiled back at him. "And thank you for the evening. I really enjoyed it."

"My pleasure." She opened the door, then paused, looking across at him. "Enjoy yourself in the States."

"I will. I'll send you a postcard."

"You'd better. . . . Okay, thanks again for tonight. See you when you get back."

"Sure. Take care."

"I will." She climbed the stairs towards the lobby door. At the top, she turned and waved; he raised his arm in reply, then drove off. He glanced back and saw her still in the doorway, watching the car, then he rounded a corner and she was lost to view. Somehow, that was symbolic, he thought: they might well never work together again after this. He had meant what he had said to her — they had made a good team and he was sorry that the partnership was over.

And it wasn't just the professional side of things that he was sorry was ending, he admitted to himself . . . but it would have been asking for trouble, one way or another, to try and take that further. Even if she had been interested — I mean, let's face it, he thought, she wasn't exactly champing at the bit about inviting you in, was she?

Forget it, Redmond. . . .

Part II

Ten

Washington, D.C.

Redmond shook his head in irritation, then turned off the computer terminal with an almost savage gesture. He leaned back in his chair, put his hands behind his neck, and stretched slowly.

"Nothing doing, eh, Steve?" said a voice behind him, startling him momentarily. He twisted round, then relaxed as he saw it was Carl Nolan, the chubby FBI man with whom he had been working for the past ten days.

"Not a thing," Redmond replied. "Eckert's death doesn't look to be any more of a deliberate killing than any of the others, as far as I can see. No suspicious circumstances, as the police would say."

Nolan nodded sympathetically. "I did warn you, didn't I? I mean, we're just not getting Defense Department scientists dying off at the same rate as you've got there — that's all there is to it."

"I know," Redmond said tiredly. "But London seemed to think it was worth following up."

187

"God knows why." Nolan perched on the edge of a desk and looked down at Redmond. "The only suspicious death we've had has been McMichaels."

"What, the one where someone might have tampered with the brakes?" Redmond shrugged. "From what I can remember, he'd been fooling around with so many wives, there was probably a queue of husbands waiting to knock him off."

"True," Nolan agreed, grinning. "But it's like we told London when they said you were coming — there just isn't anything to get excited about over here. To be honest, I don't know why they sent you."

"You and me both," said Redmond absently, staring at the blank VDT screen. Nolan was right: there was nothing for him here. He had been shunted out of the way after all; Bryceland had known all along that there was nothing doing here. It had been a classic case of glory grabbing — pack the guy who had done the real work off out of the way so that the coast was clear for someone from the upper echelons to move in and take all the credit for exposing the operation.

So here he was, twiddling his thumbs in Washington, tracking down dead-end leads and trying not to get in the way at FBI headquarters. They'd been hospitable enough, but had made no bones about their feeling that he was on a wild-goose chase.

"Fancy a beer, Steve?"

"Hell, why not?" Redmond replied, jumping to his feet. "I'm getting nowhere fast here."

Nolan took him to a bar two blocks away, where they ordered a beer apiece and went over to a corner table. Virtually everyone else in the place was watching a football game on a wide-screen TV at the far end of the bar, which suited the two of them. "Cheers," said Nolan. He sipped his Budweiser, studying Redmond intently before he put down his drink and leaned forward. "Steve?"

"Yes?"

"Level with me, will you? Do you really think there is something going on with these deaths? I mean, I know you've got proof that at least some of yours were murders, but we haven't got one solitary shred of evidence for any of ours so far."

"I don't know," Redmond admitted. "We still don't even know how many of the deaths on the Mandrake list are murders as it is. I think London wanted me to see if there were any common factors that might tie in with some of your deaths over here." It would actually have made a lot of sense to send Gail over here as well, he thought, suddenly —

then wondered why that idea had occurred to him at all.

"I thought I might have detected some sort of pattern," Nolan said hesitantly. "Three of the deaths we've had were of people who had worked on the same research project at some time — Piccolo. I gather you had a similar pattern in the UK."

"Yes, we did," Redmond said, suddenly alert. "The trouble is, we couldn't find out much about it — all the details are in the Olympus files. We managed to piece together the fact that it was probably some sort of guidance system, judging by the specialities of the people involved, but that was about all. From what we can gather, they had all sorts of problems with it, but, like I said, it's bloody impossible to get any concrete information."

"Well, if it's that important, maybe the Russians are trying to sabotage it after all. I mean, they'd hate us to develop a high-tech guidance system like that, wouldn't they?"

"They would, yes — if it worked. But why bother sabotaging something that doesn't work?"

Nolan frowned. "What d'you mean, doesn't work?"

"According to the information I have been able to get — and from some pretty expert sources — the whole thing was a flop. They closed down the research projects six months ago. They could never get it to work reliably."

Nolan shook his head, perplexed. "Well, they must have cracked it somehow. Comtex is selling the entire system to the Pentagon and your MOD and they're opening up negotiations with Boeing for the civilian applications."

"Comtex?"

"Yeah, the big multinational — they've been funding and organising the research projects. Piccolo was their idea originally — they got the Pentagon and the MOD to cough up some hard cash towards research costs."

"You're sure about this?"

"Positive. I read a report on it the other day. They've carried out field tests, feasibility studies, the lot. The Pentagon is delighted with it, by all accounts."

"Bloody hell," Redmond murmured. "Maybe the Russians knew what they were doing after all."

"Could be. From their point of view, it'd be worth trying to sabotage it, if this Piccolo is as good as everyone seems to reckon. The Russian military wouldn't want to see us get it, *glasnost* or no *glasnost*."

Redmond nodded slowly. "You could be right," he said thoughtfully. "Maybe we'd better take a closer look at this Piccolo connection." He frowned again. "But if they are trying to nobble Piccolo, then why are they knocking off scientists who've already left the project? Some of them hadn't been working on it for a year or more."

Nolan shrugged. "Do the Russians know that? And are you absolutely sure they weren't working on it in secret? All this stuff you uncovered about it being closed down and them having problems on it could just have been disinformation."

Redmond nodded reluctantly. "Yeah, you could have a point there. The whole bloody thing's certainly shrouded in enough secrecy for that." He finished his drink and stared at it glumly. "In that case, I suppose we'd better get back and take another look at these Piccolo victims, hadn't we?"

London

"Chief Inspector Redmond? Chief Superintendent Bryceland will see you now."

Redmond nodded and looked pointedly at the clock on the wall of the anteroom; the appointment had been for a quarter of an hour before. In any case, he had flown in to Heathrow less than six hours earlier and had only managed to grab a couple of hours' sleep at home before reporting in to New Scotland

Yard as ordered, so having to hang around waiting for the appointment was the last thing he wanted. This was about par for the course for Bryceland, however, an element of the power game that he seemed to enjoy playing. Redmond suspected that Bryceland had to keep reasserting his rank because, deep down, he knew that he did not deserve to have risen so high. On the other hand, maybe he did, Redmond thought sourly as he went into the modern office that had only recently been refurbished; Bryceland's knees must be sore from the crawling he had done over the years. . . .

And were you so very different up to a few weeks ago? he asked himself.

Bryceland finished reading the document he had before him, then scribbled his initials on it and placed it in his out tray. He looked up appraisingly, then inclined his head briefly in greeting. "Redmond," he said.

"Sir."

Bryceland nodded towards a seat in front of his desk, and as Redmond sat he opened a second folder. Redmond recognised it as his report of the investigations in Washington; he had been up until well after midnight typing it. "A very thorough report if I may say so, albeit somewhat negative," Bryceland pronounced portentously.

"I'm afraid we're running into a dead end," Redmond replied blandly. "There's no real evidence that anything suspicious is happening at all."

"Indeed. But even negative evidence has some value, as I'm sure you know." Bryceland nodded and turned the pages of the report while Redmond looked around the room, wondering why Bryceland had thought it necessary that he report to him in person. Not that Redmond minded the trip back to London, but the whole thing could just have easily have been done via fax machines.

"I see the FBI is stepping up its surveillance on Soviet nationals?" Bryceland commented. "Very wise, I would have thought. Very wise," he repeated absently, then closed the folder with an abrupt snap. "Anyway, you seem to be doing all you can, Redmond," he said briskly. "That will be reflected in my overall report."

"Thank you, sir."

"Indeed. You say that there are still some loose ends to tie up — how much longer do you think you will need?"

"Probably another week."

Bryceland nodded. "Take two just to be on the safe side. I gather you're flying back on Monday morning?"

"Yes, sir."

"Then enjoy your weekend, Redmond." He gestured at the pile of documents in his in tray and sighed exaggeratedly. "Some of us have to keep ploughing on, regardless — but that's what we're paid for, isn't it?"

Redmond stared at the other man incredulously. Was that all? Had he really been brought all the way across the Atlantic just to sit for five minutes while Bryceland pretended to read his report? So it seemed; that was exactly what had happened, he realised with steadily increasing irritation — but what else had he expected of the man? At least Bryceland had accepted the report without apparent demur, which was something. . . .

Redmond stood up, then hesitated. "Sir?"

Bryceland looked up at him, as if surprised he was still there. "Yes?"

"Have there been any further developments on the investigation?"

Bryceland pursed his lips judiciously, then said, "Apart from the fact that it's been given a new title — Farthingale — there have been no startling breakthroughs, I'm afraid. But we're plodding on, nevertheless." He looked up at Redmond. "If anything does happen, you'll be one of the first to know, Chief Inspector."

"Thank you, sir." Redmond did not believe a word of it.

* * *

His answerphone was flashing when he returned to his flat, so he rewound his messages as he went into the kitchen to put the kettle on for a cup of coffee. He winced as always at the deafening electronic shriek that passed for a tone on the machine — he really would have to get a quieter one — but then stopped spooning the coffee into the percolator when he heard Gail's voice.

"Sir, it's Gail Harper. I heard you were back in London for the weekend, so I wondered if you fancied another drink tonight? Give me a ring if you do." There was another squeal from the tape and the machine switched itself off.

For a moment, Redmond was aware of a surge of pleasurable anticipation — perhaps she wasn't as indifferent to him as he'd thought — before he remembered how she had started the message — "Sir." Very formal: she was letting him know this was business — but if that was the case, why all this rigmarole about going out for a drink?

As with the first time they had gone out, Gail was ready as soon as he arrived; the door opened within seconds of his ringing the bell. "Hi," she said, coming straight out and locking the door behind her. "How's America?"

196

"Still there," he said. "How's the filing cabinets?"

She chuckled. "The same. Thanks for coming round, by the way."

"It's okay. Good of you to phone me."

"Anytime. Seriously, how is it going over there?"

"So-so. We're not really getting anywhere, to be honest. It's the same story — no real evidence."

She grimaced. "We're not exactly accomplishing much over here either. Getting through miles of computer printouts and file paper, but not much else. Still, we keep grinding on at it."

"What's your team like?" Redmond asked absently, aware of the fact that she was deliberately prattling on. Was she afraid someone might be listening? It was possible. . . .

She shrugged. "Okay, but it isn't really my team — I've got Chief Inspector Graham breathing down my neck most of the time and we don't really have much freedom of action, to be honest. He says that he's just making sure I'm settling in, but I don't think they quite trust me on my own yet."

They went out into the street, but instead of heading towards the car, she paused and said, "There's a pretty good pub not too far from here. It's a nice evening — why don't we walk there?"

He glanced at her, then nodded. "Okay."

She fell in step beside him, looking casually around before she said, "Actually, sir — there is something I wanted to talk to you about."

"I thought there might be," he observed. "What about?"

"This whole investigation, sir — 'Farthingale,' as it's called now."

"Yeah, I know," he said glumly. "Bryceland told me about the change of name. What's the problem with it?"

"There are three things, really," she said slowly, as if gathering her thoughts. She drew in a deep breath, then continued. "One is that everybody seems to be convinced that the Russians are behind it and they don't seem to be considering any alternative villains. The second is that Farrington's resigned."

"Has he?" Redmond asked, pulling the corners of his mouth down in a thoughtful frown.

"Last week, apparently. The word is that he was forced out. Certain — ah — irregularities were discovered in the awarding of contracts, particularly to Comelec." She looked expectantly at him.

"Ledsham's company," he commented.

"Right. So, guess what he's doing now?"

"Farrington?" Redmond shrugged. "Tending his roses? Putting his feet up?"

"He's working for Comelec on a consultancy basis, so rumour has it. A retainer of fifty K a year. For services already rendered, I should imagine."

Redmond shook his head disgustedly. "Bloody typical. And they're just letting him do that? I mean, if that isn't confirmation that he was on the take, I don't know what is."

"Lack of sufficient evidence to justify a prosecution," she intoned formally.

"Apart from which, they don't want the scandal of a court case," Redmond nodded wearily. "So Farrington has his cake and eats it too. Nice one, Mr. Farrington. That should make up for the knighthood he won't be getting now." He shook his head, then said, "Have they tried to link him in with getting Mackinnon the job at SysCom? Do they know if he's involved with passing on information?"

She shook her head. "If they know one way or the other, they don't appear to be doing anything about it. But they seem to think that Mackinnon was passing secrets to the Russians, so if Farrington was involved in that, it seems bloody funny to let him take a job with a company working on secret research projects for the MOD."

"You could say that," Redmond agreed grimly. "You said three things. What was the third?"

"The third thing is that there is no longer any reference to Piccolo in any of the personnel files. Different project names have been substituted for all five of them — Hayward, Inchmore, Phillips, Kirk, and Aldridge." She stared intently at him, seeing the suddenly thoughtful expression on his face.

"Bloody hell . . ." he murmured. "Someone's been doctoring the files?"

"Exactly. As far as the records now show, none of them ever worked on Piccolo. In fact, there never was such a project as Piccolo." She shook her head slowly.

"It's a bloody cover-up," she said disgustedly.

Redmond came to a halt, pushing his hands into the pockets of his leather jacket and leaned against a wall, staring back in the direction from which they had come: as far as he could see, there was no sign that they were under any kind of surveillance. It was as well to be sure, though . . . "Okay, let's run through it more slowly. You reckon they're convinced it's the Russians behind it all?"

"Bryceland certainly seems to be, yes."

"So they think that even though the KGB hasn't mounted a 'wet' operation anywhere in the West for over five years, it's now killing these computer experts just in order to infiltrate people like Mackinnon into our research project — is that it?"

Gail nodded. "Bryceland's view is that this is part of some larger plan to infiltrate all of our research projects. His attitude is that it's physically impossible for the KGB to change its spots, *glasnost* or no *glasnost*. They're still capable of running an operation like this."

"It's possible, I suppose," he said doubtfully.

She stared at him. "But you don't think so?"

He shook his head. "Like I said, the results just don't justify the risks. Whatever else they might be, they're professionals in Moscow Centre — they're not going to send a full Department Eight team into the UK just to knock off half a dozen second-level computer scientists, are they?"

"They might if Bryceland is right — that this is all part of some larger operation. He did say there had been similar deaths in the States, so maybe the KGB are back in the 'wet' business."

He looked across at her. "Do you believe that?"

She grimaced wryly. "No."

"Okay, so it looks as though, if we're right, they're on the wrong track. The thing is — are they doing it deliberately?"

She nodded slowly. "I was wondering that."

"Why?"

"Farrington," she said succinctly. "Okay, he's been put out to grass, but he hasn't exactly done badly out of it, has he? Maybe all he was guilty of was doing Comelec too many favours over the years, but what if he was involved in whatever Mackinnon was up to? From what I can see, they haven't made any attempt to follow that lead at all. Okay, so maybe they've done a deal with him, like they did with Blunt after the Burgess and Maclean fiasco, but if that's the case, why let him go somewhere like Comelec?"

Redmond nodded. "It certainly wouldn't be normal practice if he was working for the Russians. What you do is put him in charge of the Queen's pictures or something, not give him another chance to pass on information." He shook his head again, "Anyway, the idea of him working for the Russians just doesn't make sense. You've seen his file, Gail — does he strike you as being a likely KGB recruit? Public school background, went to Oxford — not Cambridge, note, so he doesn't come from the same stable as Philby, Blunt, and the others. There's nothing in his past to indicate that he might be willing to work for the Soviets on ideological grounds at all."

"Maybe he's in it for the money."

Redmond shook his head. "They wouldn't involve any mercenary agent in anything as risky as this operation is — they wouldn't be able to trust him enough. No, if he's involved in this, then he'd have to be someone they can trust, which means an ideological convert. Somehow, I just can't see Farrington in that role."

She nodded slowly, thoughtfully. "So what do you think is going on?"

"Someone is behind the killings — that's obvious. Whoever is doing it must have some kind of inside knowledge, the kind Farrington can provide, so, yes, he's probably implicated — but who is he working for?" He gazed intently at her in the darkness, then looked away, staring thoughtfully across the street. "If it isn't the KGB, then who is it?" he asked, almost to himself. "Let's assume Farrington has been passing on information about the victims. Who else would be interested in that sort of data, apart from the KGB?"

"Comelec?" she said suddenly.

"Right . . ." he said softly, his face suddenly set in a thoughtful frown. "Is there any connection between Comelec and Comtex?"

"Comelec is a subsidiary of Comtex. Why?"

"Bloody hell . . . Piccolo was a Comtex project."

"Which very conveniently does not now

203

exist. Maybe that was who Farrington was really working for." Gail paused, then shook her head disappointedly. "No, that doesn't make sense. If Piccolo was Comtex's project, then why kill people who were working on it? They'd be killing their own people."

"They wouldn't, actually. None of the victims actually worked for Comtex itself —"

"Phillips worked for Comelec," Gail interrupted him.

"Okay, but he wouldn't have been for much longer. In any case, they had all left Piccolo before they were killed, so they weren't still working for Comtex on that, at any rate."

"So you're saying that Comtex is using Farrington's information to kill people involved in Piccolo, then replacing them with others who can pass them secret material?" She shook her head. "That doesn't hold up any better than the KGB theory, does it? In any case, what about the ones who weren't in Piccolo? Where do they come in?"

"Maybe they don't. Maybe they were genuine —" He broke off and shook his head, a faint wry grin on his face. "All right, you don't have to say it. I told you off about picking and choosing which victims fitted the facts, didn't I?"

"It could still be true," she said. "Maybe Barclay was a genuine accident and West a kosher suicide. So if it is just the Piccolo people being killed, the question is why?"

Redmond shook his head, then stopped abruptly as a thought struck him. "Maybe they know something about Piccolo that Comtex doesn't want made public."

"Shit . . ." she said softly, her voice appalled. "You could be right. . . ." She sighed and shook her head. "Unless this is all pie in the sky."

"Look, Gail, someone sure as hell didn't want us looking into this, did they? Think about it. Just when we were beginning to get somewhere, we were taken off it. Okay, so maybe Bryceland wants all the credit — or maybe someone decided we were getting too close. The same someone who arranged Keenan's death, maybe. And that couldn't have been Farrington either — there's no way that he could have known where to find Keenan, nor would he have been able to provide an authentic-looking MI-five pass."

"So there's a second mole?"

"Has to be. Someone in the security services — either MI-five or the Branch itself. Whoever it is, I suspect he's had us taken off this." He shook his head in angry bewilderment. "You're right, Gail. This whole thing stinks of a cover-up. Something is going on — and two of my men died as a result of it," he added bitterly.

She stared at him. "So if it is a cover-up, what are they trying to hide?"

Redmond shook his head. "God knows. It's all tied in with this Piccolo Project — it has to be," he mused. "Piccolo, Comtex, Comelec, Farrington — they're all linked in some way. Then we've got this Mister X, who has access to Special Branch operations and who doesn't want us questioning anyone involved in the killings. . . . Piccolo. I'm bloody sure that's the key. If we can find out what Piccolo actually is — or was — then we might know what this is all about."

"That's what I hoped you would say," she said quietly.

He nodded. "That's what all this is about, isn't it, Gail? You think we ought to follow this up ourselves, right?"

"By the looks of it, nobody else will."

"Very probably true," he conceded. "The trouble is that I'm in the States and you've been reassigned — we're neither of us in any position to start digging into this, are we?"

"I could," she pointed out. "I've got to wade through the files anyway, so I don't think anyone's going to notice if I take a few unauthorised detours along the way."

"If they do notice, you'll be right up the creek without the proverbial paddle."

"I know that," she said calmly. "The thing is, if I do go ahead and start digging around in the files to see what I can uncover, will I be on my own?" Suddenly, her eyes were fixed on him in an intent gaze.

Redmond blew out his cheeks slowly and shook his head bemusedly. "Hoo boy, starting with the easy ones, are you?" He thought for a moment, then said, "No, you won't be on your own. If you are caught, then I'll say you were acting under my orders, if that'll help — but it probably won't."

"Probably not," she agreed. "They'll still throw the book at me, regardless of what they do to you, won't they?"

"Very probably, yes," he agreed slowly. He thought for a moment, then said, "I could also ask a few questions back in the States, see if I can find out anything else about Piccolo or Comtex, but the point is that it'll be you taking the risks, Gail. I can always say that I was asking legitimate questions about the American deaths, but you won't have a leg to stand on if they catch you poking around in level one files — or Olympus."

"I know that," she said again. "The thing is, if I do find anything, who can I take it to? I don't know anybody high up that well — you do."

"You could take it to Selvey — he's straight

enough — but, yes, you're right. He'd probably listen to me more readily than you." He looked at her, then said slowly, "You're going to go ahead and do this anyway, aren't you? Whether I help you or not."

She hesitated, then nodded. "Yes, I am."

"Because people are getting killed out there?"

She smiled faintly at his repetition of her argument. "Something along those lines, yes, but there's more to it than that." She drew in a deep breath and looked away from him, staring across the shadowy street for over a minute. Eventually, she said, her voice so low that he had to lean towards her to hear her, "You know, I often wondered what I'd do in a situation like this, and the decision always seemed to be so easy then. There'd be no doubt in my mind at all — I'd do the honourable thing and to hell with the consequences. But when you're really confronted with it, it isn't so easy, is it? Okay, so I want to find out what's going on. . . ." She looked suddenly at him. "But do I want to risk throwing away my career over it? That, as they say, is the question, isn't it?"

"It is, yes. Nobody would criticise you if you just walked away from it, Gail, least of all me. I've been there and I know what it's like."

"Yes, but you didn't walk away from it, did you? I mean, I nagged you into carrying on with Mandrake despite the harm it might do to your career, but it was all right for me, wasn't it? My future wasn't in jeopardy, after all — but now it is. I'm the one who'll get it in the neck. The thing is, after telling you that you had to see it through, I could hardly turn round and back out when it was my turn to stand up and be counted, could I?"

He stared incredulously at her. "You're not saying you're doing this just because I kept going?"

"Well, not just that, no, but —" She spread her hands in a helpless gesture. "I just couldn't walk away from it, any more than you could."

"It's hardly the same. I could always say that I was simply carrying out an authorised assignment. The worse that could have happened to me would have been that I just wouldn't have been promoted any further. They couldn't have taken any disciplinary action. With you, losing out on your promotion will be the least of your worries. Hell, we're talking about illegal access to secret files — you could end up in prison, Gail."

"You think I haven't thought of that? That's why I don't want to have to do it alone — but if I have to, I will."

He smiled lopsidedly. "Good for you. But

you won't be on your own. I'll back you up, even if I can't actually do very much."

"Thank you," she said quietly. "Like I said, just knowing I'm not on my own helps." She looked at him, then turned her head away, as if embarrassed. After a few seconds, she said, "Sir?"

"Yes?"

"I know I've asked you this before, but . . . why did you keep Mandrake going?"

"You mean because I'm just an ambitious crawler who always toes the line? Is that what you mean?"

She flushed, but then said firmly, "Well . . . okay, yes, if you want the truth. I thought you'd have dropped the whole thing as soon as you could."

"Maybe that's why I haven't. . . ." he said slowly. "You see, whoever chose me for Mandrake thought the same as you. Give Redmond the job, he'll know which side his bread's buttered. How do you think I liked being taken for granted like that? Or of having a reputation like that?" He looked away and grimaced, shaking his head disgustedly. "Then there was pride, I suppose. You made me feel guilty every bloody time I wanted to close it down. Or maybe I thought that if I did uncover something, then I'd collect the kudos, earn a few more creep points. Maybe I remembered why

I joined the police — some half-baked notion of wanting to uphold Law and Order, or some such crap as that. It's all in there, somewhere, along with Hodge and Lennox getting killed and not wanting the bastards who did it to get away with it. I don't know. Sometimes I wonder myself."

"But you're still in there, pitching."

"Too bloody stupid to know when to quit."

"Maybe," she grinned. "Rather makes two of us, doesn't it?"

"Certainly looks like it." He smiled back at her. "Okay," he said briskly. "We'd better sort out exactly what it is we're going to do — especially what you're going to look for in the files."

She nodded. "Piccolo, Comtex, Comelec, and Farrington. Anything I can dig up on them — is that it?"

"Right. Anything at all . . ." Redmond's voice trailed off, then he said, "No, we need to be more specific. The only real link we've got is between Farrington and Comelec. Now, we can't prove that he was on the take from Comelec at the moment, so if we can establish that he was, that'll be a step in the right direction."

"Yes, but suppose I do find a link?" she said. "Suppose I find that Farrington's owned shares in Comtex for years, or he's got a num-

211

bered Swiss bank account — what then? That won't prove he's helping to set up the killings, will it?"

"No, it won't, but if you can prove that it was Comtex and not Comelec who was paying him, then that starts tying him in to Piccolo."

"That's still a long way from proving he's mixed up in murder."

"I know," he said glumly. "We've got to start somewhere, though. If we can get some proof, then we could at least bring this investigation back on the right tracks. I don't know — if we can find out what Piccolo is, maybe that'll answer a few questions, but we need to focus on Farrington and Comtex at the moment, I think."

"Okay, will do," she said. "The problem is that I don't really know what to look for. If Farrington and Comtex are involved in any financial skulduggery, then they'll have set it up pretty thoroughly, won't they? It won't be easy to establish any links between them, even for an expert — and I'm certainly not that, when it comes to stocks and shares or illicit trading. I wouldn't know a debenture from a portfolio, or whatever."

"I'm in the same boat," Redmond admitted.

"We're going to have to get someone else in on this," Gail said thoughtfully. "Someone who knows what the hell they're talking about — who knows what kind of dodges Farrington or Comtex might have pulled. We can hardly ask someone from the Fraud Squad to help, can we? Now, okay, I can hack my way into company files as well as those of banks and financial institutions. I don't suppose it's going to be any picnic, because they'll have the most advanced built-in alarm and locking systems — but I can do it, provided I've got someone telling me what to look for. Do you know of any financial geniuses who might be prepared to help?"

Redmond nodded slowly. "Actually, I do — and I think she'd be willing to help."

"She?"

He shook his head. "Don't worry about it. We'll go and see her tomorrow." He paused, then looked at her. "That is, if you're still sure? Like you said, hacking into bank and company files isn't going to be easy."

"I'm sure," she said firmly.

"Okay. Just be careful, for God's sake. You hear me?"

"I hear you." She reached out and, without realising what she was doing, put her hand on his arm and squeezed it gently. "I'll be careful, don't worry."

He glanced down at her hand, a startled expression on his face, then looked directly at her. For a moment, their eyes met, and each one saw something in the other's that made them look away hurriedly. She removed her hand, aware that her cheeks were suddenly burning and grateful for the darkness that hid her face.

His head turned back towards her and he seemed about to say something, but then he stepped back. "Right," he said, his voice unnaturally brisk. "Shall we get that drink now?"

Eleven

It was raining heavily when Gail emerged from the front entrance of the block of flats in which she lived. She glanced up at the sky, then came dashing down the steps, across the pavement, and dived into the passenger seat of Redmond's car, slamming the door behind her. "Bloody hell," she gasped. "Talk about April showers . . . It's pissing down."

"I noticed," Redmond replied laconically, looking in his mirror before he pulled out into the traffic. "Makes a change from Washington — it's in the eighties there at the moment."

"Don't rub it in," she grumbled, pulling on her seat belt. Once it was fastened, she said, "Okay — now just who is it we're going to see?"

"An old friend of mine. Her name's Julie Curren."

"And she's the financial expert who's going to help us?"

"I hope so, yes."

"Just how much of an expert is she?"

"She worked for four years in a merchant bank on their foreign investments desk, if that's any guide."

Gail nodded, impressed. "She ought to know a thing or two, I suppose. You said 'worked.' I take it she doesn't anymore?"

"No, she's her own boss nowadays. She runs a financial advisory firm that specialises in the stock market — not exactly a stockbroker, but very similar. I don't think she fancies the idea of working for anyone else these days."

"Prefers to be her own boss, you mean?"

"Definitely. Hardly surprising, though, given what she's been through."

"Meaning what?"

"Like I said, she worked in a merchant bank, but she made the mistake of marrying one of the junior partners. I wish I could say I'd known all along it wouldn't work, but I can't — he seemed a fairly decent sort of bloke, really. Very ambitious, charming, good sense of humour — and as chauvinistic as they come, apparently. 'No wife of mine's going to work for a living' — that sort of thing. They had row after row over it — she genuinely enjoyed her work, you see — but then he arranged for her to get the boot. They told her they were 'rationalising' — very sorry and all that, but there was no place for her in the new setup. The thing was, she then found out that he had been behind it all and walked out on him. It got very nasty during the divorce, and it was all she could do not to get totally screwed by him in the settlement. She couldn't prove anything about the bank, you see, so it looked as if she'd just walked out for no good reason. So there she was, on her own and with no job."

"Couldn't she have got a job with another merchant bank?"

Redmond shook his head. "Hubby had got the word out on her — the old-school-tie thing. Very sorry, Ms. Curren, but we don't have any openings for you at the present time. If you'd like to contact us a few months from now . . . You get the picture?"

"I get it," she said disgustedly.

"So she set up on her own and is now doing very nicely out of it, because she's bloody good at what she does." He grinned suddenly. "Not only that, but she got her own back on him in the end."

"How come?"

"She knew a lot more about his business dealings than he realised — enough for the Fraud Squad to nail him for insider trading. He did six months in Parkhurst. He's also finished in the City. He got caught, you see."

Gail chuckled. "Oh, I like it. It sounds as though he deserved it."

"You could say that," Redmond agreed.

She nodded thoughtfully. "I'm looking forward to meeting her."

★ ★ ★

"Here we are," Julie said, coming into the living room with three mugs of coffee on a tray. For a moment, Redmond remembered how she had looked a year ago, when she had been going through the divorce: now she seemed younger, more vivacious — more like the Julie he had known at university, in fact. Being single obviously agreed with her.

She gave them their coffee, then sat down in an armchair facing the two of them, favouring Gail with another quizzical look identical to the one she had given her when they had arrived a few minutes before. Even though Redmond had introduced Gail as one of his colleagues, it was evident that Julie had wondered if there was more to their relationship than that. After a moment or two, she turned her attention to Redmond and said briskly, "Right, Steve — you said you wanted a word with me?"

"Yes, I did," he said slowly. "I want to pick your brains, if you don't mind."

She shrugged. "Sure. What about?"

"Shareholdings and investments. Your speciality."

"I know something about them, yes," she agreed, smiling faintly.

"What we're trying to do is to see if someone has been accepting bribes from a big company.

You know, a numbered Swiss bank account, that sort of thing."

"Uh-huh," she said slowly, then looked shrewdly from Redmond to Gail and back again. "That's Fraud Squad territory, Steve — and they've got their own experts for that. Why are you talking to me?"

Redmond gazed levelly at her. "Because this is unofficial," he said bluntly. "Very unofficial."

"I see," she said thoughtfully. "I might have known, I suppose. Okay — what do you want from me?"

"Like I said, expert advice. If this someone is on the take, he'd have made damn sure the payments would be bloody difficult to trace. The payments or transfers would be very deeply hidden, and neither Gail nor I would have a clue as to where to begin looking. Gail can probably hack into any company record or document if it's on computer, but we need someone to tell her where to look and what to look for."

Julie glanced momentarily at Gail and then nodded slowly. "There are a number of ways in which stock can be held in secret. By proxy, for example, or through solicitors. The thing is that you can still trace the true ownership if you know where to look and who you're looking for, so if your 'someone' really wants to keep his involvement secret, then the link would be hidden under several layers — offshore companies, Swiss banks, front or shell companies, stockbrokers with large portfolios, things like that. The point is that if you've got the necessary time and resources you can still trace it back, but it'd take a hell of a lot of time — and that's assuming there's anything to find in the first place," she finished discouragingly. "How sure are you that this 'someone' is involved in illicit share dealing?"

Redmond hesitated, then said, "We're not. Just a strong hunch."

Julie turned to Gail. "So you're going to hack through company computer files to see if you can trace these deals?"

"If I can, yes, but I don't really know what to look for."

"No, you wouldn't, I don't suppose. It's a pretty specialised skill." She turned back to Redmond. "You didn't just come here to pick my brains, did you? You want me to help Gail track the leads down, right?"

Redmond exchanged glances with Gail, then said slowly, "I don't think we'll be able to do it otherwise. But . . . like I said, this is unofficial. I think you ought to know that we've got no authority for any of this, so you could be in trouble right up to your neck if you get involved." He hesitated, then went on, "Not just with the law, either. The company we're talking about is Comtex."

She whistled softly and shook her head. "Jesus. You don't believe in messing about, do you?" There was a faint grin on her face. "They are mean bastards to tangle with."

"There's more, I'm afraid," Redmond said, never taking his eyes from her. "It could be dangerous — and I mean that. I don't want you getting into this until you know what's at stake."

The grin had disappeared now as her eyes flickered rapidly between Redmond and Gail. "Steve . . . you're beginning to scare me. Just what the hell have you got into?"

"It's a long story, Julie."

"So tell me."

Redmond said nothing for several seconds, then looked across at Gail, who shrugged.

"You said it yourself, Steve," Gail said. "Julie's got a right to know just what she's letting herself in for."

"Okay," Redmond agreed heavily. He turned back to Julie, paused for a moment to collect his thoughts, then began to tell her the story.

". . . so if we can tie Farrington in with Comtex, we'll at least have made a start," Redmond finished.

Julie nodded slowly, thoughtfully, then let her breath out in a long sigh. "Which is where I come in, right?" she asked quietly.

"That's up to you," Redmond replied gently. "We know that they killed Aldridge, Keenan, and three policemen, so we've got to assume that they're responsible for the deaths of anything up to six other people. That's the kind of situation you could be getting yourself into. Obviously, I'll try and make sure you're kept in the clear, but if whoever's behind all this does find out you're involved, it could get nasty."

"So I see," Julie said, fighting down an involuntary shudder. "Do you think they killed the others, Steve?" she asked bluntly.

"Yes, I do," he said, without hesitation. "Certainly the people who worked on Piccolo and maybe Barclay and West as well — although God knows why in their cases."

"So that's . . . what? Seven computer experts, at any rate," Julie said, half to herself. "And nobody really knows why. . . ." She stared across the room, sipped absently at her coffee, then grimaced: it had long since gone cold. As if that had somehow prompted the action, she turned to Gail and said, "Where will you be doing your hacking? I mean, if I agree to help — if," she emphasised, glancing at Redmond to make sure he had picked it up, "then I'll have to be more or less looking over your shoulder to tell you which files to access, won't I?"

"True," Gail admitted. "I was going to do it from home."

"Then I'll have to stay at your place, won't I?"

"I suppose so, yes," Gail said, glancing at Redmond.

"How safe will that be, Steve?" Julie asked. "I mean, suppose whoever it is is watching Gail's flat?"

Redmond pursed his lips before answering. "For one thing, I don't think they've been watching Gail so far. It's been me they've been hassling, and they've got no reason at the moment to suspect that Gail's up to anything like this."

"They think we've both been bought off," Gail interjected.

Redmond nodded. "Right. If anyone does see you, we can pass you off as an old friend of Gail's — they'll have a hell of a job identifying you, because you aren't on any Central Registry or Branch file — I checked."

"No reason why I should be, is there?" Julie asked. "As far as I know, I haven't been involved in anything secret."

Redmond smiled bleakly. "You'd be amazed at some of the reasons people get onto those files. The thing is, you're not, so even if someone is watching Gail's place, they'll have a job finding out who you are."

Julie stared at Redmond in frank disbelief. "Are you trying to tell me they wouldn't be able to find out who I was if they wanted to badly enough?"

Redmond grimaced wryly. "Score one to you, Julie. Yes, they could," he admitted.

"So if they do find out who I am and put two and two together . . ." Her voice trailed off meaningfully.

"Then you're right in the shit, the same as us," he agreed heavily.

"Exactly," Julie said slowly, then sighed again. "Steve, I wish you'd asked somebody else — I really do." There was genuine regret in her voice.

Redmond and Gail exchanged rapid looks and he felt his shoulders slump fractionally in defeat. Still, he could hardly blame her; it wasn't her fight, after all. . . .

"But you didn't ask somebody else, did you?" Julie continued, her eyes fixed on his, almost defiantly. "Tell me, Steve, if I say no, what will you do?"

"Try and find another financial expert," he replied, trying not to show any hesitation.

"Oh yes?" Julie demanded disbelievingly. "And who else will you be able to trust, eh?"

She shook her head. "It's me or nobody, isn't it? If I say no, you've had it, right?"

This time, he did hesitate, looking at Gail with an expression of pure helplessness before he nodded and said slowly, "Very probably, yes. We need someone we can trust — which is why I thought of you."

"Gee, thanks," Julie said, then shook her head. She walked slowly over to the window, arms folded across her chest and stared out at the street. Neither Redmond nor Gail dared say anything. A minute passed, two . . . three. . . . Then she drew in her breath abruptly and said hurriedly:

"Okay. I'm in."

"Chanhold," Julie said abruptly. Instantly, the list of names that had been scrolling upwards on the VDT screen came to a halt as Gail directed the cursor to the file name Julie had picked out.

"Got it," said Gail.

They'd been hacking into locked and supposedly secure files and copying them directly onto Gail's hard disk virtually nonstop for five hours now. Each operation had to be done quickly before the inbuilt alarm systems in the programmes were tripped, but Gail could not guarantee that she had always been fast enough. To make matters worse, ninety-nine percent of what they had abstracted would be utterly useless — but it was the other one percent they were looking for. It was draining on the nerves because to avoid detection, Gail had decided on an arbitrary time limit of sixty seconds to study the file catalogues once they had hacked into a protected system. They had often been forced to exit with nothing at all.

"I vote we call a halt," Julie said. "You look dead beat, Gail."

"I feel it," she admitted and sat back, rubbing her eyes. "Okay. Ten minutes?"

"Gail, it's after midnight as it is. You've got work tomorrow, remember?"

"Yes, I suppose I have at that. Okay, let's call it a night. Do you reckon you've got enough to be getting on with?"

"I haven't even made a serious dent on the stuff you lifted last night," Julie said ruefully, glancing at the piles of computer paper that were strewn about the living room. While Gail had been at work during the day, Julie had been ploughing patiently through the print-outs of the files, searching for leads and cross-references. "I reckon I've got enough here for the next two weeks already." She put down the notepad on which she had been scribbling names and notes, then stood up and stretched, barely stifling a yawn.

Gail stared a moment longer at the VDT

screen, then touched a key and turned off the computer. "I think I'll have a nightcap," she said, rising from her seat. "Otherwise, I'll never get to sleep — I'll be replaying these bloody programmes in my head all night if I'm not careful. Want one?"

"I wouldn't say no. A vodka martini? Something with a bit of a kick to it."

Once Gail had brought the drinks over, the two women sat facing each other in a pair of armchairs, each one absorbed in her own thoughts. Eventually, Gail said, "You know Steve pretty well, don't you?"

There was a slight smile on Julie's face. "I suppose I do. Why?"

"Is he always as — I don't know how to describe it — as private as he seems to be?"

"You mean, has he always been a loner?"

"Something like that, yes."

Julie pursed her lips thoughtfully. "You know he's divorced, don't you?"

"I'd heard he was, but I didn't know for certain."

Julie nodded. "Five years ago. I suppose he always has been a bit difficult to get to know, but the divorce made him worse. He really went into his shell for a while. If you think he's inscrutable now, you should have seen him then."

Gail nodded. "When I first started working

for him, all he seemed to be interested in was getting promoted."

"He never used to be that obsessed about it," Julie mused. "I think it was the divorce that did it. After it happened, he threw himself into his work — probably to take his mind off what had happened, I suppose. The trouble was that he overdid it — the job became everything to him. Believe it or not, he used to have a terrific sense of humour, but there's been precious little sign of it over the past few years. When we were at university together, he was very laid-back."

"You've known him that long?"

"Oh yes. We go back a long way, Steve and I," she grinned. "We were almost engaged at one point but . . . well, it didn't happen, so let's leave it at that, shall we? We became very good friends, though — it was me who introduced him to Elaine, actually." She grimaced. "Fortunately, Steve hasn't held that against me."

"What caused the divorce?"

"Basically, Elaine got bored. I was surprised the relationship lasted more than a couple of months in the first place, knowing what she was like, but it did — until she had an affair. Steve came back from work one evening and she'd gone — just like that. He took it hard — the poor bugger hadn't a clue anything was going on."

"What happened to his wife?"

"She was living in Florida, last I heard. Married to some businessman — and probably cheating on him as well." She chuckled suddenly. "Actually, I suppose it wasn't entirely her fault — it never is, is it? — because Steve was often late back from work, that sort of thing. It can't be much fun married to a police officer, and Elaine liked having a good time." She looked appraisingly at Gail. "You seem very interested in him, Gail."

"Me?" She seemed confused at first, but then, slowly, she nodded, almost to herself. "Maybe."

Gail returned home from work at just after seven the following evening to find Julie pouring over a large chart that she had drawn over several sheets of paper taped together and spread out over the dining table. She glanced up apologetically, then went back to hunting through a list of entries on a computer printout.

"Very impressive," Gail observed, going over to the chart. On the left-hand side, Julie had written FARRINGTON in large block letters, while on the right was COMTEX with COMELEC directly underneath, a black line linking the two of them. There were also several other company names branching downwards from Comtex, with further branches extending down from each of these. Farrington was linked to a number of names and companies, as well as banks, with an ever-increasing network of branches and cross-links extending down the left-hand side of the chart. Some of the lines were in black ballpoint — these seemed to be the definite connections, Gail decided — others were in red, while a few were in pencil, presumably to indicate unconfirmed or hypothetical links. "You have been busy."

"I thought I'd better make some sort of a start," Julie explained. "We've probably got enough data to give us some indications as to where to look, rather than just having to lift files almost at random."

"Sounds sensible, but what does it all mean? Are these the shares Farrington owns?" Gail asked, pointing to the entries linked to his name.

Julie nodded. "Right — or, rather, they're the ones I've traced so far. The point is that a lot of his investments are held by his stockbroker, as you'd expect, so I've had to sift through their portfolios and then through their diversified holdings, then onto the investments of the holding companies and so on. It's like a pyramid with Farrington at the top of it, holding interests directly or otherwise at every level, but it's bloody difficult trying to trace them all. On the other side, I'm working backwards from Comtex, through their subsidiaries, bankers and investors, to see if, eventually, I can get some links between the two sides of this chart. As you can imagine, though, with something the size of Comtex, they've got holdings and interests all over the world, so it ain't easy. . . . If Steve is right and there is a link, then we'll turn it up sooner or later, but it'll be hidden pretty deeply. They'll have invested and reinvested Farrington's money so many times that it'll take ages to track down, but it has to be here somewhere."

"If Steve's right," Gail said gloomily. "If there's something to find."

"Oh, there's something to find all right," Julie said emphatically. "Farrington is hiding something. You see that red line from Trident Holdings to Gottlieb and Schuster in Zurich? They're a private Swiss bank and Trident has a numbered account with them. Our dear Mr. Farrington, either directly or indirectly, owns a good ten percent of Trident Holdings, but none of it's in his name. So, if nothing else, he's not sticking to the rules."

"That doesn't mean he's linked to Comtex, though, does it?"

"Perhaps not, but what is he hiding? I mean, if he's been having money paid into a Swiss bank account with several cutouts to cover it, then someone's paying him, aren't they? So who — and why?"

"Yes, I see what you mean," Gail said slowly.

"So — he's covering something up, which means there's something there to find." Julie sighed and stared glumly down at the chart. "The trouble is that there's no way to tell how long all this is going to take. Looking for the proverbial needle in the haystack is child's play compared to this." She shook her head slowly. "I should have known it would be when I took it on, I suppose."

Gail stared thoughtfully down at Julie, then said, "Tell me something, Julie — why did you take it on? Why did you get involved in all this?"

Julie smiled faintly. "You mean, why was I so damned stupid as to get mixed up in it?"

Gail grinned. "Something like that."

"There are two reasons," Julie said slowly. "One is that I don't think Comtex should be allowed to get away with this. I mean, okay, everyone in the City knows they bend the rules all the time to suit themselves, but when you've got as much money and clout as they have, you can get away with it. But this is different — we're talking about people's lives, aren't we? They can't be allowed to get away with that, so if I can help stop it, I will." She grinned sheepishly. "Listen to me — I sound like John Wayne, don't I? 'A man's gotta do' and all that crap."

"Don't knock it," Gail said quietly. "We're none of us in this for personal gain, after all. You said two reasons?"

Julie nodded. "I did," she said soberly. "The second one is that I owe Steve. When my own divorce was going through and it was all getting more than a little nasty, he helped me out one hell of a lot — gave me a bed when my dearly beloved husband locked me out of the house." She caught Gail's quick look and nodded, smiling faintly. "And yes, it was his bed, if that's what you're thinking, but we didn't actually share it until the fourth or fifth night — he slept on the sofa up till then. When we did spend the night together, it was my idea, not his — I mean, it wasn't as though it was the first time we'd slept together, after all, and it was more out of friendship than any wild passion, really. . . . Steve stopped me going to pieces then."

"He said you had helped him a lot, one way or another," Gail said carefully. "He reckoned he owed you, not the other way round."

Julie shrugged. "Steve is a good friend, Gail.

Even when he was tied up with his work, he always seemed to find time for me. So . . . now he needs help, I can't really refuse it, can I?"

Gail nodded thoughtfully. "I suppose not. . . ." She stared out of the window for several seconds, then seemed to collect herself. She looked at the clock on the wall and said briskly, deliberately changing the subject, "Have you had anything to eat?"

"It's okay — I'm not hungry. Well . . . maybe I am a bit, at that," Julie admitted, as though only just realising the fact.

"You're getting as bad as me. Come on, let's get something rustled up."

Fort Lauderdale, Florida

"This is the place," Nolan said, turning the car into the drive of an imposing, two-storey house that had a large, well-tended lawn in front. It was a modern building, designed as was the rule in this part of the world to withstand a hurricane, yet it still reminded Redmond of films from the fifties and sixties set in the deep South — *In the Heat of the Night* or *To Kill a Mockingbird*. Redmond almost expected to see people sitting out on the verandah sipping mint juleps. . . . He pushed the rambling thoughts aside and stifled a yawn as he followed Nolan up to the front door. He still had not really caught up with himself after the flights to and fro across the Atlantic and then down to Florida, and so he was feeling tired, to say the least. Knackered would be more like it, he decided. . . .

The door was answered by a tall, cadaverous man in his sixties with sparse grey hair who peered intently at Nolan's ID card before letting them in. He led them into a large living room that was immaculately tidy with several bookshelves lining one wall. As Redmond had expected, the books were almost exclusively electronics and computer science texts, which was hardly surprising when one considered that Professor Samuels was — or had been — one of the leading computer systems designers in the United States. Which meant the world, of course.

Samuels stared suspiciously at Redmond for several seconds before he said curtly, "You must be the British counterintelligence specialist that Nolan mentioned. Ross, he said your name was." His tone made it quite clear that he did not believe this for one minute; Redmond simply nodded noncommittally, wondering how many more half-truths he and Nolan would have to tell. They had to play this interview very carefully, because they were acting entirely unofficially at the moment

— neither Washington nor London had any idea they were talking to Samuels. If the FBI or the Branch found out what they were up to, there'd be hell to pay.

"Right," said Samuels briskly once they had sat down. "Nolan said you wanted to ask some questions about the Piccolo Project, Mr. — ah — Ross. I've agreed only because I have been specifically asked to do so by Nolan here, as a representative of the FBI. Is that clear?"

"Perfectly, Professor Samuels," Redmond said smoothly. "I understand you headed the research team for the Piccolo Project from 1985 until six months ago, when you retired."

Samuels nodded. "Yes. I took over from Professor Kratzmann."

"Am I right in saying that the project was in fact run by Comtex Industries, using funding both from their own resources and from the U.S. and British governments?"

"That wasn't really my side of it, but yes, that was essentially the situation."

"And you were officially seconded to Comtex for the duration of the project?"

"Yes. I was involved from its inception in 1979, firstly as Kratzmann's assistant, then as research director."

"Fine." Redmond glanced at Nolan, then said, "So what exactly is Piccolo?"

Samuels stared at him, then turned to Nolan.

"Is he cleared for this?"

"Absolutely, Professor. Mr. Ross has carte blanche in this matter. I'll show you the documents if you like." Redmond flashed a momentary glance at Nolan, wondering if the FBI man had overplayed his hand; if Samuels called his bluff and asked to see them, they would be sunk, because no such documents existed.

"No, that won't be necessary." Redmond let out a silent sigh of relief as Samuels paused, collecting his thoughts. "Firstly, how much do you know about it already?"

"Not very much," Redmond admitted. "All I know is that it's a computerised guidance system that uses lasers in some way and which can be used for both missiles and aircraft. The theory was that, ideally, it could allow an aircraft to land and take off automatically, so I gather."

"Exactly." For the first time, there was animation in Samuels's face and Redmond suspected that they might well have a job shutting him up now. "Piccolo itself is a navigational guidance system that uses laser pulses as well as radar. The resulting data is fed into an on-board computer along with inertial navigation data, wind speed, and so on to give an accurate geographical fix and altitude reading, whether at night, or in zero visibility, with a precision that no other computerised system can match. If used by a cruise missile, for example, we could pick out a particular church spire as a target in thick fog at a range of three thousand miles — and hit it. We would not even have to programme in a course as such, which is the case at present. We could simply tell the system where it is intended to go, and it would automatically take the missile around any obstacles — hills, buildings, power lines, and so on, because it would detect them either on radar or visually by laser, and take the missile round them while then setting up a revised course to take it on to its target. The problem with the present computer-guided systems is that it only takes one slight error early on in the flight to end up with a major deviation by the time it reaches its target — this would not occur with Piccolo, because the system would constantly be checking its geographical location and correcting the course accordingly in the same way as a human operator would do if he were controlling it from its launch site — which was the method used in the Gulf War. With Piccolo, however, you would not need any human operator. In addition, the system would also enable incoming aircraft or missiles to be detected and evasive action taken — automatically. Thus, any missile or aircraft equipped with Piccolo would virtually be able to fly itself, under any conditions, and to adopt evasive manoeuvres if under attack, but at a far faster rate than human reflexes would allow."

"An automatic plane, you mean," Redmond murmured.

"Exactly. Eventually, the idea was to make the system so sophisticated that, in an emergency, the aircraft would be able to land itself, either by remote control from the ground, or fully automatically, without any outside assistance at all."

Redmond stared at Samuels for several seconds, then seemed to collect his thoughts. "You said 'the idea was.' Is the project still running?"

Samuels looked at Nolan, evidently surprised, then back at Redmond. "Of course it isn't. It was closed down six months ago. That was when I took my retirement."

Redmond glanced at Nolan. "And was the project successful?"

Samuels shook his head slowly, his eyes now fixed appraisingly on Redmond. "No, it wasn't."

"You mean — Piccolo doesn't work."

"No, Mr. Ross. It doesn't."

Redmond heard Nolan mutter something under his breath that sounded like "Jesus H. Christ," but he did not take his eyes from

Samuels. "Is there any way that Comtex, or anyone else for that matter, could have found a way to make it operational since the project was closed down?"

Samuels glared at him. "Mr. Ross, or whatever your real name is, we had been working on that project for over a decade, using the best computer and electronics experts on both sides of the Atlantic. We tried every approach imaginable, plus a few that were pure shots in the dark, and if there was any way to get it to work at an acceptable level of reliability, then we would have found it, believe me. That was why the project was terminated — we finally admitted defeat."

"Reliability? That was the problem?"

Samuels nodded. "We never managed to top eighty percent reliability, which was nowhere near good enough, of course."

"Did you ever identify the reasons?"

"There were a number of factors involved, the basic one being that it was probably too ambitious. Piccolo was originally based on projections of computer capabilities in the future — we were designing systems to be driven by computers that hadn't even been built at the time. The project had built-in computer evolution, to use the buzzphrase we had in the beginning. The intention was to put us ahead of the competition in that respect —

in 1979, we were designing a system that would use the computers of the late eighties and early nineties."

"Only you didn't get the computers you predicted?"

"Not completely, no, although there were basic flaws in the designs that were not apparent for some time. Some of the components and subsystems could not be tested until sufficiently powerful and sophisticated computers could be developed to run them, so that by the time we found out that they did not function optimally, we'd already spent five or six years on them in some cases."

"As well as investing a good deal of money in them, I suppose."

"What? Oh, yes, naturally. Millions, in some cases. That was why Piccolo was kept going as long as it was. We all knew by 1988 that, short of starting over from scratch, it was not a viable proposition, but they kept asking us to try again."

" 'They'?"

"Comtex."

"But they eventually gave up six months ago?"

"Yes. They closed it down and disbanded the team. Several of us took early retirement, with substantial gratuities, I may add."

Redmond nodded slowly. "Who would have

received your progress reports, Professor?"

Samuels shrugged. "The Scientific Division in Houston."

"Comtex, you mean?"

"Of course."

"And they would have forwarded them to the Pentagon?"

"Presumably."

"But you never reported to anyone but Houston?"

"No."

"Uh-huh," Redmond said slowly. "So, in your professional opinion, there is no way that the Piccolo system could now be a viable proposition — correct?"

"That's what I said," Samuels said testily. "Not without completely redesigning and re-developing it."

"And how long would that take?"

"I'd estimate five years minimum. Probably nearer ten."

"I see," Redmond said slowly. He rose to his feet. "Thank you for your help, Professor."

They went back out to the car and climbed in, wordlessly, but Nolan made no effort to start the engine. He simply sat in the driver's seat, staring through the windscreen. "Steve — just what the hell is going on?"

Redmond looked back at the house, his expression grim. "If I were you, Carl," he said quietly, still watching Samuels's house, "I'd put him under permanent surveillance." He turned and gazed bleakly at Nolan. "I think we just met our next victim."

London

Julie shook her head wearily, then put down the printout sheet and leaned back in her chair. "I don't know," she muttered. "I just don't know."

"Nothing?" Gail asked. She was in front of her computer console as always, staring glumly at a list of names and figures on the VDT screen.

"Not a bloody thing," Julie agreed morosely, then looked around the living room, which was littered with printout paper and handwritten sheets of notes and diagrams, the end result of ten days' solid work. They had finished abstracting the raw computer data five days ago and had been collating the results ever since, but there was still no identifiable link between Farrington and Comelec or Comtex beyond his knowing Comelec's managing director. While such an acquaintanceship had hardly been desirable or entirely ethical, given their relative positions when the one had been in a position to award contracts to the other's firm, there was no hard evidence to point to any impropriety, except, perhaps, the offer of the consultancy post — and even that could be argued away as the prudent move of a firm wishing to benefit from his experience and expertise in the field of defence contracts.

Evidence — that was what they needed. Good, hard evidence that would stand up in court if necessary, but they had found nothing untoward about Farrington. True, they had uncovered enough dubious transactions elsewhere to keep the Fraud Squad happy for months, but Farrington was still in the clear. . . .

Gail pushed her chair back from the console, then swivelled it round to face Julie. "Are there any more files you could pick out for me to lift?"

Julie sighed. "Hundreds of them, Gail. There are scores of loose ends on that thing we haven't chased up yet." She gestured irritably at the large chart, which was now crisscrossed by a bewildering network of lines and symbols. "The trouble is that they'll take weeks to track down, let alone collate."

"And we don't have weeks, do we?"

"No," Julie admitted. "I can't afford to take much more time off from the business, to be honest. I've still got bills to pay. . . ." She stared helplessly at the pile of paper in front of her. "It's just that I thought we had enough here. I didn't think anyone would go as deep as this." She shook her head. "I still don't believe it. . . . Nobody would go to this much trouble, just on the off chance that someone would hunt as obsessively as we have — I bet even the Fraud Squad would be packing it in about now. Maybe there isn't anything else to find after all. Maybe Farrington was just trying to hide some of his loot from the tax man." Her voice sounded infinitely weary, despairing.

"He wouldn't have to go to that much trouble." Gail nodded at the chart. "Even I know that."

"I know, I know. So he's up to something, but I'm damned if I can find out what, or who's paying him. I was just so certain that if there was anything here, it would show up on that bloody chart. Only it hasn't. I suppose we could always take another look," she added unenthusiastically.

"Forget it — it's late enough as it is. I don't know about you, but I'm about ready for some kip."

Gail never knew just what it was that woke her up, but she immediately noticed the light under the door of her bedroom. What the hell? She slipped out of bed, pulled on a dressing gown, and opened the door into the living room.

Julie was sitting at the dining table, also in a dressing gown, and she was studying a printout sheet intently. She glanced up at Gail, then nodded sheepishly. "Couldn't sleep."

"It's nearly two o'clock," Gail protested weakly.

"Just an idea I had — something I hadn't tried yet," Julie explained absently, her attention once more on the printout. "Ah — thought it was here," she murmured, then circled an entry on the sheet. Then, she looked around the room with a faintly mystified air.

"What are you looking for?"

"The Calgram file."

Gail thought for a moment, then said, "Over there." She went over to a neat stack of paper and brought it over, wondering why the hell she didn't just go back to bed and leave Julie to this latest wildgoose chase. Julie muttered her thanks, then began leafing slowly through page after page of fanfold paper, her face set in a frown of concentration.

She tensed and placed her pen next to an entry. She circled it, then checked back to the original sheet she had been studying. She stared almost disbelievingly at it, then murmured, "Bloody hell . . ." She scooped up the large chart from where it had been strewn on the floor. Slowly, carefully, she drew a black line across the central dividing line linking up the two halves of the diagram for the first time.

She stared down at the chart, then looked up at Gail, her eyes now excited, triumphant.

"I think I've found it."

Twelve

Hampstead Heath, London

"So that's it," Redmond finished quietly. "Piccolo doesn't work and, according to Samuels, it never will."

Gail stared up at him, then shook her head slowly. "Shit. . ." she muttered, appalled, then turned away from him to stare out over the panoramic view of London. They were standing on the top of Parliament Hill and it was a clear evening; in the distance, she could see the tall spire of the Post Office Tower and the silver dome of St. Paul's. Yet her eyes were unfocused, not taking in any of the magnificent vista. She shook her head again. "So that's what this is all about. . . ." she said, half to herself, then looked back at him. "That's what Comtex is covering up, isn't it? The fact that they're selling both the American and British governments a lemon. Anyone they don't think they can trust is being killed off. . . . Jesus Christ. It's obscene!"

"That's about it," Redmond said, nodding heavily. "Just one huge cover-up, like you said. A bloody great con trick."

248

"But . . . how the hell do they expect to get away with it? It's bound to come out sooner or later."

"How? There won't be any expert witnesses to testify against them, will there?" Redmond replied sourly. "They'll be able to wheel out their own tame scientists to say that of course the bloody thing works. Comtex has got more than enough clout to do that, Gail. Not only that, but will the U.S. and UK governments want to admit that they've been taken for a ride? They'll want this swept under the carpet as well."

She nodded unhappily. "I guess they will at that." She looked away again and a heavy silence fell as they brooded on the implications. A young courting couple came towards them, and Redmond stared suspiciously at them, wondering if they formed part of the surveillance he had been unsuccessfully looking for since he had landed at Heathrow early that morning. But they were too young, not even out of their teens, and they were totally engrossed in each other: they passed by without even a glance in his direction. Slowly, Redmond looked around, but there was still no sign of anyone watching him. Of course, that was hardly conclusive because given high-tech equipment such as directional microphones and image processors, it was relatively easy nowadays to maintain surveillance on a subject without revealing one's presence.

So . . . either they were satisfied he was no longer a threat and were leaving him alone — or they were making damn sure he did not know he was being followed, which meant that they were suspicious after all. The thing was, he could not rid himself of the feeling he was being watched, although that could simply be because of the enormity of the knowledge he now possessed. It was the old cliché: he knew too much.

Unfortunately, it was too late to worry about that now. . . .

"Okay," he said suddenly, bringing Gail out of her own reverie. "So now we know what this is all about, what else do we have? You said you and Julie had found something."

She nodded. "We did indeed. First, Farrington does hold secret shares in both Comelec and Comtex — and has for the past five years. Since he joined the Research Co-ordination Unit, in fact. None of the shares are in his name and he's gone to such lengths to conceal his ownership of them that he must have had professional help to do it — even Julie was barely able to follow the trail. The point is that he started acquiring the shares a month after being transferred to the unit. Since then, the value of the Comelec shares

250

has increased fivefold — and seventy-five percent of Comelec's business is through the MOD. Interesting, eh?"

"You're sure about this?"

"Well, Julie is anyway — she lost me about halfway through her explanation. You were right, though — she really does know her stuff. Apparently, Farrington's ownership of the shares — and he's got a fair-sized holding in Comelec — is through a long chain of stock-brokers, proxy shareholders, Liechtenstein lawyers and bankers, numbered bank accounts, offshore companies and so on, but at a conservative estimate, Julie reckons he must have made something like half a million out of his Comelec shares alone."

Redmond whistled softly. "You mean he must have invested a hundred grand to begin with?"

"Or just been given the shares for nothing. We haven't been able to sort that out yet."

Redmond shook his head thoughtfully. "So Comelec has prospered because of the MOD and so has Farrington. Rather looks as though he was on the take, doesn't it?"

"It does," she agreed. "The point is, what was he being paid for?"

"Right." Redmond nodded grimly. "Was it just for putting contracts Comelec's way — or was it for setting up contracts of a different sort? Did you get anything on Comtex or Comelec?"

"Julie did," Gail replied. "She chatted up some acquaintance of hers in the City and got some fairly detailed information." She reached inside her jacket and took out a notebook, which she opened. "Okay. For starters, for Comelec, read Comtex. Although Comelec is officially a fairly autonomous subsidiary of Comtex, in practice it's not much more than a department of the parent company specialising in computerised weapons and detection systems. Ledsham, the CEO, has to get approval for virtually everything from Comtex in the States, even down to hiring and firing his own departmental heads. That's all he is himself, really, while the so-called board of directors are all Comtex appointees. Comtex owns something like seventy or eighty percent of the stock."

"You said that they have to check with the States before hiring anybody important," said Redmond. "Would that apply to consultants as well?"

"Probably."

"What about Comtex itself?"

"Comtex is big, very big. It's up on a par with Exxon, ITT, and the others, but is probably more diversified. It's into virtually everything, but particularly in the electronics and aeronautical fields. The head office is in Houston, but they've got operations all over the world — London, Paris, Tokyo, Hong Kong, Singapore, Bahrain, the lot. They tend to adopt a steamroller approach to business — anyone in their way just gets flattened, because very few people can really afford to take them on, not when their annual turnover is on a par with the GNP of some Western countries. Not even the U.S. government can afford to upset them too much." She laughed harshly. "Neither can ours, come to that. Maybe you've heard about the four factories they're building in the north of England?"

Redmond nodded. "I heard something about it, yes."

"They've ridden roughshod over trade union legislation as well as local conservation interests — and they've been given huge government grants to do it. The factories are all in unemployment black-spots, you see."

"I do see," said Redmond, nodding thoughtfully. "So they aren't too bothered about legal niceties?"

"You could say that. They're involved in anything that's profitable, legal or not. And they don't mind who gets hurt. Julie was told that at least two promising computer firms have gone bankrupt because they were competing with Comtex subsidiaries. They got

Cocom to blacklist them and that was it."

"Cocom?" Redmond asked. "Isn't that some sort of U.S. government setup? They put the boot into computer firms who want to export to the Soviet bloc, don't they?"

Gail nodded. "Right. Although it's based in Paris, it's effectively a part of the U.S. government, whose role, as you said, is to control the sale of American technology to the Eastern bloc. For 'control,' read 'prevent,' especially if we're talking about computer technology. If any firm is even suspected of selling computer hardware — or software, come to that — to the Eastern bloc, then Cocom blacklists it and, from that day on, there is no way that the firm can buy any further equipment, or even export what it's already got. The U.S. government invokes its Export Administration Act, which controls the use of all U.S.-developed technology. For example, no matter how many times a computer changes hands, it still remains subject to U.S. export laws if more than five percent of it consists of American technology — which means virtually every microcomputer ever made. You could be the tenth owner of the bloody thing and if you tried to sell it to a computer buff in Warsaw, let's say, you'd be blacklisted."

"And this blacklist is pretty potent?"

"You bet. What it means is that if you're

254

on it, then not only U.S. companies but also about eighty-five percent of European high-tech companies will not touch you with a barge-pole, or they'll be blacklisted as well. You go out of business — end of story."

"Jeez," said Redmond softly. "This Cocom's got that much power?"

"It has. And Comtex wields a hell of a lot of influence in Cocom — and in Washington." Gail shrugged. "Like I said, you just don't take them on if you've got any sense. They're ruthless."

Redmond nodded briefly, then said, "They don't sound as though they'd be too morally outraged at the idea of bribing government officials."

Gail smiled grimly. "Comtex? By the sound of it, that's almost the first thing they include in the estimates for any operation or project they set up. When you're talking the sort of money they deal in, they could bribe a civil servant like Farrington out of the petty cash — no questions asked. They're as bent as a nine bob note."

Redmond rubbed his chin thoughtfully, then said slowly, "You and Julie've done bloody well, Gail." He sighed. "The trouble is, we still don't seem to be that much further forward."

"At least we know what's really going on

now," Gail pointed out.

"True — but all we've got is proof that Farrington has been on Comtex's payroll for years, but we still don't have any proof that he was setting up the Piccolo deaths, do we? Okay, so he was on the take, but it could have simply been to make sure Comelec got more than its fair share of contracts from the MOD. We're going to need more than this if we're going to get Bryceland or Mayhew to switch Farthingale onto this tack."

"I wouldn't bank on Mayhew doing anything of the sort, whatever you gave him," Gail said, her expression grave. "That's something else we found out — why you and I were reassigned when we were."

Redmond stared intently at her. "Go on."

"We were getting too close for comfort. You see, once we knew what we were looking for, Julie and I managed to track down other secret shareholders in Comelec and Comtex, and the list makes very interesting reading — top civil servants and politicians, for example. And one of them is MI-five's deputy director general — Sir Ronald Mayhew."

Redmond checked his watch yet again — it was almost nine — then looked across the street at number 44, an expensive Georgian house he had been watching for the last hour

256

or more. Farrington and his wife were supposed to be visiting friends that night, according to the information he had been given, but there was still no sign of them so far. Redmond was in his car just along the road from the Farringtons' home, but the problem was that you could not sit for that length of time in a Kensington street at night without attracting suspicion. He had already noticed more than one curtain being twitched back to watch him; all it needed was for some resident to telephone the police and he would have some explaining to do, either now or later. So where the hell was Farrington?

As if to confirm his fears, Redmond saw a policeman walking down the street on the far side, and he was looking over at the car. There was no doubt that he had seen him, despite the fact that Redmond had deliberately parked in the shadows. The policeman came to a halt, now looking directly at the car and its solitary occupant, then crossed the street.

Redmond sighed and wound down the window, holding up his Special Branch pass, trying not to smile at the sudden change of expression on the policeman's face. He said nothing, however, just nodded apologetically and walked on past without a check in his step.

Redmond grimaced: it was very likely that,

sooner or later, the report that he had been maintaining a watch on Farrington's home would filter through to Bryceland and he would want to know just what the hell he had been playing at, especially as he was supposed to be on leave. If all this proved to be a wild-goose chase — as it could well do, if he were honest about it — then he would have some explaining to do. Bugger . . .

Less than two minutes later, however, a taxi pulled up outside number 44; the front door opened and Farrington and his wife appeared. Mrs. Farrington looked impatient, as if they should have left some time ago. Redmond looked at his watch — 9:08 — and his lips tightened. There might not be a lot of time now, because he would have to assume they would be back by midnight, since it was a normal workday tomorrow.

The Farringtons went to the taxi and climbed in; the cab drove off and in less than half a minute had disappeared from view, turning right into Knightsbridge. Redmond gave them five minutes to get clear before he climbed out of the car, closed the door, then walked unhurriedly across the street, his hands pushed deep into his pockets.

As he reached number 44, he glanced casually around, then mounted the steps to the door, taking a key from his coat pocket. He inserted it in the lock, turned it — it was a little stiff — and was inside within a minute of leaving the car. He pocketed the key, wondering how Farrington would react if he knew Special Branch had a duplicate key to both his town and country houses — as they had for virtually every high-ranking official who had signed the Official Secrets Act. Then, he began his search, flicking on a pencil torch.

He already knew the layout of the house by a study of its plans on file, and it took him less than thirty seconds to check the alarm system — which had not been switched on. Presumably, they had left in such a hurry they had forgotten to set it, but it made his own task that much easier. Now he could begin in earnest.

Redmond's search was rapid and thorough, but, despite this, he was at pains to replace everything exactly the way he had found it. He started downstairs in the living room, then worked his way methodically through each room but without result. There was nothing incriminating anywhere in the house, not even the odd document that had been brought home overnight to work on against regulations. Nothing in the cistern or under the carpet, no false panel — a complete blank. The problem was, of course, that he really needed much longer than he actually had. To turn a house over properly needed a team of experts working for several days, but Redmond was looking for the kind of evidence that Farrington would want to have within easy reach. Something that would not be concealed in the attic or under the floorboards — a list of names or phone numbers, coded or otherwise, cryptic entries in a diary. True, Farrington would be asking for trouble if he were to leave anything incriminating lying around, but you never knew; even trained deep-cover agents had been known to do so, especially after they had been in place for a while. They became over-confident, too convinced that they were in the clear and that, as a result, their homes would not be searched. In any event, Redmond doubted that Farrington would have had much instruction or experience in espionage trade-craft; he might just get careless.

If he was implicated at all, Redmond thought sourly, returning to the study, a pan-elled room in the back of the house on the first floor. If there was anything to be found, it would be here in Farrington's inner sanctum. But where? He had already searched the wall safe behind the portrait of Wellington and found nothing, so now he worked his way along the bookshelf, opening books to see if any scraps of paper fell out. But there was still nothing except an awareness that Farrington was keen on golf and cricket, judging by the contents of his library.

Redmond checked his watch. It was 12:30, already half an hour beyond the deadline he had set himself, but he still could not bring himself to leave empty-handed. He stood in the middle of the room looking around aimlessly, trying to think of where he would hide, say, a sheet of paper. There simply wasn't anywhere else he could look, not unless he was going to start probing into the leather upholstery of the armchairs or prising up floorboards. So where would be the most secure place to hide anything? The safe of course, but he had already looked there. Ah, to hell with it, one more look and then he'd go.

Feeling distinctly like the proverbial drowning man clutching at straws, Redmond went over to the portrait, removed it once more from its hook, then, consulting the slip of paper he had brought with him, dialled the lock's combination. He pulled open the door and removed the documents, resisting the impulse to leaf through them just once more — he had already done that three times. Shining the pencil torch into the safe, he meticulously examined its interior, tapping cautiously on its sides. Then, he removed the rubber gloves he had been wearing and ran his fingertips over the surfaces, very delicately.

There. He stopped abruptly and moved his fingers back, locating the tiny hairline crack. He shone the torch into the safe again and, now that he knew it was there, he could see a dead-straight line running vertically up the back of the safe. Next to it was a very shallow indentation; he pressed it and a section of the safe's inner wall clicked smoothly open.

Inside was a small red notebook.

Redmond snatched it out and opened it, feeling his heartbeat accelerating as he saw columns of letters and figures arranged in five character groups: they had to be in code. Checkmate, Farrington, he thought exultantly, then went over to the desk. He turned on the anglepoise lamp and took a tiny camera from his pocket. Carefully, he photographed each page of the notebook twice.

He was just in the act of replacing the camera in his pocket when he heard the sound of a car engine outside. He went to the window and swore under his breath as he saw a taxi parked in the road — and the Farringtons were climbing out of it.

Moving rapidly now, he turned off the lamp and returned the notebook to the concealed compartment, swinging the flap shut. The documents went back into the safe, which he closed, spinning the combination dial. Finally, he replaced the portrait on its hook.

Redmond stood in the centre of the room again, forcing himself to check that everything was back the way it had been, even though he could hear the Farringtons' voices in the hallway downstairs. Redmond eased open the door, emerging onto the landing. He pulled the door shut behind him, straining his ears to hear what was happening downstairs. Their voices were plainly audible — they were having a row.

"You know very well I wanted to be back before this," Farrington was saying. "I do have to be in Slough at nine tomorrow, you know."

"Well, if you hadn't dragged your feet earlier, we could have left on time. One can't be the last to arrive and the first to leave."

"One can, you know. I never wanted to go in the first place."

"A fact that must have been patently obvious to everyone there. I doubt if we'll ever be invited again, thanks to you."

Their voices faded as they went into the drawing room and closed the door, but Redmond could still hear the argument raging on. That suited him fine: if they were shouting at each other, they would be less likely to hear him. He descended the stairs rapidly, paused as he reached the bottom step, listening to the voices, then noiselessly crossed the hall, opened the door, and slipped out, pulling it closed behind him. He smiled as he realised he could still hear them: whatever would the neighbours think?

He walked back to his car, totally unaware of the broad grin on his face.

"It's code all right," Gail said, a tone of quiet triumph in her voice as she pushed back her seat from her computer console. "Quite a simple one, actually."

"And what does it say?" Redmond asked, going round behind her to look at the VDT screen.

"It's a list of names, addresses, and biographical information," she replied unnecessarily; Redmond was already reading them off the screen. There were seven names at the top of the screen: Hayward. Barclay. Inchmore. Phillips. West. Kirk. Aldridge.

These were the ones whose coded entries Farrington had neatly crossed out; these were the dead scientists. Five of them had also been marked with an asterisk: Hayward, Inchmore, Phillips, Kirk, and Aldridge — the ones who had worked on Piccolo. But what were Barclay and West doing on the list, in that case?

"Oh, bloody hell . . ." he murmured in dawning realisation.

"Barclay and West?" said Gail, as if reading

his mind. "Decoys, that's all they were. It's the Piccolo ones they were really after." She touched a key and five more names appeared; three of them had asterisks.

"Presumably, those three are all ex-Piccolo scientists — only they're still alive. So far." She shook her head angrily. "This is their fucking hit list. They killed Barclay and West, and they're going to kill those two at the bottom just so it won't look too obvious that Piccolo was the common factor."

"And it worked," Redmond said bitterly. "I damn nearly discounted it altogether after West."

"But you didn't," she reminded him. "If you had, we wouldn't have got that." She nodded at the screen. "I mean, look at it this way — we've got Farrington now, haven't we?"

Redmond nodded slowly. "Yes, we have. I'm going to nail the bastard to the wall."

Thirteen

Saturday Afternoon

"Look, are you sure this is the only way?" asked Gail. She was standing by the front window of her flat, looking at Redmond, but, silhouetted as she was against the light he could not see the expression on her face.

He nodded. "We've got to force the issue, Gail, like it or not."

"But why?" she persisted. "Surely if we take what we've got to Selvey or whoever, they'll have to act on it, won't they? I mean, okay, it won't stand up in court, but there's enough to initiate an investigation, isn't there?"

"More than enough," Redmond agreed. "But where will that get us? You saw the names on that shareholder list — how many others are there we haven't uncovered yet? Once we get an investigation underway it's going to take weeks, months maybe, to get enough evidence to start making arrests — and somebody's bound to tip them off. They'll disappear, one by one, before we can pick them up — we know damn well they've got enough contacts to manage that. What we need is something that will force the Deputy Assistant Commissioner to move now, before they can all make a run for it."

She shook her head and moved towards him. "Yes, I can see that, but — well, suppose it all goes wrong? I mean, confronting Farrington's one thing, but how do you think Comtex will react?"

He hesitated, then replied quietly, "I'm not saying there isn't a risk involved, but this is honestly the only way we can get anywhere. They're not going to do anything too drastic, because that would be asking for trouble, but I think this is going to scare the living daylights out of them. And especially Farrington — it's his head on the block, after all. He's almost certain to give something away, because I don't think he'll have the nerve to bluff it out."

"I hope you're right," she said. "Just take care."

"I will, don't worry — it's my neck, you know."

"I just hope to hell you know what you're doing, that's all."

"I'll be all right. Don't you think I can handle Farrington or something?"

"It's not Farrington I'm worried about. It's who's behind him."

"You let me worry about that." Redmond wished he felt as confident as he sounded. She had a point, because he was sticking his neck out a long way, but it had to be done, like it or not. . . .

"Just be careful."

"I promise." He looked at his watch. "I'd better be going." He looked intently at her. "Now just make sure you do exactly what I've told you, right?"

"I know what I have to do," she said with a faint air of irritation. "I ought to — we've been through it enough times."

"It's for your own good, Gail, believe me. Right, let's get this show on the road," he said with an attempt at lightheartedness. "I'll see you tonight, let you know what happened, okay?"

"Okay." She saw him to the door. "Just take care, sir," she said again.

"Gail?"

"Yes?"

"Do me a favour, will you?"

"What?"

"Stop calling me sir, okay?"

She stared at him in surprise, then nodded, smiling faintly. "Okay — Steve?"

"That's better."

Totteridge, Hertfordshire

Redmond smiled to himself as he turned

268

into a wide gravel drive that led up to the rambling house. Farrington clearly was not short of a few bob. This place had to be worth five hundred thousand at least, and if you added it to the value of his town house, there would not be much change out of a cool million. Admittedly Farrington had been a very high-ranking civil servant, and he had also married into wealth, but how much of this had come out of backhanders from Comtex over the years? Had Elizabeth Kirk and the others helped pay for his house?

Redmond brought his car to a halt in front of the large, panelled door, then climbed out, looking around him. Although the action was apparently casual, he was wondering if Farrington was under surveillance, as was entirely possible. If he were running the operation from Comtex's point of view, then it would make sense, now that Farrington had been exposed — albeit only to a small extent — for them to keep an eye on him. If this was so, then Redmond knew he was putting his head into a noose, but, as he had said to Gail, he had little choice in the matter.

Well, actually, he did, he thought suddenly: he could just turn his back on all this and walk away. If he had any common sense, that would be precisely what he would do. The trouble was that he couldn't walk away from himself. . . .

He pressed the doorbell firmly and within a quarter of a minute the door was opened by a short, middle-aged woman whom Redmond knew was Mrs. Jukes, the Farringtons' part-time housekeeper/cook: Mrs. Farrington was seemingly averse to housework of any kind. "Good morning," Redmond said affably. "Is Mr. Farrington in? I'd like a word with him, if I may."

"Er — yes. Come in, Mr. — ?"

"Redmond."

"Come in, Mr. Redmond." She stood aside to let him into the hall, then said, "Is Mr. Farrington expecting you, sir?"

"No, but I'm sure he'll see me. Tell him it's in connection with Comtex and Piccolo."

"I'll see if he's about. If you'll excuse me a minute?" She disappeared through a door to the right, at the foot of the stairs, but emerged again less than twenty seconds later. "If you'll come in, Mr. Redmond?"

The door led into a drawing room, expensively furnished, which ran the full length of the house: Redmond could see the back garden through the patio doors on his left. Farrington, a stockily built man with iron grey hair cut *en brosse*, was standing in front of a large fireplace, and his face was blazing with fury. Despite this, he controlled himself until Mrs.

Jukes had closed the door, leaving them alone.

"Just what the hell do you mean by this, Redmond?" he exploded. "Barging in here like this. What right do you have —"

"I didn't barge my way in at all," Redmond pointed out, reasonably. "You invited me in."

"Don't you adopt that attitude with me!" Farrington protested. "I'd be quite within my rights to phone the police and have you thrown off my property."

Unruffled, Redmond pointed to the telephone on a low table. "There it is. Go ahead."

Farrington glared at him, then said tautly, "Just say what you came here to say, then go."

"That could take a little while, Mr. Farrington," Redmond said. He walked over to an armchair and sat down. "You might as well make yourself comfortable."

"Get on with it!"

Redmond reached inside his jacket and took out a folded sheet of paper, which he held out to the other man. Farrington stared at it suspiciously, a puzzled frown on his face that abruptly gave way to dawning realisation. He snatched the paper from Redmond's grasp and opened it hurriedly, his shoulders slumping as he saw its contents. "Where — how did you get this?" he demanded angrily.

"Does how I got it really matter?" Redmond

asked tiredly. "And as for where — you know damn well where it came from, don't you? And in case you think I don't know what it is, I've had it decoded, Farrington. It's a list of scientists, both the ones who have already been killed and the ones you and your pals haven't got round to yet — the ones you've still got to silence. And it's all in your hand-writing, isn't it? So, the way I see it is this: I've got you by the proverbial short and curlies."

Farrington's face had gone pale. He began to speak, but had to clear his throat before he said, "I see. I take it you intend to blackmail me?"

"Something like that, yes."

"With this?" Farrington said, his eyes suddenly lighting up as he turned quickly and threw the paper onto the fire behind him. As it burst into flames, he glared triumphantly at Redmond.

"Photocopiers are wonderful machines, don't you think?" Redmond said, smiling faintly.

Farrington's eyes blazed in fury, and, for a moment, Redmond was convinced that he was about to attack him, but, with a visible effort, Farrington brought himself under control. "What do you want from me?" he asked, his eyes glittering. "How much?" he asked, putting a sneer into his voice.

"Oh, it won't be cheap, believe me," Redmond said impassively. "And you've nothing to be so bloody superior about, Farrington. How many deaths is it now? Seven?" He stared at Farrington, his eyes cold. "And you have the nerve to look down on me."

"We're not so different," Farrington snapped. "You're selling out Special Branch, aren't you? Isn't that what you're doing?"

"And why not?" Redmond demanded, allowing his urbanity to crack now. He rose to his feet and began to pace impatiently. "All I did was try and do my job properly and what happens? I get kicked in the teeth. Somebody else gets the credit. I've had enough of bucking the system. If you can't beat 'em, join 'em. I might as well get something out of all this — hell, everyone else is, by the looks of it, so why should I be the only sucker around?"

"All right, you've made your point," Farrington said sourly. "As I said, how much do you want from me to keep quiet? I take it that's what the arrangement will be? If I pay you, then you won't show those photocopies to the police — is that it?"

"That's part of it, yes. But you're not the only one I'm after. There are bigger fish for me to fry, after all."

"What do you mean?"

"I mean that I know who you're really working for, Farrington. It was very neat, I'll give you that, letting us go off on a wild-goose chase, when we thought it was the Russians behind it all. But we both know that wasn't the case at all, don't we, Farrington? And I can prove it."

Farrington shook his head, but there was a look of fear in his eyes as he said, "I don't know what you're talking about."

"Yes, you do, Farrington, or you wouldn't have let me in when I mentioned Comtex to Mrs. Jukes. That was your first mistake. By letting me in, you more or less admitted you knew what I was talking about — and that I was right. I've got evidence implicating Comtex in all this. Not to mention Sir Ronald Mayhew, by the way. I can prove it's Comtex behind the Piccolo killings, not the Russians."

"I still don't know what the hell you're talking about!" Farrington protested, but the fearful expression was still in his eyes, giving the lie to the words.

"Farrington, didn't I get through to you?" Redmond demanded. "Listen — read my lips: I — can — prove — it. I've got enough evidence to blow Comtex wide open, and I'll do it if I don't get what I want. I want you to tell them that. If they want me to keep my mouth shut, then Comtex has to make it worth my while, and, like I said, it won't be cheap."

Farrington stared at him, aghast. "You're insane! You don't know what you're saying!" he said in a strangled voice. "Do you know who you're taking on? You can't go threatening an organisation like Comtex! They'll —"

"I just did," Redmond said, without inflexion. "And I am not bluffing, either. Tell them that as well. If they don't come up with an acceptable offer, then I hand over everything I've got to the relevant authorities. And don't think Mayhew will be able to block it this time, because it will go over his head. Way over."

Farrington shook his head incredulously. "They'll destroy you, Redmond!"

"They can try, but they'd be stupid if they did. I've got contigency plans in the event of anything — untoward — happening to me. Make sure they realise that when you pass the message on, Farrington. And do it quickly. They'll know where to find me."

Bakerloo Line: Saturday Evening

Redmond was certain now that nobody was following Gail — although, as he had said to Julie, there would not have been any particular reason why anyone should. She had arrived at the Baker Street underground station exactly on schedule, taking up a position on the platform about thirty yards away from where he himself had been waiting, apparently engrossed in an evening paper. She had not once looked in his direction, nor shown any awareness of his presence. When the northbound train arrived, Redmond moved towards her so as to be in the same carriage, but his attention had been focused on the other passengers. It would be impossible for anyone to be observing either of them under these circumstances without Redmond noticing, and the only sign of any interest had been on the part of a young man who had been eyeing Gail up with little attempt at concealment. He had disembarked at Willesden Green, however, and Redmond was now satisfied that the "drop" could go ahead.

As the train pulled into Neasden, Gail stood up and went to the door. Redmond took up position slightly behind and to one side of her, swaying momentarily against her as the train came to a halt. In that fleeting contact, he slipped a small package into her coat pocket before he regained his equilibrium. He allowed Gail to move ahead of him as they emerged onto the platform and headed for the exit, looking around him all the time. Nobody was paying either of them any attention at all, and as he watched Gail disappearing through the station entrance, Redmond let out a sigh of relief. It had been almost a textbook handover.

He hoped everything else would run as smoothly.

It was nearly eight o'clock when Redmond reached home. He turned his car into the underground car park beneath the block of flats in which he lived, driving slowly along the aisle between the rows of cars before he parked in his usual place against the wall about twenty yards from the lift door. He climbed out and turned back to lock the car door.

"Redmond." The one word, spoken very quietly, had him pivoting round, his body crouching reflexively into a defensive judo stance until he saw the speaker, a stockily built man who emerged from the shadows next to a Ford Sierra. It was only then that Redmond recognised the other man; his name was Turner and he was a member of MI5. . . . Oh shit, Redmond thought feelingly, but seeing that Turner had his hands pushed deep into his coat pockets, he slowly straightened up, watching Turner intently. This couldn't be coincidence: they had reacted bloody quickly.

"Turner," Redmond said flatly. "What's all this about?"

"You're to come with me, Redmond," Turner replied. As he spoke, two burly men climbed out of the Sierra and took up position on each side of Turner in what had to be a deliberate display of intimidation. "Orders, Redmond," Turner added quietly.

"Orders? Whose?"

"Does it really matter?"

"Turner — what the hell is this all about?"

"You really ought to know better than to ask questions like that," Turner replied impassively. "My orders are that I've to deliver you to a particular address and that I've not to take no for an answer." He shrugged. "It doesn't really look as though you have any choice in the matter, so just get in the car, will you, Redmond?"

Redmond looked at Turner's two companions and shrugged in turn. "Okay," he said. "Let's get on with it." He walked over to the Sierra and climbed into the back, with one of the "heavies" taking the seat next to him while Turner took the front passenger seat. The other man was already behind the wheel and started up the engine. He had just put the gear lever into first when Redmond said quietly, "Seat belt."

The driver glared at him in the mirror, but

made no attempt to fasten the safety belt. Redmond caught a glimpse of a brief smile on Turner's face, instantly suppressed, but the momentary display of solidarity made Redmond wonder if Turner was entirely happy with the assignment he had been given.

But what exactly had his instructions been? The question nagged at Redmond as the car emerged from the car park and drove off; within a few minutes it was obvious that they were heading east, towards the City, but Redmond suspected that they would be going further than that. This had to be connected with the confrontation with Farrington — three hours ago now, he realised, surreptitiously checking his watch. So, if nothing else, going to see Farrington had achieved its desired effect in that it had stirred up the opposition and forced them to react, but — what the hell was going to happen next? The mere fact that they could mobilise MI5 in under three hours gave a pretty good indication of their influence behind the scenes. In all probability, Redmond decided uneasily, Mayhew could not have managed that single-handedly, deputy DG of MI5 or not: Redmond knew as well as anyone how much paperwork and authorisation that would entail. So — Mayhew was not the only one high up in the security services who was involved. . . .

The journey lasted twenty minutes, taking them across London and into dockland before the Sierra turned into the yard of a warehouse in Wapping. Within seconds of the car coming to a halt, the main door of the warehouse was wheeled aside as several arc lamps on the roof came on, bathing the Sierra in a bright light. Two men stood in the warehouse entrance, staring impassively at the car, each with a tell-tale bulge under his left armpit that betrayed a shoulder holster and each with his right hand resting casually across his stomach within easy reach of the gun.

"Right, out," said Turner.

Redmond stared at him for a moment, then opened the door. He waited for a moment before he realised that none of the car's occupants were making any move to get out, then swung the door closed. The car immediately drove away, leaving him alone with the two armed men.

"Right, Redmond. This way," said the taller of the two, and Redmond glanced at him in surprise; he had a faint, but perceptible, American accent. "Come on, move," the American said impatiently, and Redmond moved forward and past him into the warehouse, which was brightly lit inside as well. He looked quickly around, seeing rows of packing cases neatly stacked and noting that the floor was swept clean; it was evidently in regular use. But then, it would be, if it were owned by one of Comtex's subsidiaries. To his left was a flight of metal steps that led up to an office overlooking the warehouse floor. The office itself was in darkness, but Redmond had an uneasy suspicion that he was being watched from there.

"Through there, Redmond," said the American, pointing to a door halfway along the left-hand wall, just along from the flight of steps. Redmond glanced back at him and, with a start of recognition, realised that he had seen the other man's photograph in a file somewhere — but what was his name? He had to be CIA, though — so what the hell was he doing here?

The door led into a long corridor with several doors on each side that, presumably, led into storerooms. They went along the corridor until the American said, "The end one on the right." The other man went past and unlocked the door; inside was a bare, brick-lined room with a single packing crate against the far wall and a light bulb suspended from the ceiling to provide illumination, but that was all. There was no window, and the door looked heavy and solid.

Redmond paused in the doorway and looked thoughtfully at the American, memorising his features. The American grinned easily, as if unconcerned about what Redmond was doing, and said, "You know, that was a pretty dumb thing to do, going to see Farrington like that, wasn't it?"

Lansky: the name seemed to pop into Redmond's mind from nowhere. Greg Lansky — and definitely CIA. He realised that Lansky was studying him intently, a calculating glint in his eyes, and said, shrugging, "It told me what I wanted to know, Lansky."

There was an undeniable reaction on the other man's face. Lansky's eyes seemed to bore into his, and Redmond was struck by an almost palpable sense of menace; he knew that he was looking at one of the most dangerous men he had ever met. It was in the way Lansky held himself, the coiled tension that made the gun in his shoulder holster seem almost superfluous. And yet there was something else in Lansky's eyes, a hint of respect, almost, in the way he looked at Redmond, as if he were weighing up a worthy adversary, before he smiled again and the moment was gone.

"Very good, Redmond. But recognizing me isn't going to make much difference, is it?"

Redmond shrugged again and went into the room. He did not turn round as the door was closed and locked behind him.

"— they'll know where to find me."

Gail reached out and turned off the cassette player, shaking her head slowly in a combination of awe and despair. There was no doubt that Redmond's plan to rattle Farrington had succeeded — that much was evident from the tape — but had he been too successful? Had he been told too much for his own good?

She checked her watch for what had to be the fiftieth time, then stood up abruptly and paced slowly over to the window, trying not to look at the telephone on the bedside table. Instead she looked down at the street below, wishing she were at home and not in this anonymous Bayswater hotel. Redmond had insisted she stay here tonight: "I want you safely out of the way, Gail — then I won't have to worry about you."

But what about me? she wondered bleakly. How do I cope with sitting around here wondering what the hell's going on? She shook her head again and turned away from the window. Come on, she pleaded silently, staring at the telephone, willing it to ring. It was now four hours since Redmond had passed the package to her on the Tube, and he must have been in the clear then or he would not have come anywhere near her. The package had contained a minicassette tape of his conversation with Farrington from which she had taken several copies onto normal-sized tapes, trying to close her mind to the reason for doing so: if Redmond was not in touch with her by noon tomorrow, she had a list of high-ranking security and police officers to whom she was to send the tapes. Simply playing safe, he had said, trying to reassure her.

She tensed suddenly as she heard a car pulling up outside and sprang towards the window, her heart racing. . . . Her shoulders sagged in disappointment as she saw a stranger emerge from the car below.

She grimaced as she stepped back and turned away. This was getting her nowhere. But what else could she do but wait — and worry?

Fourteen

Redmond heard the sound of footsteps approaching along the corridor and checked the time on his watch — it was just after eleven, two and a half hours since he had been brought here. There had been some far-off unidentifiable sounds an hour or so before, but, apart from that, there had been no signs of any activity in the warehouse. He had virtually resigned himself to having to spend the night curled up on a crate, but it looked as though they had not yet finished with him. He took several deep breaths to key himself up: he would have to be in optimum condition, physically and mentally, ready to face whatever was coming next.

The door opened and a single, prematurely bald man stood in the entrance, gun in hand. Redmond had not seen him before, but he held the silenced automatic pistol as though he were accustomed to using it. Redmond made a mental note: possibly this one was more reliant on a weapon than Lansky had been, because there had been no real need to produce it.

"Come on, Redmond."

Redmond suppressed a smile at the other man's tone — he seemed to be enjoying the power the gun gave him. "Okay," Redmond replied equably and walked out as the gunman stepped backwards. He gestured along the corridor, and Redmond saw a second man standing at the door into the main part of the warehouse. He was also unfamiliar — how many of them were there, for God's sake? Or was this intentional, letting him see just how many men they had at their disposal so that he would know exactly what he was taking on?

They walked across the warehouse, the second man leading the way with the gunman behind Redmond. The floor was still brightly lit, but this time, as he glanced up at the office, Redmond could see shadowy outlines of people inside. This was probably what his captors had been waiting for — the leaders, or at least some of them.

But they did not take him there. Instead, the second man led him through another door on the far side and into a small room that had a table and a chair in its centre, facing an unmanned closed-circuit TV camera and a single loudspeaker. Two bright, but not overpowering, spotlamps illuminated the table and chair, though Redmond had no doubt that this was all intended to emphasise his situation. He was on his own, and they were not going to let him forget it. . . .

As he looked around the room, the second man went out and closed the door, locking it. Despite this, however, Redmond felt strangely calm as he turned back to the table. This was where some, at least, of his questions would be answered — there could be no other explanation for this setup.

He looked directly into the camera and said, "Shall I sit down?"

"If you wish," said a voice through the loudspeaker. Redmond nodded almost imperceptibly; the voice was refined, with the same lack of accent as a BBC newsreader, but it had been subtly distorted electronically, rendering it flat and metallic — and therefore unrecognisable. The actual speaker would be up in the office in total security.

Redmond sat down and addressed the camera. "I don't suppose you'd like to tell me who I'm talking to?"

"Hardly, Redmond. But you may as well think of me as Beresford. It's not my real name, of course, but it will suffice."

"Okay, Beresford. Shall we get on with it?"

"They said you believed in the direct approach. I can see they were right. Very well. As you have no doubt realised, you've presented us with a bit of a problem. I have been

287

listening to a recording of your conversation with Farrington and it is evident that you know far more about us than you should. One of the things that we would like to find out is where you came by this information." There was an expectant pause.

"I'm sure you would," Redmond replied, folding his arms.

"Never mind. We'll get round to that later, perhaps. The point is, Redmond, did you really think that we could afford to let you run around free, knowing what you know? Did you honestly think you could blackmail us, that we would let you put us under that sort of pressure? Or was the blackmail threat simply a ploy to panic Farrington into talking?"

"Does it really matter now?"

"Possibly not, although I would like to know if you really do have those documents you claim to have. I don't suppose it would be telling you anything you didn't already know if I admit that they could cause us some embarrassment if they are as comprehensive as you say they are. In any case, I need hardly tell you that the last thing we would want, whether the documents exist or not, would be for you to pass on what you have already discovered to the various authorities. It would complicate the issue tremendously."

"Rather an understatement, isn't it? If I reveal all my evidence about Piccolo, Comtex, Comelec, Farrington, Mayhew, and the rest, it'd blow the whole thing wide open and you know it."

"Perhaps. I'm not sure that you really appreciate just what is at stake here, though, Redmond. Suppose you tell me what you think the situation is?"

Redmond stared at the camera for several seconds, then shrugged. "Okay, we'll play it your way. It's a cover-up, isn't it? Comtex is selling a pig in a poke to the Pentagon, the MOD, and eventually to Boeing, because the Piccolo system just doesn't work. It's using contacts in both the CIA and MI-five to cover up this fact. All these 'successful' field tests and feasibility studies are probably very carefully staged fabrications designed to mislead the Pentagon and the MOD into believing that the various problems have been overcome. That's if either of them ever knew what the real problems were, considering the fact that Comtex processed all the progress reports anyway. The problem has been the Piccolo scientists who know bloody well that it doesn't work, and never will, so those who can't be bought off are being killed to keep their mouths shut." His lips twisted momentarily into a grimace of disgust, before he leaned forward slowly and resting his elbows on the table, stared intently into the camera lens.

"So the deals will go through and no doubt there'll be all sorts of escape clauses written into the contracts allowing Comtex to avoid any liability when the damn thing goes wrong, as it inevitably will, or at least to hold up any litigation for years, by which time their contacts in the CIA will have all the necessary documentation either shredded or classified so that any legal action won't have a snowball's chance in hell of succeeding. Even if it ever gets to court, Comtex will have a battery of tame 'experts' saying how wonderful the system is and how it must have been operator error or something, while all the scientists who might have testified on the plaintiff's side will be dead and buried.

"The point is that Comtex has invested too much in Piccolo, probably billions by now, to let it go. They've got to recoup their losses somehow, so they've got to sell it and the only way they can do that is to pull off this scam. And, of course, to do that, they've got to have the connivance of British and American government officials, members of the various intelligence services and so on. With the sort of money Comtex can afford to pay, it wouldn't be any great problem to bribe officials in sensitive positions, would it? It's about par for the course for Comtex anyway, judging by what I've heard."

There was a pause, then the voice said, "Very good, Redmond, but you still have not grasped the complete picture. You see, there is more than just money involved. Consider what would happen if Comtex was obliged to cancel Piccolo. We would be talking about a total loss of billions of dollars, which would affect not just Comtex, but also its subsidiaries and dozens of other companies who have been given orders for the various hardware, software, components, and so on, not to mention the various banks, financial institutions, and investment companies who are also involved. These would all suffer losses to a greater or lesser extent. You may recall that four factories, all in the Comtex group, have been built in the north of England, which have been geared up to produce subsystems and components for Piccolo. If it is cancelled, these four factories will close, with the loss of over three thousand jobs in areas already crippled by unemployment — but even that will only be the tip of the iceberg, if you consider all the possible applications of the system and the factories, installations, and marketing apparatus that have been set up all over the world. We are talking about economic and political dynamite, Redmond. Unemployment on a large scale, as well as Comtex shares falling sharply in London, New York, Tokyo, Hong Kong — everywhere. Imagine the effect on our own stock market if, say, ICI's shares were to plummet — half the stock exchange would go with it. The same will happen with Comtex. We'd have Black Monday all over again. At best, a recession. At worst, another Wall Street crash. That is how important Piccolo has become, Redmond — through no choice of our own, I might add. That is why it must go ahead."

"Bollocks," Redmond said scathingly. "You're asking me to believe that you're solely motivated by altruism, is that it? The fact that Comtex stands to make billions out of all this doesn't come into it at all, I suppose." His voice was heavy with irony. "Comtex is only interested in preserving jobs and maintaining stability in the money markets and so all the profits will go on feeding the Ethiopians or saving the whale. Aren't we lucky to have such a benevolent multinational corporation? Bullshit, Beresford! You're all in it for whatever you can make out of it."

There was a pause, and then the voice said, "I'm afraid I do have to acknowledge that our motives are not entirely untainted, but what I am saying still stands. Surely you can see how serious the consequences would be if Piccolo were to be scrapped?"

"Who to? Comtex? The U.S. and British governments, perhaps? Stock market speculators? They'll all survive, or at least the people at the top, the ones really responsible for the mess in the first place, will, once they've served up a few scapegoats. But what about the fighter pilot who's using Piccolo for low-altitude night flying and ends up hitting a mountain at seven hundred miles an hour? Or the passengers of a plane descending through thick fog to land because of this wonderful new system, only to find they're five miles off course and two hundred feet too low? What about the consequences to them, Beresford? What'll Comtex be doing then, beyond saying that it couldn't possibly be a failure in the Piccolo system?" Redmond shook his head in disgust. "You're selling shoddy goods, and that's all there is to it, except that your goods will kill people — and they will, won't they, Beresford? They're bound to, seeing as how the system will fail once every five times it's used — but you really couldn't give a damn about that, could you?"

There was a long silence, then Redmond thought he heard a sigh from the loudspeaker. "Very well, Redmond," said the voice resignedly. "I think you've made your position clear. I had hoped you could be persuaded to accept our view of the situation, but evidently not.

We would rather have had you, if not on our side, then at least as a silent neutral, but I can see that either is too much to hope for. I'm sure you can appreciate, however, why the effort had to be made, because one of the possible alternative courses of action, that of simply eliminating you, would provide us with a number of problems we would rather avoid."

"I can see that," said Redmond, smiling faintly, infuriatingly. "It would be rather awkward to explain, wouldn't it? You can't just knock off a Special Branch officer without causing a few ripples, can you? Killing me would rather confirm to others that I was on the right track, so when the documents surface — as they will, Beresford, and I strongly suggest you bear that in mind — when they surface, you'll have even more problems than you've got at the moment."

"If those documents exist."

Redmond shook his head amusedly. "Can you really afford to take the chance? I'm not a complete idiot."

"No — just regrettably misguided. But I think that you should be in no doubt that if we have to resort to such extreme measures, we will not hesitate to do so. However, we do have other options. We don't have to kill you, Redmond. We can destroy you. We can ruin your career, arrange for your flat to burn down, put you in prison — dammit, Redmond, you don't need me to tell you what MI-five can do if it really wishes. We can make your life a living hell, Redmond — yours, and Miss Harper's if necessary."

Redmond tensed involuntarily, despite himself, as his stomach seemed to turn over. Oh, shit, no . . . "Inspector Harper? What has she got to do with it?"

"It occurs to me that she might well have given you the help you would have needed to acquire the information you have evidently amassed. Frankly, as you have been in the United States for the past few weeks, I don't see how you could have uncovered any of it without some help, and if this is indeed the case, then Miss Harper would seem to be a very strong suspect, wouldn't you say? That is her special strength, isn't it? Hunting through computer files, extracting cross-references, gaining access to restricted files — I can think of few people better qualified in that respect. So if she is involved — and, believe me, if she is, then we will find that out — then I'm afraid she will receive the same treatment as you, Redmond. Except that with a woman, we can always make things a lot — ah — messier, wouldn't you say? Faked pornographic photographs, that sort of thing.

Very unpleasant, but effective."

Redmond forced himself to shrug. "If you say so, Beresford."

"I do say so, Redmond. However, be that as it may, I hope we have made it clear exactly what we would do if you were to reveal what you have already uncovered. On the other hand, if you were to see sense and say nothing, the benefits to you would be quite substantial. Rapid promotion, payments into bank accounts of your own choosing, plus the freedom for you and Miss Harper to pursue your own lives.

"Be practical, Redmond. As the Americans say, we hold all the aces. Did you really think you would be allowed to sabotage our efforts with impunity? Yes, you are in a position to cause a good deal of disruption to our plans, I grant you that, but if you do, you will regret it for the rest of your life. As will Miss Harper, if she is involved — and, possibly, even if she isn't. That I promise you, Redmond.

"Think about it. Use your own common sense."

Redmond did not look up as the door behind him opened and the balding gunman came in, the silenced automatic aimed levelly at the slumped figure in the chair.

"Come on, Redmond. Up."

Slowly, Redmond twisted round in his seat and focused his eyes on the gunman before he nodded dully and stood up. The gunman gestured with the automatic and Redmond headed towards the door back to the store-rooms without being told. He did not even bother to look up at the office — not that it would have made much difference, because the lights had been turned off again — but seemed instead to be lost in a brooding pre-occupation. They crossed the warehouse floor and went through the door opposite, the gun-man holding back momentarily in case Red-mond tried to slam it back in his face, but the man ahead just walked straight through, his eyes fixed on the floor.

They walked slowly along the corridor and had almost reached the end door on the right when Redmond suddenly checked in his stride, as though hesitating. Impatiently, the gunman prodded the automatic's silencer into Redmond's back a fraction of a second before he remembered his training instructor's warn-ing. . . .

With a sudden, convulsive surge, Redmond pivoted and chopped viciously downward with his right hand onto the gunman's wrist. The gun slipped from the bald man's suddenly nerveless fingers but still had not reached the floor when Redmond's right knee exploded into the gunman's groin with the force of a sledgehammer. The gunman clutched at himself, fighting for breath as Redmond bunched his hands together and brought them whipping across in a vicious blow to the side of the other man's neck. The gunman sprawled limply sideways and lay still.

Redmond waited, chest heaving from the sudden exertion, his eyes on the door into the warehouse, then he bent over the guard and dragged him into the storeroom. Quickly, he searched the gunman, taking out a door key and a Vauxhall car key from his pockets. He went back out into the corridor, closed the door behind him, and locked it with the single key before he scooped up the gun, a Walther P38, and checked it rapidly. Now, he forced himself to take several deep breaths to drain away the adrenaline and only then did he head towards the skylight window high up in the end wall. He unscrewed the silencer and pocketed the gun before he clambered up and opened the window. Shit, it would only just be large enough. . . . He scrambled awkwardly through and then dropped to the ground outside, taking up a crouching position as he listened intently for any sign of an alarm. From here, he could see one end of the warehouse yard, with the boundary wall of the premises just to his right. Four cars were parked thirty yards away, facing the wall — and one of them was a Vauxhall Astra.

There were no shouts, no sign that he had been heard or seen, but he probably had only a few minutes before the guard was missed, so he could not afford to hang about. He moved forward to the corner of the stores block and peered round it, so that now he had a view of the entire yard. There was a large van parked directly in front of the main warehouse door, fifty yards or so away — it had been backed up to the entrance and Redmond suspected that it had been used to bring the TV and sound equipment. Beyond the van were two more cars, one of them facing outwards.

There were also two men standing in the wash of light from the main door, each one smoking a cigarette, and several seconds later, Redmond also spotted a third in the shadows by the street gates. Redmond ducked back out of sight and swore inwardly; there was no point waiting for the two men to finish their smoke, because it looked as if they had only just lit up and the alarm would be sounded long before they finished.

Moving in a low crouch, Redmond came out of his cover and headed towards the cars, freezing into immobility when one of the smokers suddenly turned towards him. In fact,

Redmond was less worried about them than the one by the gate; their night vision would be more restricted by their standing in the light than the one in the shadows, but one of them might still see a movement out of the corner of his eye. The smoker turned back to his companion and Redmond moved off again. Moments later, he was crouched behind the nearest car, peering over the boot at each of the three men in turn.

Still no reaction.

The Astra was the third car along; Redmond scuttled over to it using the cars themselves as cover, until he was crouching next to the Astra's driver's door, praying that this was the right bloody car. . . . He had a moment of panic when the key seemed to stick, but then he felt it turn and heard a click as the door unlocked. He froze: it had sounded deafening to his hypertaut nerves, but there was no response from any of the guards. Redmond was about to ease the door open and slip quietly into the driving seat when he remembered the interior light — they'd have to be blind to miss that coming on, especially the one by the gate. . . .

Shit.

Oh hell, here goes. . . . He pulled the door open and dived in, hearing a startled shout from behind him as his left hand reached for the choke and his foot for the accelerator. The starter motor whirred, but the engine wouldn't catch and there was a shot from somewhere behind him and as the windscreen shattered he was shouting "Come on, you cow!" before the engine fired and a second shot slammed into the car's body just behind the door. Redmond whipped the gear lever into reverse and took off, crouching down, yanking the wheel hard over to the right. He felt a jarring impact as the front wing clipped the car next to him; simultaneously, he heard the next shot. There was nothing to indicate where it had gone — presumably, the car's sudden movement had thrown off the gunman's aim.

Redmond slammed the gear lever into first while the car was rolling backwards and rammed his right foot to the floor. He punched his left fist through the starred windscreen and then the rear window exploded as the fourth shot ploughed into it. Redmond spun the wheel and the car raced towards the exit — and the third man was pulling the left-hand gate closed. Redmond turned the wheel slightly to the right, aiming for the gap, still keeping his right foot down, only distantly aware of another shot ripping into the back of the car.

Once again, the car shuddered as it hit the

gate a glancing blow that slewed it round in a rending screech of tortured metal, then he was clear, spinning the wheel to the left, sliding out in front of an indignant taxi only twenty yards away, the rear swinging round as he applied opposite lock, then the tyres gained traction and he was screaming away up the street. He glanced into his mirror and swore loudly as he saw a car hurtling out from the yard; it was coming after him.

It was only then that he became aware of the high-pitched squeal from the front of his own car. The front wing had been pushed back by the impact and was scraping against the tyre; it was only a matter of time before it blew out. He had only minutes to lose his pursuer; there was no way he would be able to handle the car in a high-speed chase if he had a punctured tyre.

He took the first turning on the left, and then went right then left again with no particular plan in mind beyond trying to fool the chasing driver. No go; he was still there and, if anything, was closing up. The drag on the tyre was slowing Redmond up as well as making steering difficult; there was now no chance of losing the following car. It was too close; all that remained to be seen was what they would do next.

Looking in his mirror, Redmond saw the

passenger leaning out of the car — and he had a gun in his hand. Jesus Christ, they certainly weren't messing about. . . . He flicked the wheel to one side then the other, zigzagging to throw him off his aim, praying for a sight of a police car but suddenly he had no time left. He felt the wrenching pull to the left as the tyre blew, but managed somehow to keep the car moving straight. The headlights of the pursuing car were suddenly very close.

He slammed on the brakes, jamming his foot down to the floor, fighting the lurch to the left as the car came screeching to a halt. He wrenched the gears into reverse and stamped on the accelerator, sending the Astra leaping backwards, straight at the car behind.

The pursuing car was braking but he was far too late; the two cars smashed into each other at a combined speed of over forty miles an hour. Redmond was thrown backwards by the impact, but he had been braced for it; he was already in first gear again and revving up; there was an agonising moment when nothing happened, when the car remained stationary, then the rear bumper disentangled itself from the other car's mangled front and he was able to drive off, accompanied by a deafening clamour as what was left of his rear nearside wing clattered along the road.

The pursuing car did not follow; the passenger was lying across the bonnet, his face and shoulders a mass of blood, his head sliced open by the glass as he had been catapulted through the windscreen. The driver was unharmed physically, but was shaking uncontrollably, stunned by the suddenness of the crash, oblivious to everything but the vision of the Astra coming straight back towards him.

Redmond drove on for a mile or so, his teeth gritted against the jolting and juddering from the flat tyre, before he brought the car to a halt. He climbed out, frowning in surprise at just how unsteady his legs were, then he began looking for a Tube station.

Fifteen

The insistent knocking on the door brought Gail awake — although her initial reaction was surprise that she had fallen asleep at all — then she threw back the blankets and jumped out of bed, reaching the door in two rapid strides. For a moment, she fumbled with the key in the lock, then she managed to open the door. "Steve!" she gasped. "Where have you been? I've been worried sick and —"

"Can I come in?" he said gently.

"What?" she asked confusedly. "Oh — of course." She stood aside to let him in, then closed the door, flicking on the light as she did so. Only then did she see the lines of strain on his face, the tense look in his eyes. "What happened?"

He shook his head tiredly, but there was a faint smile on his face now. "They bought it, Gail," he said softly. He looked around the small room. "I don't suppose you've got anything to drink, do you? I sure as hell could do with one at the moment."

She stared at him for a moment, a confused expression on her face, then nodded and turned away to the tray of drinks on the bedside table. "I got them earlier," she said, her voice curiously distant, as if she were not really concentrating on what she was saying. "Whisky?"

"Beautiful."

As she poured his drink, she frowned, trying to come to terms with the realisation that her first impulse on seeing him had been to fling her arms around him. She had only just managed to stop herself in time.

What the hell was happening to her?

She took the drink over to him, then perched on the edge of the bed, looking intently at him. "Okay," she said quietly. "What happened?"

". . . so that's it," Redmond finished quietly. "Now we know what they're up to."

She shook her head slowly, incredulously. "So you were right after all," she said softly. She walked slowly to the window and looked out into the darkness, which, in a way, was entirely appropriate. Suddenly, all of it — Piccolo, Comtex, Beresford — seemed to belong to a different world. "Have you reported it yet? To Selvey, or whoever?"

"Not yet," he said, and she heard near exhaustion in his words. "I'm not doing anything until we've talked this out."

"Talked this out?"

"Look, Gail — we're both involved in this. This Beresford, whoever the hell he is, already suspects you, and it won't take them long to find out you've been digging through the files."

"Well, that was always on the cards, wasn't it?"

He shook his head. "That was before I knew exactly what we were up against — and it scares the shit out of me." He saw her startled expression and grinned without humour. "I'm not kidding, Gail — we really have come up against the big boys. It isn't just a case of Comtex bribing a few civil servants. To get away with the kind of stunt they pulled tonight, they must have genuine clout that probably amounts to at least tacit approval from some government departments. I mean, it's entirely possible that the MOD knows the bloody thing doesn't work and is being forced to buy it anyway because it's politically expedient to do so — that's the kind of power we're taking on, Gail. And they're not going to thank anybody who exposes this can of worms. There's too much at stake, too many careers on the line."

She stared at him. "You mean we've bitten off more than we can chew — is that it?"

"I just want you to know the situation before we decide what we're going to do. I want you to know the risks, Gail, because you're going to be caught up in this as well. I was hoping I could keep you out of it but —" He shrugged helplessly. "Sorry."

"Sir — Steve — I'm a big girl, in case you hadn't noticed. It was my idea to go digging in the files, remember? I knew what I was getting into. You said you wanted to talk this out, so I take it we've got different options available?"

Redmond nodded. "Three, really. The first is the one Beresford put to me: we just keep our mouths shut and take the money. He's promised us promotion, Swiss bank accounts, the lot."

"The Farrington treatment, you mean."

"Right."

She pursed her lips thoughtfully. "Sounds tempting, I suppose — except that we couldn't trust them, of course."

He nodded encouragingly. "Go on."

"There's no way that they're going to let us stay alive and free with what we know — they're not going to have a sword of Damocles hanging over them like that. Oh yeah, they'll hold off awhile until the sales have gone through, then they'll clobber us, one way or another, no matter what safeguards we took out. They'll cook something up to discredit us and have their side of the story so immaculately documented, we wouldn't have a prayer. And even if by some improbable chance they didn't put the boot in, we'd spend all our time looking over our shoulders waiting for it, wouldn't we? I don't think I fancy that very much, thank you. In any case, didn't you rather put the kybosh on that option by escaping tonight?"

"I didn't have much choice, did I? I could have promised them anything tonight and they'd still have held me there for several days just to be on the safe side — and you'd have sent everything to Selvey and the others in ten hours' time. Once they'd got to hear about it, I'd have ended up in a concrete overcoat. I could still probably sell them the idea, though, if you wanted. It'd be their preferred choice, after all."

"You said three options. What are the others?"

"The second is that we do the knight-in-shining armour bit and take them on. We pass this all on to Selvey, with duplicates to the Deputy Assistant Commissioner, the DG of MI-five, the Home Secretary, and anyone else we can think of just in case Selvey's involved as well and we expose the whole bloody lot. We've probably got enough to torpedo the Piccolo deal, so we'd win this battle, anyway."

"But not the war?"

"Be serious, Gail. Comtex is huge. Even if we got Farrington, Mayhew, and a few others, even if we found out who Beresford was and nailed him as well, we'd only be scratching the surface. Sure, it'd be a start and we'd probably hurt Comtex a lot, but — well, they'd get their own back sooner or later. Probably sooner. They wouldn't let us get away with it, would they?"

She shivered involuntarily. "No, they wouldn't. We wouldn't have any sort of hold over them at all, then, would we, if we'd already exposed Piccolo."

"Right. So we'd probably have an even shorter life expectancy than with the first option."

"And the third?" she asked, her voice almost inaudible.

"We just walk away from it all," he said simply. "We disappear — head for Rio or Morocco or wherever and go into hiding."

"But they'd just come after us."

"Maybe — but maybe not. We'd still have a hold over them with what we know, and they might decide it's not worth the effort of hunting us down and then wiping us out, especially as we won't be that much of a danger to them if we're that far away. We could make it bloody difficult for them to find us as well, because, let's face it, we know all the

310

dodges for moving around undetected. It'd give us the best chance of survival out of the three options — I'd say an even chance, anyway."

She nodded slowly. "And even if the worst came to the worst, we'd probably still last longer than with either of the other two, right?"

"Probably, yes."

She looked intently at him. "I think I know which one you prefer, Steve."

"Forget about that for the moment. Which do you want to go for?"

She turned back to the window and stared down at the street below for almost a minute. Then, she shook her head gently. "I just can't walk away from it, Steve. I don't think I could live with myself if I did, not once the first plane crashed because of a Piccolo failure. I couldn't have that on my conscience, knowing I could have prevented it but chickened out." She shrugged quickly, nervously. "Anyway, I don't see why those bastards should be allowed to get away with it, not if we can stop them." She turned back to him. "I say go for it. Which is what you want, isn't it?"

He nodded slowly. "Yes, it is." He sighed. "Someone has to stop them."

"Okay," she said softly. "Let's nail the bastards."

He reached out and took both her hands in his, squeezing them gently. "Thanks, Gail."

She glanced down at his hands, and smiled to herself. "I reckon we both need our heads examined."

"Probably. But I don't think either of us could have done anything else, could we?"

"No, I suppose not. But thanks for giving me a choice. I appreciate that." She squeezed his hands in return.

He looked down at them, a startled expression on his face, then raised his eyes to hers. "Gail?"

"Yes?"

"This probably isn't the best time . . ." he said, a wry grin on his face, "but when this is all over —"

She nodded emphatically. "You bet." For a moment, their eyes held each other's, then, slowly, she moved closer to him, bringing her arms up around his neck. Their kiss was slow and lingering, before her lips slid away from his and began to nuzzle at his neck. "Steve?"

"Mmm?"

"Your timing is abysmal."

"It could be improved, I suppose," he chuckled, gently stroking her hair.

They kissed again, but then moved reluctantly apart. They stared wordlessly at each other, hands clasped, then, slowly, she removed her hands from his. "Okay," she said, her voice deliberately brisk. "So what's the next step?"

He nodded as if in appreciation of her businesslike manner. "I telephone Selvey and get things moving. There'll be no turning back after that. It'll be all or nothing."

She nodded and took a deep breath. "Then let's do it."

Selvey answered the phone on its fifth ring, but Redmond gave him no time to speak. "It's Redmond."

There was a momentary pause, then Selvey said, "Steve? What the hell are you doing calling at this time of night?" There was an unmistakeably peevish note to his voice, which was perhaps understandable; it was nearly two-thirty in the morning, after all.

"I can't tell you, sir, not over the phone. It's a Priority Alpha matter."

"Steve, you don't have enough authority to initiate Priority Alpha."

"I haven't initiated it, but — believe me, this is that urgent."

"I see." Redmond could hear the change in Selvey's voice. "Is there anything you can tell me now?"

"There are one or two things I'd like you to do, sir. Firstly, get in touch with Deputy

313

Assistant Commissioner Pemberton and get him into your office —"

"The DAC? Have you taken leave of your senses? Just what —"

"Sir, this is absolutely vital, believe me. Would I be calling you at this time of the night otherwise?"

"Well — perhaps not, but you cannot possibly expect me to do all this without some indication of what is going on."

"I know who's behind the deaths of the Piccolo scientists, sir — and it isn't who we thought it was."

"I see. . . . Can you prove whatever it is you've found out?"

"Sir, they tried to kill me tonight to prevent me passing on what I know. Of course I can prove it."

"Right," said Selvey briskly. "I'll certainly get things moving down here. You want to see the DAC and myself once you get here?"

"Yes, sir — but nobody else is to know. This is important, sir."

"I'm beginning to appreciate that. This sounds rather ominous, Steve."

"Yes, sir. One more thing. Could you look up someone called Lansky? We've got a file on him, but I can't remember the details, although if he isn't in the wet section, I would be very surprised."

"Will do — and I think you could be right about where we'll find him. The name certainly rings a bell, anyway." There was a pause and then Selvey said, "Steve?"

"Yes?"

"Whatever you've turned up, well-done."

London

There was silence for almost a minute after Redmond finished speaking; both of the other two men present in Selvey's office seemed to be absorbing the implications of what they had been told. When Redmond had arrived, thirty minutes before, he had found Deputy Assistant Commissioner Pemberton, the head of Special Branch, waiting with Selvey; the latter had been as good as his word.

Suddenly, Pemberton sighed, the sound abnormally loud in the tense silence; then he stood up and went over to Selvey's desk. He pulled open the top drawer and took out a bottle of brandy. "With your permission, Bill?" he asked, glancing at Selvey.

"Certainly, sir. There are some glasses in the bottom drawer."

"I know," Pemberton said. He was a stocky man of below-average height, but he radiated an intense energy, even at this ungodly hour of the morning. He had been in Special Branch

for nearly thirty years and had seen it all —
Philby, Blunt, George Blake's escape — but,
as he watched him pouring out the drinks,
Redmond had the feeling that the action was
simply Pemberton's way of covering the fact
that what he had heard tonight had shaken
him to the core; this was worse than anything
that had gone before.

Pemberton handed glasses to Selvey and
Redmond, then said quietly, "I think we could
do with this. I know I certainly could." He
stared at his glass thoughtfully. "I take it that
there's no doubt it is Comtex and not an elab-
orate KGB ploy?"

"It's Comtex," Redmond said flatly.

"In any case, the Reds wouldn't dare act
so openly," Pemberton said, rebutting his own
argument. "So we have Comtex involved,
along with Farrington and probably Mayhew." He broke off and shook his head disbelievingly. "Is he really involved?" he asked,
his voice bewildered. "I mean, I've known
Ronald for years. I can't believe he'd do anything like this."

"It's not as though he's betraying his country, is it, sir?" asked Redmond.

"No, I suppose not," Pemberton said
doubtfully. "This is a new kind of treason.
. . . And although I hate to say it, this would
certainly explain why he sent you to Wash-

ington, Redmond." He nodded slowly, as though the pieces were beginning to fall into place. "Who else is involved? Do we know?"

"The CIA, in all probability," Selvey said succinctly. "Or at least parts of it. Steve — er, Chief Inspector Redmond — recognised one of the men at the warehouse. It was Lansky." Pemberton frowned slightly at the name, so Selvey explained, "Grigori Lansky, also known as Greg or Gregory Lansky." He glanced at Redmond. "You were right, Steve — he was in our files. His parents were Lithuanian, but they emigrated to Canada in 1938, so he was born in Ottawa. He worked for the CIA for a while as a hit man, especially behind the Iron Curtain, because he speaks fluent Russian. He left the Company eight years ago. That's when the CIA started getting rid of most of their 'dirty tricks' personnel, but our information is that he still works for them on a free-lance basis. He dropped out of sight about a year ago, so it all ties in."

"You're certain it was Lansky?" Pemberton asked Redmond.

Redmond bit back an angry retort and said firmly, "It was Lansky, sir."

"Right," said Pemberton with a sigh. "Comtex, a CIA hit man, a high-ranking civil servant and the deputy director general of MI-five. You really have stirred up a hornet's nest, haven't you, Redmond? And all this is simply to conceal the fact that Piccolo is a dud? How the devil did they get it all organised?"

"They already had Farrington in place — they'd bought him years ago. He was arranging for contracts to go Comelec's way, and when they didn't, he was telling Comtex how best to undermine the firm that did get it. So when they needed someone to provide them with background information for Lansky's hit men to go after the Piccolo scientists, he was ideal. They had Mayhew handle the security angle — he could monitor our efforts. Mackinnon was a bit of luck for them, because it started us looking in the wrong direction, but I think that once we knew someone was definitely killing our scientists, Mayhew probably decided it was safer to take over the investigation himself. That way, he could keep it under control."

"So that was why you didn't report any of this when you got back from the States?" asked Selvey.

"Yes, sir. I didn't know who I could trust."

"So what made you decide to trust me in the end?" asked Selvey.

Redmond stared levelly at him. "Put it this way, sir — if DAC Pemberton had not been waiting here with you, then I'd have known you were with them. And, with respect, if both you and the DAC are involved, I've still taken precautions."

"The devil you say," said Pemberton angrily. "You've got a damned nerve." He glowered at Redmond and seemed about to say something else, but then he took a deep breath and shook his head. He said slowly, "On the other hand, given the circumstances, I suppose I have to say that you behaved very professionally." He turned to Selvey. "Right, Bill. What do you suggest our next move should be? I mean, apart from what Redmond and Inspector Harper have managed to find, how much actual proof do we have? Or leads to any other individuals who might be involved?"

"Not much at all, sir," Selvey admitted. "Under normal circumstances, our best course of action would have been to place the suspects we do have — Farrington, Mayhew, and the other secret shareholders that Harper found — under surveillance. Unfortunately, what happened to Steve tonight has made matters rather more pressing."

"Exactly," said Redmond. "With respect sir, we've gone past the surveillance stage. Comtex knows by now that we're onto them and I think they'll have to act fast. They tried to kill me, so how many more will they take out to cover themselves? If we want to avoid any more deaths we've got to act now. We've got to arrest Farrington and Mayhew and find out what they know."

"Yes, I see your point," Pemberton said doubtfully. "All the same —"

"Look, sir, if we don't move now, I don't think we'll get another chance. Farrington and Mayhew will either disappear or be eliminated. Comtex is certainly ruthless enough for that. Then we'll have nothing to go on at all. We'll probably never find out who else is involved, or if we've already got the kingpins. I mean, we don't have any leads at all on this Beresford character, to choose just one example."

Pemberton rubbed his chin thoughtfully, then shrugged. "Very well, Redmond, we'll do it your way." He stared intently at Redmond, and there was a steely glint in his eye now. "And I hope, for your sake, that you know what you're doing."

Farrington replaced the telephone and stared at it, his mouth set in a grim line. So it had come after all. He was going to have to run for it — but how long did he have? He could hardly say that it had come as a surprise, not after what Redmond had said yesterday, but Beresford had said that Redmond was being dealt with, that he would no longer be a threat. So what had gone wrong?

He shook his head impatiently. Brooding about that would not help at all — he had to move fast if he were to escape. He went upstairs and lifted a suitcase from the bottom of the wardrobe in his bedroom and threw it on the bed. Next, he began snatching items almost at random and hurled them haphazardly into the case — shaving equipment from the bathroom, shoes, socks, shirts — until he realised he was panicking, had stuffed in far more than he would need. He'd do far better to get dressed, for one thing.

As he pulled on his clothes, he caught sight of his wife's photograph on the dressing table and hesitated momentarily. She had been in the country over the weekend and had not yet returned, but he knew he would not miss her, nor she him. The marriage had only ever been one of convenience and so the break would be clean, without regrets or second thoughts.

The doorbell rang and he froze, realising that he had delayed too long. For a moment, he contemplated trying to escape through the back door, but they would have stationed men there. The doorbell rang again, insistently. He started to move towards the bedroom door, then changed his mind and went over to the dressing table. He unlocked the bottom drawer and took out a Walther PPK automatic pistol, along with a silencer, which he screwed onto the barrel as he made his way downstairs. When he reached the hall he took a deep breath, then placed the silenced gun in the pocket of his crombie coat that was hanging beside the door. Then, one last check in the hall mirror to make sure his features were composed and he opened the door.

There were two raincoated men on the doorstep. "Yes?" he said, trying to look as irritable as anyone would be at being wakened this early in the morning.

"Mr. Farrington?" said the older of the two men.

"Yes?"

"I'm Detective Inspector Moore and this is Detective Constable Hartley." He held up his identification card. "May we come in?"

"Er — yes. Of course." Farrington stood aside to let them in, but looked beyond them as he did so. Before he closed the door he saw a Ford Orion parked opposite with two men inside. He turned to Moore and Hartley. "Well, Inspector, what can I do for you?"

"We'd like you to accompany us, sir."

"I beg your pardon?" Farrington demanded angrily, looking from one man to the other. "You're not serious, are you?"

"I'm afraid we are, Mr. Farrington."

"But — but — there must be some mistake!

Am I under arrest?"

"We are empowered to detain you under section two of the Official Secrets Act," Moore said formally.

"What the devil are you talking about?"

"Just come with us, Mr. Farrington. You know as well as I do that you don't have any choice in the matter."

Farrington glared at him. "No, I don't suppose I do, but once this has all been cleared up, Inspector, I shall be demanding a full explanation."

"That's up to you, Mr. Farrington."

"Is it all right if I get my coat? Or isn't that allowed?" Farrington's voice was scathingly ironic.

Moore seemed unruffled. "Of course."

Farrington muttered something under his breath, then went to the row of pegs beside the door. He selected the crombie and put it on, but, while his back was turned to the two policemen, he took out the gun. For a moment he hesitated at the thought of what he was about to do, but then he turned and shot Moore in the chest at point-blank range. Farrington pivoted round and fired his second bullet into Hartley before the young DC had even begun to react. Moore was thrown back against the wall, then slid slowly downwards, leaving a smear of red on the wallpaper, while

Hartley doubled up, clutching at his stomach, before he toppled slowly forwards, groaning feebly.

Farrington spared him only a glance as he went into the living room and looked out of the front window. The Orion was still there, but there was no sign of any other police presence; presumably there would be someone round the back, but Farrington was not concerned about that. He ran back upstairs, grabbed the case, then came back downstairs and ran through the kitchen and out into the conservatory that led directly into the garage. Inside was his Mercedes 230SE, parked facing outwards. He threw the case into the boot, then pressed the button that activated the electronic door's lifting mechanism. As the door began to move upwards he jumped into the car and started the engine. As soon as it caught he jammed his foot down on the accelerator, the Mercedes's wheels spinning before they gained traction, throwing the car forward and out onto the gravel drive. Farrington had a momentary glimpse of an expression of surprise on the Orion driver's face as he came out through the gate, then he spun the wheel, turning left, the opposite direction to the way the Orion was facing. Looking back in his mirror as the Mercedes pulled away, Farrington saw the Ford come roaring out of its parking space, the driver sending the car into a perfectly executed 180-degree sliding turn, so that the Orion was in pursuit before the Mercedes had travelled a hundred yards.

Farrington's mouth tightened as he saw the Ford coming after him, then took the next corner at speed, the Mercedes's tyres screeching in protest. He had to lose the Ford, or find a stretch of dual carriageway — his superior speed would count for little in a built-up area, especially with a trained driver pursuing him. Again, he twisted the wheel over, but he was travelling too fast this time and the Mercedes' rear end slewed sideways, smashing into a parked car with a sickening metallic crunch. He swore but kept his foot down, changing up rapidly through the gears until he was doing over sixty. Not fast enough, though, he realised as he looked in the mirror: the Orion was still there. Clearly, it was no ordinary production model. . . .

But then he saw a set of traffic lights a hundred yards ahead — and they were just changing from green to amber. His foot lifted momentarily from the accelerator almost reflexively, before he pressed the pedal down again, swerving outwards to avoid the car in front, which was slowing down. The red light came on, fifty yards to go, the engine roaring as he raced towards the junction.

An articulated lorry was coming out from the left, moving slowly across his path. . . .

Farrington flicked the wheel to the right and hurtled past the front of the lorry, hearing a deafening blast from the horn as the lorry driver hit it in protest, but then he was past and through the junction.

The Orion's driver saw Farrington's manoeuvre and tried to follow him, but at the last moment, he realised that he was not going to make it — there was not enough room now. He jammed his foot on the brake, but it was too late — the lorry was only feet away. The Orion's wheels locked as it skidded on past the malevolent red eyes of the traffic lights, and then the driver wrenched the wheel to the right in an instinctive urge for self-preservation. The Ford slewed round and smashed into the trailer, sideways on, the impact hurling both men to one side in their seats as the car's right wheels lifted off the road, then crashed back down.

The driver looked around incredulously, conscious of only one thought — he was alive. Somehow, he had survived. With an effort, he focused his eyes, which wouldn't seem to work properly, and looked across at his passenger, who was slumped against the door. Blood was pouring down from his head where it had struck the door, but he was breathing.

They had both made it. . . .

The driver leaned back in his seat and closed his eyes briefly as he let out a long sigh of relief. Thank God they had both been wearing seat belts, he thought distantly. It was almost a prayer, as were the words he muttered in a shaking voice:

"Jesus Christ . . ."

Sixteen

Sunday Morning

Superintendent Nicholls of Special Branch rubbed his unshaven chin in distaste and stared blearily at his reflection in the car's rearview mirror. God, he looked bloody awful. Although this was not surprising as, half an hour ago, he had been fast asleep; indeed, he was still not quite sure what was going on. The phone call that had awakened him had not explained anything beyond the bald fact that he was to arrest Sir Ronald Mayhew. But why, for God's sake? You didn't go around arresting deputy director generals of MI5, even if they were working for Moscow Centre — you did deals with them, put them out to grass, made them the ambassador to Outer Mongolia, but you never arrested them.

Until now. Just what the hell was going on? Whatever it was, it had to be serious for Pemberton to drag Nicholls out of bed at 6:30 in the morning — or even for Pemberton to be awake at such an ungodly hour. The shit must really have hit the fan, Nicholls thought, and for that reason, he had signed out a gun from the armoury, which he was hoping he would not have to use. He vaguely recalled that Mayhew had been a prize-winning pistol shot in his army days and so Nicholls was not taking any chances.

His car turned the corner and pulled up behind an unmarked police Granada. Inspector Lane, his number two, climbed out of the Granada and joined him in the back of his Rover.

"Right, Dave," Nicholls said briskly.

"That's the house there, number eighty-six," Lane said, indicating a three-storey Edwardian terraced house opposite.

Nicholls nodded. "Anyone else there?"

"We don't know, sir."

"Oh, great . . ." Nicholls said resignedly. "How many men have we got?"

"Two round the back and two more in the Granada."

"You're sure he's in there?" He nodded towards number 86.

"According to Five, yes."

"Well, they should know. Let's get on with it, shall we?"

Nicholls led the way up the steps, with Lane just behind him, and pressed the doorbell. When there was no response, he pressed again, then a third time. Eventually, the door opened and Mayhew stood in the doorway, wearing a dressing gown and blinking vaguely at them.

"Nicholls?" he said finally. "What the devil are you doing here?"

"I'm sorry, Sir Ronald, but this is important. May we come in?"

"Nicholls, do you know what time it is? Can't it wait?"

"I'm afraid not, sir."

Mayhew stared at Nicholls in frank hostility for several seconds, then said irritably, "Oh, very well, then. Come in."

As Nicholls went into the hall, he heard a woman's voice call out from upstairs. "What is it, Ronnie darling?"

Mayhew suddenly went brick red with embarrassment. Obviously, the woman was not his wife — had MI5 known that? Nicholls wondered. They might have bloody well mentioned it if they had. "I shan't be a moment," Mayhew called out. He turned to Nicholls. "This had better be damned important, Nicholls."

"It is, sir, believe me. I'm afraid you're under arrest, Sir Ronald."

Mayhew stared at him disbelievingly. "I beg your pardon?"

"You're under arrest."

Mayhew shook his head. "You — you're insane, Nicholls!" he protested. "Under arrest? For what?"

"We are detaining you under section two

330

of the Official Secrets Act."

"But you can't! You don't have the authority!"

"I do, Sir Ronald, as you well know. In any case, I'm acting under the specific instructions of Deputy Assistant Commissioner Pemberton."

"Harold?" Mayhew echoed, then shook his head again. "I — I don't understand."

Neither do I, thought Nicholls. He said, "You'll have to come with us, Sir Ronald. Now if you'd like to get dressed, we'd better be going. Lane, go with him, will you?"

"Yes, sir."

Mayhew stared levelly at Nicholls, his earlier discomfiture disappearing. "You're making a big mistake, Nicholls. Once all this has been sorted out, you'll regret being involved, I can promise you that." He glared at Nicholls a moment longer, an undeniable warning in his eyes, then turned and headed for the door.

Before he had reached it, however, a young woman appeared in the doorway, a slim brunette with dishevelled hair who was dressed in a red silk dressing gown that was barely long enough to be decent. "What is the matter, Ronnie?" she asked, giving Nicholls an appraising look.

"Nothing, Michelle. Something's come up at the office — I'll have to go in and sort it out." He looked meaningfully at Nicholls with these words.

"Oh, I see," she said, looking again at Nicholls. "Will it take long? We're supposed to be going down to Sussex today, aren't we?"

"I'm not sure how long this will take," Mayhew said, but he was still looking at Nicholls. "I'll phone you later."

"I see," she said coldly. "In that case, I'll be going." Her voice was hard, calculating, and, for a fleeting instant, Nicholls almost felt sorry for Mayhew, getting caught up with a bitch like that. But only for an instant, because it was obvious that Mayhew did not expect to remain under arrest for long. So why was he so bloody confident?

More to the point, if he was right and he was quickly released, presumably after some intervention by friends in high places, where would that leave the arresting officer?

Lansky checked his watch and saw that it had been four minutes now since the two Special Branch men had gone in, and there was still no sign of anyone coming out. Carefully, Lansky surveyed the scene once more, although he knew that McClelland, the man sitting next to him in the driver's seat, would be doing the same, but there was still no sign that they had been spotted by anybody in

332

the police vehicles.

Lansky and McClelland had arrived twenty minutes earlier and had immediately spotted the unmarked Granada parked outside Mayhew's town house. Lansky had known there and then that his original instructions to warn Mayhew of his imminent arrest would now be impossible to carry out. Stupid bastard, he thought; Lansky had tried phoning Mayhew several times, but each time he had heard the engaged tone — presumably Mayhew had left the phone off the hook. Probably did not want to be disturbed while he was screwing his current mistress, but it meant that he could not be tipped off the same way as Farrington. So it would have to be the contingency plan.

Lansky bit his lip. Things were falling apart, that much was obvious. God only knew what had gone wrong at the warehouse, but all hell had broken loose since then. Once an operation began to come off the rails, the way this one patently was, Lansky knew from long experience that it took a lot of pulling back onto the tracks. By the look of it, someone was pressing the panic button and Lansky didn't like that. He was having to operate off the cuff, rather than making careful preparations — and that was when mistakes were made.

On top of that, there was another, more personal anxiety for Lansky to ponder. Redmond had recognised him, so there would be a full-scale police search underway for him right now — and he was sitting within thirty yards of Special Branch officers, for Christ's sake!

They could not see him, however, he reminded himself. He had chosen his present position carefully. Mayhew's town house was situated in a square that had a rectangular area of vegetation in the centre, with several trees and bushes. McClelland had parked on the far side of the square with several bushes between them and the Granada. On the other hand, Lansky had a clear view of the front door of number 86 through the rolled-down window.

He looked down at the rifle that was resting across his knees, grimacing in distaste as he saw the bulbous shape of the silencer. Lansky never liked using them, because they reduced the bullet's velocity and impaired accuracy, but at a range of no more than fifty yards, he could hardly miss, while the soft-nosed dum-dum cartridges actually worked better at a lower velocity and would certainly have the desired effect. His objection was purely professional — using a silencer almost smacked of cheating, somehow.

How much longer were they going to be, for God's sake?

There. The front door was opening and he

had the rifle up to his shoulder before anyone came out. He peered through the telescopic sight and lined up the crosshairs on the first man to emerge, but it was the police officer, so he shifted to the second man and saw Mayhew's unmistakable silvery hair. Lansky tracked him down the steps, then, as his victim reached the pavement and presented a steady target, he centred the sight on Mayhew's forehead and squeezed the trigger. There was a soft *phut!* and then Mayhew's head jerked backwards. Lansky just had time to see a spray of blood and brain erupt from the back of Mayhew's skull before he brought down the rifle and yelled, "Go!"

McClelland turned the key in the ignition, and the engine caught first time. The car surged out of its parking space, skidded round the corner into the main road, and raced away, its engine screaming.

Nicholls had thrown himself flat to the ground in an automatic reflex, and he was still lying full-length on the pavement as he watched the car accelerating away, swearing in anger and frustration as the Granada started up and pulled out — but it had to make a U-turn before it could take off in pursuit and Nicholls knew intuitively that the escaping car had too much of a head start. They'd never catch it. Nevertheless, he watched the Granada roar off around the corner and out of sight before he turned back to the motionless form on the pavement.

He did not bother feeling for a pulse. Mayhew had to be dead. Nobody could live with that much of the back of his head blown away.

The telephone rang. Selvey reached it first, but only by a whisker and then only because he had been closer than Redmond. "Yes?" he said, barking the word out, his eyes staring at Redmond without seeing him so that Redmond saw his expression change suddenly: Selvey's shoulders slumped and Redmond knew it was bad news. "I see," Selvey said slowly, heavily. "Thank you. . . . Yes, call me at once." He replaced the receiver and stared gloomily at Redmond, dimly aware of the other man's exhaustion; Redmond was grey-eyed through lack of sleep, which was hardly surprising, Selvey thought vaguely. . . . "That was Nicholls," he said dully. "Mayhew is dead."

"Oh, shit . . ." Redmond muttered. "How?"

"He was shot as they brought him out. Someone had a rifle in a car on the other side of the square. He took out Mayhew with one shot, then the car went off like a bat out of hell. They lost it," he added, as if that did not need to be said at all.

336

"Any more word on Farrington?"

"None. They're still looking for him." Selvey shook his head as if in defeat.

"First Farrington and now Mayhew," said Redmond. His expression was grim. "There must have been a leak somewhere. Farrington might just have got lucky and made a run for it, but they had a hit man waiting outside Mayhew's. They must have been tipped off."

Selvey nodded reluctantly. "I'm afraid you're right, Steve. It certainly looks as though we have another leak somewhere. Unfortunately we had over a dozen Special Branch members involved, one way or another — any one of them could have tipped them off." He shrugged. "The only way we'll be able to find out for certain, I suspect, will be by asking Farrington — or Lansky."

"Some chance," said Redmond disgustedly. "The bastards could be anywhere by now."

Sunday Afternoon

It was almost four in the afternoon when Farrington turned the Lada off the road and up a narrow lane that led past a small cottage. The Lada had obviously seen better days, but Farrington had to admit that Smethurst had still done well at such short notice, because there was nothing wrong with the engine at

337

all: Smethurst had tuned it up himself. Also, it had the added virtue of being utterly inconspicuous, unlike the Mercedes — which was probably no more than a mangled cube of compressed steel in Smethurst's scrapyard by now.

Farrington drove carefully through a narrow gate and parked it in front of the cottage, which was a single-storey two-bedroom building that dated from the thirties and was now used as a holiday home, although it was in need of a lick of paint around its woodwork. He parked the car and climbed out, then looked around. About a quarter of a mile away was a low dyke, beyond which were the grey waters of an estuary, while to his right he could see the masts and yards of a marina only about two hundred yards away. Although he could not see it from here, he knew that tied up to one of the jetties in the artificial harbour would be a twenty-five-foot cabin cruiser that would be fuelled up and ready to sail. He would check that but there would be no problem: he had to wait until tomorrow night, anyway. For a moment, he felt a surge of impatience, but forced himself to calm down. Considering the situation, a delay of only one day was not bad at all, especially as everything had been carefully set up now. Twenty-four hours, thirty-six at the most and he'd be free, on his way — where? Switzerland first, then to the States, probably, to see what they had arranged for him.

He could never come back but that would be immaterial. He had more than enough money to live as he pleased and there were no ties to bind him; his wife would probably be glad to see the back of him so that she could spend more time with her current paramour, while his son would be more concerned about the scandal and the effect it would have on his chances of becoming an MP than anything else. Farrington would not miss them.

There was a faint smile as he took a key out of his pocket and unlocked the cottage's front door. They would never find him here.

Monday Morning

Redmond was staring absently at a report on his desk when Selvey came in. He nodded to Gail, who was sitting at the computer console, rapidly typing in commands and scanning the displays that came up before keying in further instructions. She looked up briefly, nodded vaguely in reply, then returned her attention to the VDT.

"Any news?" Selvey asked Redmond.

"Nothing at all. We haven't even found

Farrington's car yet. We've been through the usual procedures, a watch on all airports and docks, ferries, and so on, but — well, put it this way, Comtex can get Farrington and Lansky out of the country without too much bother, one way or another."

Selvey nodded slowly. "They're certainly a professional organisation, you've got to give them that." Redmond could hear the grudging approval in Selvey's voice, but he could not argue with the assessment. "So all we've got left is that list of shareholders Gail dug up."

"Who might or might not be able to give us the information we want." Redmond shook his head. "I suspect that if we want to get anything worthwhile on Comtex, we have to find Farrington or Lansky. And even if I were a betting man I wouldn't like to put any money on that."

"You're probably right," Selvey agreed gloomily. "Anyway, keep at it."

Beresford grimaced with distaste as he climbed out of his car and looked around. He had parked in a garage driveway behind a parade of shops in Brentford, and although he had deliberately chosen an anonymous Ford as opposed to the car to which his position entitled him, he still felt distinctly conspicuous in his three-piece suit as he walked through

340

a tiny square of garden to a weather-beaten door at the back of the parade; this was not the most salubrious of areas. He took out a key and unlocked the door. Inside was a flight of steps that led up to a two-storey flat above one of the shops.

Lansky was waiting for him, leaning against the frame of the door into the living room. He nodded slowly, almost insultingly, at Beresford. "So you finally got here, then?"

"I came as soon as I could," Beresford said impatiently, squeezing past the other man. "I do have more to worry about than your personal problems, you know."

"I can imagine," Lansky said drily. "All hell must be breaking loose."

"Quite," Beresford snapped. He looked around the small but adequately furnished room. "Are you all right here?" he asked. "It was all we could manage at such short notice."

"It'll do — I've known worse." Lansky suddenly threw aside his offhand manner. "I'd appreciate knowing what the hell is happening, though."

"The situation is under control at the moment — just," Beresford replied. "You and Farrington are the only ones they are actively searching for."

"Figures — we're the ones Redmond can actually implicate. The thing is, how much more does he know?"

"Difficult to say. Redmond is keeping this very close to his chest, which is understandable, if damned awkward, but we must assume that if Harper succeeded in uncovering links between Farrington, Mayhew, and Comtex, then she will also have a list of the other shareholders."

"You think she's involved?"

"I shall be surprised if she isn't — I don't see any other way that Redmond could have uncovered so much. We're notifying those on the list, of course, but, as you say, we really need to know what else Redmond and Harper have discovered."

"You're the one with the contacts, Beresford — use them."

"Oh, I'll find out, but, at the moment, you and Farrington are my chief concerns." He stared at Lansky, then shook his head suddenly in disbelief. "That really was abominably stupid, wasn't it, allowing Redmond to identify you? What on earth possessed you? Was it some quaint, old-fashioned notion about meeting your enemy face to face?" He nodded slowly, answering his own question. "Yes, that would be it, wouldn't it? Your colossal ego got in the way again, didn't it? You just had to confront him, to have your moment of triumph — and look where it got you." He gestured at the room. "Hiding away in some poky little flat above a dry cleaner's."

"Okay, so it wasn't the best idea I've ever had, but it wouldn't have made any damn difference if your men hadn't let him get away — what the hell were they playing at, for Chrissake? They were your men, Beresford, remember — not mine. You insisted on taking care of him, giving him the Big Picture — and how did that work out, eh? I could have told you he wouldn't play ball. You should have let me deal with him before it got too late, but no, you knew better, didn't you?" Lansky shook his head. "There are some guys you just can't buy at any price — or frighten," he said, his voice unexpectedly quiet. "Redmond's one of them. He isn't the gutless crawler you all thought he was — anything but, in fact."

Beresford stared at him in surprise. Lansky almost sounded envious. . . . Then, Beresford collected himself and said, "This is not really getting us anywhere, is it? Neither of us is entirely without fault in this matter, but that's water under the bridge now. The point is that you were the one he saw, not I."

"Right — so what the hell am I doing sitting here? I want out."

"You're hardly in a position to make de-

343

mands, are you? You're a wanted man, remember? You've got every policeman in the country looking for you."

"Don't remind me. What I want to know is, what is being done about it."

"Don't worry. Arrangements are being made to get you out of the country within a few days, but in the meantime, we want you on standby, just in case they locate Farrington before we can get him out tonight. It's not likely they will, but it's possible — I'm not sure how well Farrington has covered his tracks. If they do locate him I shall know immediately and I'll want you to get to him."

"What do I do — hold his hand?"

"Come now, Lansky, you know as well as I do how much he can tell them. We cannot possibly allow him to be taken prisoner and interrogated. I have no illusions at all as regards his loyalty — he'll betray the lot of us inside five minutes. You'll have to ensure that doesn't happen. Get him out if you can, but if not . . . Well, you know how much is at stake, for all of us. I'll do what I can to slow things down at this end, but the rest will be up to you."

Lansky nodded heavily and sighed. "Okay, I get the picture."

"I thought you might."

Monday Afternoon

"Steve?" Gail said suddenly, taking Redmond by surprise. It was the first thing she had said for at least two hours, so total had been her concentration on the computer displays in front of her.

"Yes?"

"I think I might have found something." Her voice was a combination of hope and timidity: she did not dare believe it yet.

Redmond stood up and went round to stand behind her, looking at the VDT screen. He rested his hand on her shoulder and squeezed it gently; she glanced up at him in surprise, then smiled. "Go on," he said.

"It's a very long shot, but —"

"Gail, we don't have any shots at all at the moment, long or otherwise. Whatever you've got, let's have it."

"It struck me that if Farrington wants to get out of the country he'll have to do it by small boat or light aircraft — we're watching all the airports and so on. He might try to get out through Heathrow, say, in disguise, but I should imagine he'll feel safer by more secret routes. Am I making sense so far?"

"Perfectly."

"Now, he'll probably use Comtex as much as possible, so I did a check of all the ships owned or run by Comtex or its subsidiaries — there aren't all that many, actually. One of them, the *Triton V*, was diverted from Rotterdam to Dieppe yesterday. The signal was sent out to her two hours after Farrington ran for it — and it originated from London."

"Did it?" Redmond asked, suddenly interested.

"The new orders mean that she'll be sailing down the East Anglia coast tonight. All Farrington would need to do would be to find a boat and she could pick him up out at sea."

"Very true," said Redmond doubtfully. "The trouble is that there's an awful lot of coastline to patrol, and the change of orders might mean nothing at all, anyway."

"That's what I thought at first." There was animation in her face and voice now: clearly, she thought she was onto something — or was it wishful thinking? "I did a search for all references to East Anglia in our files on Farrington and came up with the address of a holiday cottage near Bradwell-on-Sea on the Blackwater estuary in Essex. Farrington went there for a week's fishing holiday in April last year, but that's the only one he's ever been on. He also used a fake name when he booked it."

Redmond shrugged. "So maybe he took a girl with him."

346

"That wasn't in the file. It just referred to a fishing holiday. Notice the date, though — five months before the Piccolo deaths started. Might he have been planning his escape route, just in case?"

Redmond nodded slowly. "Yes, he could have been."

"He could have had a duplicate key cut — and it would be a perfect hideout. Miles from anywhere, deserted, especially at this time of year, and right on the coast. He could take a boat out and be picked up outside the twelve-mile limit within a couple of hours. Not only that, he probably thinks there's no record of his previous visit there on file."

Redmond rubbed his cheek thoughtfully. It could fit, yes, but was she reading too much into it? On the other hand, they had damn-all else to go on. He went back to his own desk, opened the bottom drawer, and took out a road atlas, flicking through the pages until he found the relevant map. Yes, it would be an ideal hideout, he decided — and damned near untraceable. "It's worth a phone call to the Essex police, anyway," he said. "Get them to see if anyone's there."

"It's rather flimsy, Steve," Selvey said dubiously, looking down at a 1:25000 scale map of the Blackwater estuary that was spread out

347

on his desk. "I mean, how much evidence do you actually have?"

"Just about bugger-all," Redmond admitted. "But it makes pretty good sense as a bolt-hole, doesn't it? It's secluded, but still within fifty miles of London, and there's a marina at Bradwell Waterside here." He indicated the place on the map. "The cottage is within a quarter of a mile of it at the most, which means that if Farrington's got a boat there waiting to take him out to the *Triton V,* he doesn't have to worry about the tide, not with a dredged harbour virtually next door. Anywhere else in the estuary — or anywhere around that coast where you could moor a boat, you've got mud flats to contend with at low tide, but, with that marina, he can run for it anytime he likes."

"If he's there," Selvey pointed out. "He could be anywhere in the UK by now — and that's assuming he's still in the country at all."

"Yeah, I know," Redmond said glumly. "But he had to leave in a hurry and we've been watching all the ports and airports he might use. Maybe he's had to hole up for a day or so. If that's the case, this cottage is as good a bet as any."

"Ask the local police to take a look," Selvey suggested.

Redmond shook his head. "I've already

been on to them and they've taken a long-distance look. There's a car parked in front of the cottage, but they haven't been able to read the number. The only plate they can see is covered in mud, apparently, so we don't know who the owner is. They're trying to contact the cottage's owner, but he's not at home at the moment. The thing is, these bastards have probably already killed at least ten people — twelve, if you count Keenan and Mayhew — so do you think they'll stop at a policeman who knocks at their door? Remember what Farrington did to Moore and Hartley — killed one and put the other in intensive care, and that was without Lansky. If we send the local bobby to take a closer look and Farrington is there, then we could have one more dead policeman on our hands and Farrington will be halfway to the continent by the time we get there. We need to go in armed, if we go in at all."

Selvey nodded thoughtfully. "What do you suggest then?"

"We'll need to get an armed party up there as soon as possible, if only to cut off his escape if he makes a run for it. In the meantime we contact Hereford and get them to send a team."

"The SAS? Isn't that going over the top rather?"

Redmond shook his head grimly. "Farrington on his own is bad enough, but if Lansky's there with him, then they won't be messing about. He's good — too bloody good."

"That's assuming they're there at all, Steve. This could all be a wild-goose chase."

"Then we put it down to an exercise. I shouldn't think Hereford'll mind — they're always going on about being on their toes and being able to respond to emergencies, so let's take them at their word. But if Lansky is there, and he's got backup, then we could have a very nasty situation indeed."

Selvey nodded slowly. "Very well — take one of the crisis teams and get up there. If nothing else, get a cordon around the place, but if you can also find out for certain whether Farrington's there, get word back to me. I'll start getting things moving as regards getting some backup there. As soon as you know what the situation is, get in touch."

"Right. Do we have a chopper handy?"

Selvey smiled faintly. "I'll get one laid on for you."

"Thanks." Redmond was already halfway to the door, but then Selvey's quiet voice stopped him.

"Steve?"

"Yes?"

"Good luck."

Seventeen

Blackwater Estuary, Essex

"Nearly there, sir," the pilot called out above the din in the Jet Ranger's cockpit.

Redmond nodded in acknowledgment and looked out of the window at the countryside below. On the left, half a mile or so away, was the broad expanse of the Blackwater estuary, fringed by mud flats and marshes, while, almost directly ahead, a mile or so away, were the squat, somehow sinister structures of Bradwell Nuclear Power Station. It was a desolate area, with few trees to break up the flat landscape, and Redmond suspected that, in winter, the winds would be strong and bitingly cold.

Redmond turned to the other four passengers, the members of one of the crisis teams that the Branch had on standby for situations like these. "We should be able to see the cottage any minute now" he yelled to them.

They nodded in reply, and peered intently out through the perspex. Redmond wished that he had had time to get to know them better; all he knew about them were their

351

names: Briers, Harris, Milne, and Sellars. Like himself, they would have undergone a training course with the SAS at Hereford and so would all be well-versed in the use of firearms, but this was no substitute for getting to know their strengths and weaknesses, when they might well be having to use their expertise within the next couple of hours. Not that there was anything he could do about it now. . . .

Half a minute later, they flew over a narrow road on the left that led to a farm — Westwick Farm, according to the map — then Redmond pointed at a single building about two hundred yards off the main road. "That's it," he shouted to Briers, who nodded again, then grimaced.

Redmond understood the reason for the gesture. The terrain could not possibly be worse from their point of view — flat, with no effective cover close to the cottage. It would be impossible to approach unobserved from any direction, unless they waited until dark, which would also make it easier for Farrington to slip away unseen.

"He's chosen a good place if he is here," Briers observed, echoing Redmond's thoughts. "No way of getting close under cover and he's only a couple of hundred yards from the harbour."

Redmond nodded, but said nothing as they

flew over the village itself and on towards the power station, where there was a disused airstrip. A minute or so later Redmond saw two police cars parked on the pitted runway. The helicopter came in to land about thirty yards away from them. Redmond and the crisis team emerged from the cockpit and, crouching low, ran over to the cars to be met by a dark-jowled man who held out his hand as Redmond approached.

"Chief Inspector Redmond? I'm Sergeant Merrick."

Redmond stared at him in surprise. "Where's Inspector Crosby?" Crosby was the local Special Branch officer.

"In London, sir. Training course. Started today, in fact."

Redmond looked over at the two police cars, full of a sudden unease. "Are these the only men you've got?" There was only one policeman in each car.

"There are two more in Bradwell itself," Merrick said defensively, but it was plain that he was wondering what all the fuss was about.

"Are they armed?"

"Armed?" Merrick exclaimed.

"Oh, shit . . ." Redmond groaned. "Didn't they tell you this was a grade one alert?"

Merrick stared at him incredulously. "No, they did not, sir. All they said was that I was to put Pewet Cottage under observation and then to meet you here. Nobody mentioned any grade one alert."

"So none of you are armed?"

"No, sir." There was a dawning comprehension on Merrick's face now.

Redmond closed his eyes and took a deep breath: it was not Merrick's fault. There had obviously been a failure in communications somewhere between London and here, perhaps understandable in view of the haste with which everything was being set up, but infuriating all the same — and dangerous. What it meant was that there was only a handful of armed men available to stake out the cottage — and they would have to be split up. "Briers?"

"Sir?"

"Do we have any reserve firearms with us?"

"Yes, sir. One."

"Give that to the sergeant, will you?" He turned back to Merrick. "We'd better get moving. I'll brief you in the car."

"Yes, sir. There is one thing, though. There's been a big pileup on the A-twelve just outside Chelmsford. If you're looking for reinforcements, that's where they'll have to come from."

"Oh, great," Redmond said bitterly, shaking his head slowly. "That's all I bloody well need."

Just under three minutes later, the two cars entered Bradwell Waterside, turning sharp left to follow the road round to the pub, which was where Merrick had set up his observation position. Redmond approved of the choice: according to the map the rear of the pub would command an excellent view of the cottage.

The cars pulled up in the pub car park, and Merrick led the way inside. "We're using the upstairs bedroom at the back," he said, taking them into the pub, then up a flight of stairs and into a south-facing bedroom. Two constables were stationed at the window, but, at a signal from Merrick, they moved aside to make way for Redmond. From the window, Redmond could see the cottage clearly, a quarter of a mile away. He surveyed the scene carefully, memorising the lie of the land, knowing that he might have to find his way around it in pitch darkness. Behind him, he could hear Briers talking to Merrick in a low murmur, presumably completing Redmond's sketchy briefing, but he ignored the sound and concentrated on the landscape.

Pewet Cottage was almost due south, with the B1021, the road leading to Maldon, over to the left. To the right was Bradwell Marina, a rectangular-shaped harbour about 250 yards long and 150 wide, with a long spit of land separating it from the estuary itself, except for a fifty-yard-wide entrance in the northern corner of the harbour. Beyond this gap was Pewet Island, a low, marshy strip of land. The southern corner of the harbour was only some two hundred yards or so from the cottage, while there was a boatyard all along the south-eastern side of the harbour that could provide plenty of hiding places for Farrington if he made a run for it. There were also a dozen or more vessels moored in the harbour, any of which could be fuelled up and ready to go. There was no way they could watch them all.

It did not look very good at all.

Redmond picked up a pair of binoculars he had brought with him and lined them up on the cottage. He had seen the Lada parked out-side when they had flown over, but it was invisible from here. There was no sign of any-one inside the cottage — the net curtains ob-scured any view from this distance.

"Okay," Redmond said quietly and turned to one of the constables. "Has there been any sign of life since you've been watching?"

"No, sir. Nobody's been in or out, and I haven't seen anyone moving around inside. But then I don't suppose I would, not with those curtains."

"True." Redmond turned to Merrick. "Do we know how long that car's been there, Sergeant?"

"The Lada arrived at around four yesterday afternoon. It was driven by a stocky man with short grey hair who was on his own."

"You're sure about the description of the driver?" Redmond asked, exchanging glances with Briers. It could well be Farrington.

"It's unconfirmed. Mrs. Burrows of Westwick Farm saw the Lada arrive, but nobody else has seen anything at all. And no, we don't know if the cottage has been hired out yet," said Merrick, anticipating Redmond's next question. "I got Colchester to get someone round to the cottage's owners, a Mr. and Mrs. Patterson, but there's nobody there. According to the neighbours, they went off on a motoring tour two days ago and aren't expected back for a week at least. We're still trying to trace them."

Redmond looked out of the window and shook his head. "So whoever's in there could simply be on a fishing holiday, for all we know."

"The description matches Farrington's," Briers observed.

"Hardly conclusive, though, is it?" He stared over at the cottage for several seconds, then turned back to face the others. "We'd better get into position. Harris, I want you at the eastern end of the track leading up to the cottage — where it joins the road. Milne, get to the southern corner of the harbour. Sellars, I want you in that farm to the south of the cottage — Westwick Farm. Get moving, all of you — and make sure nobody spots you from the cottage. Only use the walkie-talkies if you have to — I don't suppose anyone'll be listening in over there, but you never know."

He turned to Merrick as the others left. "Where's the phone?"

"Downstairs, behind the bar."

"Then we'd better see what the hell's going on in London."

Selvey's number was engaged.

Redmond muttered a curse, then pressed down the telephone cradle to dial again, his lips set in a grim line, even though he knew that Selvey was most likely frantically phoning round various people in Whitehall — and probably Hereford — to arrange the backup he had promised. It was infuriating, nevertheless. Redmond finished dialling, then swore out loud this time as he heard the engaged tone once more. He glanced at his watch — it would be dark in two hours or less — and dialled yet again.

This time, he sighed in relief as he heard the ringing tone, but several seconds passed before the phone was picked up at the other end. "Selvey here."

"It's Redmond."

"Good. What's the situation?"

"Bloody awful. We've only got half a dozen men here, including me — there's been some sort of pileup outside Chelmsford. I need that backup fast."

There was a pause, then Selvey said slowly, "I'm afraid there's been a bit of a problem over that. Hereford is reluctant to send anybody without some fairly definite indication that it is actually Farrington. Can you confirm that it is?"

Redmond closed his eyes and spat out a silent oath. He drew in a deep breath, then said, "Not definitely, no, sir. We've got a description that matches his, but — well — we don't have any photos of him with us, so we can't check with the witness for a positive ID."

"I see. Have you sighted him at all?"

"No. We're not even sure he's in the cottage at the moment. There's a car outside, but that's the only indication we've got."

"I see," Selvey said again. "Well, I'm afraid that's the situation, Steve. The SAS will not move unless they've got more definite evidence. Our lords and masters don't want them running loose all over the Essex countryside, not until we know exactly what is going on."

"Look, I only want them here on the scene — they're not being asked to stage a helicopter gunship assault on the bloody place! Once they're here, their CO can decide what to do — they're the experts at this sort of thing, after all."

Selvey's voice sounded weary. "I know, Steve. That is precisely what I have been telling everyone here, but it's like banging my head against a brick wall. The SAS will not be allowed to move without a definite identification of Farrington. I don't like it any more than you do, Steve, but there it is. If you can get some definite proof that it is Farrington, then they'll move immediately."

Redmond hesitated, then said slowly, "Sir, nobody had told the police up here that this was a grade one alert, and now we find we can't get any support from Hereford. Is someone higher up putting obstacles in our way?"

There was a pause, then Selvey replied, "It's beginning to look that way, but there's no way of knowing at the moment, is there?"

"Shit . . ." Redmond murmured. Comtex's invisible power again; they ought to have foreseen this. . . . Spilt milk, though. "So they're still at Hereford?"

"Yes. On standby."

"Which means they won't actually take off for another fifteen minutes, if I recall their procedures properly. It's a hundred and fifty miles or more to here, which is over an hour in a Wessex — so, unless I can get confirmation within the next thirty minutes, they still won't get here until after dark, in all probability."

"I know, Steve. But if you can get that confirmation . . ."

"I see. It's down to me, isn't it?"

"Use your own discretion, Steve."

"Thanks very much," Redmond muttered ironically as he replaced the telephone. He stared unseeingly at the wall, his expression thoughtful, then turned to Merrick. "We need a positive ID," he said slowly.

"So I gathered, sir," Merrick replied drily. "How do we get that?"

"We don't really have much choice, do we?" Redmond said quietly. "We can't afford to piss about here hoping that Farrington or whoever it is will show himself. So somebody is going to have to go up to the cottage, knock on the door, and see who answers it."

"And if it is Farrington, sir?" Merrick answered. "Seems to be a good way to get your head blown off, especially if he's got a bodyguard with him. Just because Mrs. Burrows only saw the one man doesn't mean to say that he's the only one in there, does it?"

"I know, but do you have any better ideas?" Redmond asked, grimly. "It'll be dark in two hour — less than that, probably — so that's all the time we've got."

"I suppose so, sir," Merrick agreed reluctantly. "Who gets the short straw?" he asked.

"It has to be me, doesn't it?" Redmond said softly, but he was not looking at Merrick as he spoke. Merrick had the curious impression that Redmond was talking to someone else, but there were only the two of them in the room. "I'll need someone to cover me, though — Briers, I think."

"Cover you? Where from?"

"The car. There's no way we can get within a hundred yards of the place without being seen anyway, so we might just as well drive up to it."

Merrick stared at him, then shook his head slowly. "It's your funeral, sir," he said softly.

"I bloody well hope not."

Redmond brought the car to a halt by the gate and looked intently at the cottage, twenty yards away. There was no sign of anyone watching from the windows, but that proved nothing: anyone inside would have seen the car coming from the moment it had turned off the road. He turned to Briers and nodded slowly. "Right, Briers," he said quietly. "If you see anything at all suspicious, yell out."

"Right, sir," Briers said grimly. "I wish you'd let me come with you, though."

"We've been through all that. I need you watching my back — right?"

"Right, sir," Briers said reluctantly.

"Good." Redmond reached inside his jacket, taking the Browning automatic from its shoulder holster. Quickly, he checked the magazine, then replaced it, nodding briefly as he saw Briers doing the same with his own weapon. The two men exchanged glances, then Redmond said, "Let's get on with it, shall we?" He opened the door and climbed out, slamming it behind him. For a moment he looked towards Westwick Farm, two hundred yards away, where Merrick and Sellars would be watching through binoculars; Merrick would have a telephone next to him — just in case. Redmond took a deep breath, then walked through the gate and up the path towards the cottage, trying to ignore the sudden sensation of being centred in a rifle's crosshairs. He flicked a glance behind him and saw Briers leaning against the far side of the car, his arms folded, apparently casually, on the roof, but Redmond knew he would be holding the gun out of sight and would be able to fire in less than a second.

He focused his attention on the cottage and realised that he still had twenty yards to go — what had happened to time? It seemed to be dragging by. . . . Still no sign of life from inside though, but what difference did that make? Ten yards. At this range, they could hardly bloody miss. . . . Redmond pushed the thought aside, but still involuntarily looked over at the low boundary wall over to his left, twenty yards away, the nearest available cover. Five yards . . .

Then, he heard the sound of a car engine behind him and spun round, dimly aware of Briers shouting a warning, but the next second, a car — a Jaguar — came into view, hurtling along the narrow track towards the cottage. Redmond saw the driver wrenching at the wheel and the car turned into the narrow gateway, but too fast: the rear end slewed sideways and smashed into the gatepost, flattening it. As the car skidded to a halt, Redmond had a momentary glimpse of Lansky in the passenger seat before he turned and sprinted, head down, towards the low wall.

Behind him, three men came piling out of the Jaguar. Lansky and the driver ran towards the cottage, with Lansky firing off a snapshot from a handgun at Briers as the third man lined up a sawnoff shotgun at Redmond's running figure. There was a deafening blast as he fired, but he was a split second too late, Redmond was diving over the wall, out of sight. The gunman swore and then broke into a run after Lansky and the driver, who were scrambling through the cottage's door, but he had only taken three or four steps when Briers loosed off two rapid shots from behind the car. The first bullet slammed into the gunman's side just below his ribs, throwing him against the doorjamb before the second took him in the chest. He stood for a moment as though impaled, then toppled slowly forwards, clutching frantically at his chest, his eyes rolling upwards in his head as he crashed to the ground.

Redmond saw none of this. He was pressed flat to the ground on the far side of the wall. He twisted round to face the cottage, pulling his walkie-talkie from inside his jacket. "Merrick?" he yelled.

"I saw it," said Merrick's voice. "You were right, sir."

"Get on to — Jesus Christ!" The last exclamation was wrenched out of him as the cottage's right-hand front window suddenly exploded outwards in a welter of flying glass. A split second later, Redmond heard a rapid staccato as someone inside opened up with a submachine gun, a Skorpion by the sound of it, he decided with a detached part of his mind

— where the fuck had that come from? — then winced as the windows of the car disintegrated in a hail of bullets. Redmond saw Briers disappear from sight.

"Briers!" Redmond shouted into his radio. "Briers!"

"Here," Briers replied. "I'm okay. I got down in time."

"Good. Merrick, tell Selvey to get some reinforcements in here. These bastards are armed to the fucking teeth." Redmond ducked reflexively as a second burst of fire carved chips out of the wall a foot above his head. As the Skorpion fell silent, he heard Merrick's voice over the radio. "Say again!" Redmond yelled.

"London says —" Merrick began.

Again, his voice was drowned by the Skorpion's deafening clamour, but this time the car was the target once more. It was obvious what the gunman was doing — pinning Redmond and Briers down, which meant that Farrington was probably slipping out through the back door right now. There was nothing Redmond could do about it, because the wall ended abruptly ten yards to his left so that he could not head off in pursuit without exposing himself to gunfire from the side windows. A range of twenty yards with a Skorpion shooting at him at a rate of six hundred rounds a minute . . .

Suicide.

Unless . . . He snatched up the radio again. "Briers?"

"Here, sir."

"How many are shooting at us, do you reckon?"

There was another burst of fire above Redmond's head, but as soon as it finished, Briers replied, "Just one. He's taking turns to have a go at each of us."

Despite the situation, Redmond found time to smile at Briers's voice: calm, unhurried, he might have been talking about the weather. "Reckon you're right. Now —"

Another voice cut in. "Milne here. Two men have just come out the back. They're heading my way."

Redmond swore. Milne was the man stationed at the harbour, and he would be on his own unless someone could get over there fast to join him. "Briers?"

"Here."

"We'll have to take this bloke out. You cover me — okay?"

"Okay."

"Get loaded up."

"Wilco."

Redmond took out his pistol and flicked off the safety catch.

"Ready," said Briers.

"Give him the full magazine when I give the word."

"Okay."

Redmond twisted round until he was crouching up on one knee, his head just below the level of the wall. Take a deep breath, then another, visualise the cottage, three, two, one —

"Go!" he yelled. A split second later, he heard Briers's gun begin to fire, aiming at the cottage's front window. Redmond came up over the wall in a surge of movement, then pelted towards the cottage. A second later, he flattened himself against the wall next to the side window. He raised the radio to his mouth again.

"One more time, Briers!"

Briers opened up once more, still aiming at the front window. Redmond swung his pistol hard at the window beside him, but, as the glass shattered, the Skorpion opened up again, spraying the car in a withering burst of fire. Redmond had a vague impression of Briers falling out of sight again, but then he struck a second time at the glass with the pistol. He moved outwards, turning to aim the Browning through the shattered window at the gunman ten feet away. The gunman pivoted round, his finger still on the trigger, but before he could bring the weapon round far enough, Redmond fired three rapid shots. The first took the gunman high up on his left arm, the impact spinning him round so that the second shot struck him in the side, just above the hip. The third hit him in the ribs and threw him to one side so that he crashed down onto a coffee table, flattening it. But he still had the Skorpion and was trying to bring it up again when Redmond squeezed the trigger a fourth time, placing this shot into the other man's chest. The gunman jerked convulsively, his body arching in agony, then, slowly, he settled back down into the growing pool of blood on the floor, his head lolling tiredly to one side as the Skorpion slipped from his lifeless fingers.

It was only now that Redmond remembered the gunman's last burst of fire, directed at Briers — and how he had fallen back. He looked over towards the car, but there was no sign of Briers; almost before he was aware of it, Redmond was running towards the bullet-riddled car.

Briers was lying motionless on his back, spread-eagled, a line of bullet holes stitched across his chest; he must have died instantly.

Redmond stared down at him, his eyes glittering, then spun on his heel and jumped into the car.

* * *

Lansky stood just inside the open back door, looking quickly around, ignoring the gunfire from the front of the cottage. He held a sawn-off shotgun in one hand, almost nonchalantly, with the safety catch off; he turned to Farrington and said, "I'll go first. If nothing happens, you come after me. Got that?"

"But —"

"Listen, either you come after me or you stay here, it's up to you, but I know what the hell I'm going to do." He turned back to the door, took one more rapid look, then launched himself through the doorway and out, sprinting towards a wooden shed thirty yards away in a low crouching run, zigzagging at random intervals. At any moment he expected to hear a gunshot, but nothing happened and he skidded to a halt next to the shed almost with a feeling of anticlimax. He beckoned to Farrington to follow, then glanced around again. Farrington came running up, his face already flushed with exertion and tension.

"There isn't a marksman out there," Lansky said briefly. "He'd have had his sights lined up on the door and he'd at least have had a go at me when I came out." He peered around the corner of the shed towards the harbour, then said, without looking round,

"Right — stay close behind me. We're heading for the boat. Let's go."

The two men set off in a jogging run, although Farrington stumbled as he looked back at a renewed burst of gunfire from behind. "Keep going!" Lansky yelled.

They were approaching the harbour now, with the boatyard on their right and a footpath coming in towards them from the left. The harbour itself was deserted and Lansky guessed that the police had cordoned off the area. The cabin cruiser was moored at the end of the nearest jetty, only fifty yards away now as they skirted the road along the quayside. Christ, they were nearly there! Only another —

"Freeze!" yelled a voice from behind them. Farrington skidded to a halt, looking around confusedly, but Lansky threw himself to the left, twisting around in midair. As he hit the ground he rolled once, then lined up the shotgun on the man who had shouted, standing behind an upturned boat only ten yards away. Lansky squeezed both triggers simultaneously and the impact of the shells lifted the other man bodily into the air, hurling him backwards, arms outflung, with half his chest shot away. He crashed heavily onto the gravel and lay there, unmoving.

Lansky scrambled to his feet in time to see

Farrington glance briefly at the dead man, then take off running towards the jetty. Lansky was about to follow when he heard a shot from somewhere behind him. He spun round and saw two more armed men running towards him along the footpath, only fifty yards behind. Beyond them, he could see Redmond's car lurching across the grass from the cottage — it was evident that McClelland had been dealt with. Lansky reached inside his jacket for his pistol, then loosed off two rapid shots at the approaching men. As they dived flat to the ground, Lansky ran towards the boatyard, taking cover behind a wooden paint store. He peered round it just as the nearest pursuer scrambled to his feet, and in less than a second, Lansky had aimed and fired, hitting the man in the shoulder, the soft-nosed bullet all but tearing his arm off. The policeman collapsed, screaming and clutching at his shattered shoulder, his face contorted in agony, but Lansky had to duck back out of sight as the remaining pursuer fired.

Lansky flicked a glance towards the boat and saw that Farrington had already reached the end of the jetty. As he watched, Farrington cast off the bow rope and jumped down onto the deck. The next moment, he had cast off the stern mooring, and it was only then that the realisation struck Lansky — Farrington was leaving without him.

The bastard . . . But what else had he expected?

Lansky raised his gun in a two-handed grip and lined it up on Farrington. Although he knew the range was probably too great, he swore as he saw Farrington crouch down out of sight, as if he knew what was happening. Lansky heard the engine cough into life and saw the cruiser begin to move away from the jetty. For a moment, as the boat turned towards the harbour entrance, Farrington's head was silhouetted and Lansky squeezed off a rapid shot. The cockpit glass shattered a foot to Farrington's left, and Lansky saw him duck out of sight again.

"Shit!" Lansky shouted, then glimpsed a movement out of the corner of his eye. He pivoted round as the third policeman sprinted towards the upturned boat the first man had used for cover; Lansky fired twice and the other man went down, blood pouring from his thigh. Desperately, he tried to crawl away, but Lansky knew that he had plenty of time to finish him off — and there were still four shots left in the magazine. Carefully, almost lovingly, he lined up the barrel and began to squeeze the trigger.

And froze.

Suddenly, the sound of Redmond's car was

ominously close, the engine roaring above the sound of spitting gravel as it accelerated. It sounded as if it were coming straight at him. . . .

Lansky turned in sudden, horrified realisation, and then the paint store seemed to explode as the car ploughed through it at nearly forty miles an hour, throwing the timbers aside like so many matchsticks and scattering the tins of paint before it smashed into Lansky. He pitched forward onto the bonnet, screaming in agony as both legs were broken at the knee, then he was hurled over the roof before he slammed down into the ground, rolling over and over in a limp, boneless fashion behind the car as Redmond slammed on the brakes.

Redmond hit the door release with his right hand, scooped up his gun with the left, and jumped out of the car almost before it had come to a halt. Holding the Browning two-handed, he lined it up on Lansky's motionless figure as he walked slowly towards him, never once taking his eyes from him. There was a growing pool of blood under Lansky's torso, but he was still breathing stertorously through his half-open mouth — and, when Redmond was only five yards or so away, he could see that Lansky's right hand was still holding his gun. . . .

A split second later, Lansky twisted round, yelling incoherently in rage and defiance as he brought the gun up, but Redmond reeled off a rapid succession of shots, each bullet slamming into Lansky's chest and shoulders. Lansky jerked and writhed convulsively with each impact, and then Redmond's gun fell silent. For a moment, Lansky's pain-filled eyes met Redmond's, and his mouth opened as though he were about to speak, but then his head lolled to one side and he slumped tiredly over onto his back, staring sightlessly up at the slate grey sky.

His gun was still gripped tightly in his right hand.

Slowly, Redmond let out his breath in a sigh that was a mixture of triumph and relief; then he turned to watch the cabin cruiser as it surged through the harbour entrance, picking up speed.

Farrington.

Redmond balanced himself on the foredeck of the speedboat as the police launch came alongside, then stepped unhurriedly across to the launch, nodding his thanks to the young PC who had grasped his hand to help him aboard. He turned to the speedboat's helmsman and raised his hand. "Thanks, Mr. Harrison."

"Anytime," the other man called, then spun the wheel and opened up the throttle. Moments later, the speedboat was heading back towards the marina four miles away. Redmond checked his watch and nodded in silent approval. A mere thirty minutes had passed since the first shots had been fired at the cottage. Merrick had had a police launch standing by at Brightlingsea, which Redmond had called up before persuading Harrison, a local boat owner, to take him out to the mid-estuary rendezvous. Apparently, Farrington's cabin cruiser, the *Kestrel*, could do twenty-five knots, but Harrison had estimated it would not be able to make more than about twenty in this sea, so, by that reckoning, he could only have managed seven miles or so by now, probably less. Subtract the four miles Redmond had already covered in the speedboat and Farrington was probably no more than three miles ahead, although Redmond had seen no sign of his boat so far in the gathering twilight. Nor could he now, as he peered over the launch's bow. Already, the launch was picking up speed as it headed off in pursuit.

The PC led the way to the wheelhouse, where Redmond found a helmsman and an impossibly young-looking police sergeant. "Chief Inspector Redmond?" asked the sergeant. "I'm Sergeant Walford, sir."

The two men shook hands, then Redmond pointed to the radar screen that Walford had been studying. In its centre, dead ahead, was a single blip. "Is that him?"

"It certainly is," Walford replied. "Three miles ahead, give or take a yard or two, and doing eighteen knots on a southeasterly course."

"You're sure it's him?"

"Nobody else it could be." He twisted a dial below the screen, and the single blip was joined by a second, on the edge of the screen. "He's heading straight for that larger blip further out, sir. At a guess, that'll be the *Triton V* waiting to pick him up."

"How far has Farrington got to go?"

"Another ten miles yet, and we'll overhaul him before that. We've a good seven- or eight-knot advantage over him in this sea."

Redmond nodded absently. "But what if the ship sends out a high-speed boat to pick him up — a fast inflatable, say?"

Walford's expression changed. "Then we'd have a very different kettle of fish, sir." He looked at Redmond. "How likely is that?"

Redmond shrugged. "Search me. Until half an hour ago, I wasn't even sure Farrington was here at all. Your guess is as good as mine."

"Then we'd better wind up the elastic a bit, hadn't we?" Walford grinned. "Give it all we've got, Jameson."

"Right, Sarge."

Redmond clutched at a handhold as the launch surged forward, pounding through the waves as Jameson gave the powerful diesels their head. Walford picked up his binoculars and began quartering the sea ahead, seemingly oblivious to the corkscrewing motion, but then lowered them with a self-conscious smile at Redmond.

"Won't see a bloody thing yet, of course," he commented. "It's getting too dark. We'll have to use the searchlight once we come up to her."

For the next twenty minutes or so, Redmond's gaze was fixed on the radar screen and on the blip that moved steadily towards the centre of the screen as the launch inexorably closed the gap. Despite this, he found his thoughts wandering as he recalled Merrick's face, pale and drawn on the stretcher, just before they had lifted him into the ambulance; he had almost bled to death despite the tourniquet Redmond had tied around his thigh. Yet Merrick had been lucky, more so, probably, than Sellars, who might well never be able to use his right arm properly again. And far more lucky than Briers or Milne, of course . . .

Farrington was going to pay, Redmond

thought, his lips set in a grim line. This time, the bastard wasn't going to get away with it. . . . He forced his attention back onto the screen.

Presently, Walford said quietly, "Let's have the lights on then, Stevens."

The third member of the crew, the one who had helped Redmond aboard, nodded and stepped up onto a raised platform behind Jameson. He flicked a switch, and a blinding beam of light stabbed out into the gloom.

"Dead ahead," Walford said, not taking his eyes from the screen. "Range eight hundred."

Stevens nodded and aimed the searchlight accordingly, moving it from left to right in a narrow arc on either side of the bow, but the illuminated circle of water remained obstinately empty.

"Come on," Walford muttered. "She's got to be out there somewhere." He glanced at Redmond, then looked back at the screen, almost guiltily. "Bugger," he said softly. "She's turning to port. He must have seen the light. Port ten, Jameson."

"Port ten, Sarge."

"Got her," Stevens said calmly, and Redmond looked ahead, grinning triumphantly as he saw the cabin cruiser caught squarely in the searchlight beam. As he watched, the other boat suddenly heeled over as Farrington altered course again, zigging and zagging in a frantic, but futile, attempt to escape. All his twisting and turning accomplished was to enable the launch to close the gap more rapidly, until the *Kestrel* was only fifty yards away.

Walford picked up an electronic loudhailer, switched it on, then called, "Ahoy, *Kestrel*. This is the police. Heave to and allow us to come alongside."

By way of answer, the *Kestrel* swung round again, heading straight out to sea, but, at a nod from Walford, the launch altered course to intercept, closing the distance between the two craft rapidly.

"I say again, heave to, *Kestrel*," Walford called out. "There's no point running anymore."

For several seconds, there was no response from the fleeing cruiser, but then, abruptly, the *Kestrel* lost way as Farrington cut the power. Within moments, she was lying virtually stopped, wallowing uncomfortably in the swell as the launch slowed in turn and moved closer. Redmond could see Farrington in the other boat's cockpit, facing him, one hand held in front of his eyes against the searchlight's glare.

"We're coming alongside," Walford announced. "Stand by to receive a line."

Farrington waved his hand resignedly in acknowledgment, and at a signal from Walford, Stevens went forward to throw across a line. It fell across the *Kestrel*'s aft well-deck and Farrington climbed down from the cockpit, bending down to pick up the line.

But he seemed to be crouched down for longer than was necessary: suddenly, he straightened up and Redmond saw that he was holding something in his right hand — a bottle. With a convulsive heave, Farrington lobbed it across the ten-yard gap between the two boats and, as it curled lazily towards the launch's stern, Redmond saw the burning wad of paper that had been stuffed into the bottle's neck.

It was a Molotov cocktail.

The next instant, it exploded, showering burning petrol over the stern, and within seconds, the after part of the launch was ablaze. Redmond heard Walford swear loudly and saw him snatch up a fire extinguisher, but then he forgot the young sergeant as he reached inside his jacket for his pistol. Farrington was crouching down again in the cruiser's well-deck and, as Redmond lined up his gun, Farrington rose to his feet once more, a second bottle in his hand. He pulled it back behind his head, and his arm was just starting to come forward in a throwing action when Redmond fired three rapid shots.

The second bullet struck Farrington in the shoulder, throwing him back against the wheelhouse ladder and knocking the bottle from his grasp. An instant later, it shattered at his feet and the petrol ignited, enveloping Farrington in flames. He screamed in agony, slapping frantically at the flames that were engulfing him, then lurched towards the side of the boat, as if to throw himself over the side, still shrieking in hideous torment. Before he could reach the gunwale, however, he pitched heavily forward into the leaping flames.

Somehow, he managed to drag himself back onto his feet, but now he was on fire from head to foot, an animal-like howl coming from what had once been his mouth. He stumbled blindly around and fell against the ladder; he grabbed hold of it, then twisted round so that he was facing Redmond as though transfixed.

Redmond took careful aim at his chest, then squeezed the trigger, again and again, pumping bullet after bullet into the burning man. Farrington reeled backwards as they slammed into him, jerking convulsively with each impact. Then, as if in slow motion, he slumped tiredly forward and disappeared from view.

Slowly, Redmond brought his gun down, his face ashen as he watched the blazing *Kestrel* drift away, the fire spreading rapidly. Redmond stared at the doomed vessel for almost a minute, then let out his breath in a long sigh before he turned to help Walford and his crew fight the fire astern.

It was over.

Epilogue

There was a very fine drizzle in the air, and so both men were wearing military-style raincoats as well as carrying the obligatory furled umbrellas for their walk along the terrace overlooking the Thames. Each man was almost an archetype of a pillar of the Establishment, an image that was reinforced by the Houses of Parliament behind them. Neither had spoken for at least a minute, but now the slightly shorter of the two men looked around to see if anyone was within earshot and said:

"Well, a right bloody fiasco that was. Do you know how much I stand to lose if this Piccolo deal doesn't go through? Which, to be frank, now seems extremely unlikely. I don't think we can keep the lid on it much longer. A week at the most before the Opposition brings it up in the House, I would think. And God only knows what Houston will say." He paused and looked appraisingly at the other man. "This was your responsibility — to ensure that nothing came up to jeopardise the sale. I don't think Houston is going to be too impressed by your performance."

The man Lansky had known as Beresford sighed gently and said, "With respect, I was assured by Mayhew that he had the matter well in hand, that he had successfully diverted Redmond and Harper. I did have other pressing matters on my plate at the time."

"No excuse. It was still your overall responsibility."

Beresford inclined his head, but said nothing. The first man turned away and stared absently across the river. After a few moments, he said musingly, "Redmond and Harper."

"Yes?"

"We can't allow them to get away with this, can we?"

Beresford shook his head. "Certainly not."

"Precisely." Big Ben struck behind them and the first man glanced at his watch. "I shall have to go. I have to be in the House for Question Time." He looked intently at the man next to him. "See to it, Selvey. And make sure there are no slipups this time."

Selvey nodded. "Leave it to me." He looked out over the river, then added, almost as an afterthought, "Home Secretary."